Knit Your Own Murder

Berkley Prime Crime titles by Monica Ferris

CREWEL WORLD
FRAMED IN LACE
A STITCH IN TIME
UNRAVELED SLEEVE
A MURDEROUS YARN
HANGING BY A THREAD
CUTWORK
CREWEL YULE
EMBROIDERED TRUTHS
SINS AND NEEDLES
KNITTING BONES
THAI DIE
BLACKWORK
BUTTONS AND BONES
THREADBARE
AND THEN YOU DYE
THE DROWNING SPOOL
DARNED IF YOU DO
KNIT YOUR OWN MURDER

Anthologies

PATTERNS OF MURDER
SEW FAR, SO GOOD

Knit Your Own Murder

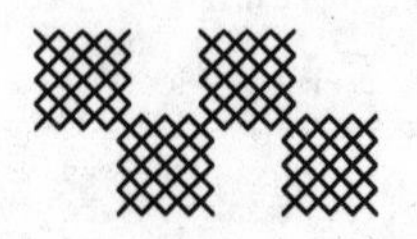

Monica Ferris

BERKLEY PRIME CRIME, NEW YORK

An imprint of Penguin Random House LLC
375 Hudson Street, New York, New York 10014

This book is an original publication of Penguin Random House LLC.

For more information, visit penguin.com.

Library of Congress Cataloging-in-Publication Data

Names: Ferris, Monica, author.
Title: Knit your own murder / Monica Ferris.
Description: First edition. | New York : Berkley Prime Crime, 2016. | Series: A needlecraft mystery ; 19
Identifiers: LCCN 2016009072 (print) | LCCN 2016015743 (ebook) | ISBN 9780425270127 (hardcover) | ISBN 9781101638309 ()
Subjects: LCSH: Devonshire, Betsy (Fictitious character)—Fiction. | Murder—Investigation—Fiction. | Women detectives—Fiction. | Needleworkers—Fiction. | Needlework—Fiction. | BISAC: FICTION / Mystery & Detective / Women Sleuths. | FICTION / Mystery & Detective / General. | GSAFD: Mystery fiction.
Classification: LCC PS3566.U47 K57 2016 (print) | LCC PS3566.U47 (ebook) | DDC 813/.54—dc23
LC record available at https://lccn.loc.gov/2016009072

FIRST EDITION: August 2016

PRINTED IN THE UNITED STATES OF AMERICA

10 9 8 7 6 5 4 3 2 1

Cover illustration by Mary Ann Lasher.
Cover design by George Long.

Acknowledgments

I want to thank Maru Zamora, Alicia Vázquez-De-Ortiz, and Ricardo Ortiz-Nava for language help with the intense quarrel in Spanish that is described in this book.

Dr. Michael Austin of the University of Minnesota's Safety and Environmental Protection Facility was extremely helpful about poisons. He even showed me how, under extraordinary conditions, including coincidence, someone might bypass their safeguards.

Thanks to the Davisson people Allan and Lief, who deal in coins, for selling me an Edward the Confessor early medieval silver penny—and thereby giving me the information I needed to allow Rafael Miguel Antonio de la Valencina Zamora Soto (isn't that a great name?) to add one to his own collection.

Thank you, Bill Staines, for permission to quote the chorus of your song "River (Take Me Along)" in this novel.

And of course, thanks to Diane Davis, the talented needlework artist who created the little knit pattern of Sophie in the back of this book.

Knit Your Own Murder

Chapter One

JOE Mickels sat alone in his big old car. He was a thick-bodied man with a harsh face set on either side with long, old-fashioned sideburns. It was the last Tuesday in March, near the end of winter in Minnesota. The sky was overcast, the sun showing its location by a light spot in the clouds. The temperature was above freezing by two degrees.

Joe was tired; not just physically tired, but spiritually tired. Tired to his bones, tired to his soul. He had worked hard all his life, and what did he have to show for it?

There was the money, of course. Lots of money, actually. Once, that was enough. Every time he worked a deal successfully he got paid, so it became a way of keeping score. It was a game he was good at, and he had played it for a long time, racking up points, until he was so far ahead the numbers had become almost meaningless.

The problem was—and who would have thought it?—

the money itself had also become meaningless. He'd never married, had no children, so there was no one standing by, eager for him to die and leave it to them—so they could blow through it in a couple of years and wind up on welfare. Or to rebel and go all anti-money and declare they didn't want any of it. Or to be grateful for his ability to earn money because they'd inherited that trait themselves. Or to give him grandchildren to tease and love and spoil. There was no one to give a damn.

When he died, his money would dissipate like fog on a sunny morning.

He'd finally thought of a way to leave his mark, a good, solid method. He'd tried and tried and tried to make it happen—and failed. Two days ago he'd failed at what he thought was his last, and best, chance to build the Mickels Building right here in his hometown. A building that would stand for at least a century, maybe two, with his name proudly spread across the lintel. Now it was never going to happen. And he was tired, maybe too tired to care.

Today was his birthday. He was eighty years old. A really big number, eighty. Until two days ago he hadn't felt eighty. Hell, he hadn't even felt seventy. But today he felt every year—every minute—of eighty.

When Joe Mickels was a kid, fifty was old. One foot in the grave, the other on a banana peel was how he would have described it. But nowadays fifty was still middle-aged.

On the other hand, even today eighty was old. The chance to put his permanent mark on the world was almost certainly past. Eighty was summing-up time, not make-your-mark time.

He'd had one last shot at it, a beautiful shot, and almost

succeeded. But he was spread a little thin right now, unable to convert holdings to sufficient cash quickly enough to get that property, to raise his bid past the soaring bids of Maddy O'Leary and Harry Whiteside.

He was almost depressed enough not to be angry.

Almost.

Chapter Two

On Friday afternoon, the Monday Bunch was in session at Crewel World. They had met on Monday earlier that week but were eager to complete a group project and had been meeting two, sometimes three times a week. They were sitting around the big library table in the middle of the shop. The Bunch was a long-standing group of women—and two men—who normally met weekly at the needlework shop to stitch on a wide variety of projects and to gossip. But all seven people in attendance today were knitting, and all were working on toy animals. A heap of excelsior stuffing was in the center of the table.

"I always thought Harry Whiteside would come to a bad end," said Bershada, a handsome black woman. She was casting off the last row of a small Paddington bear she'd been knitting.

"Yes," said Connor, his tone just a little remonstrative, "but murdered? Surely that's a bit harsh."

Harry Whiteside had been found in the kitchen of his fine Wayzata home, his skull broken and his house vandalized.

Bershada responded coolly, "I knew his second wife, poor thing, and helped her pack the day she left him. I thought at the time—that was, what, three years ago?—that he deserved worse."

"I'm surprised she stuck with him as long as she did, knowing what a bast—pardon me—what a hard man he was," said Phil, who was knitting, of all things, a large fruit bat. "But I thought it would be bankruptcy doing him in, not murder. He started small, built slowly, then all of a sudden he's rich. Happened so fast, it seemed bound to fall down around his ears. But he wasn't actually a crook, was he?"

"No," admitted Bershada. "Well, not completely a crook," she amended. "But a lot of people thought they got taken by his methods of doing business." She glanced around the table and added in a quieter voice, "Not excluding our own Maddy O'Leary."

Maddy wasn't exactly one of Crewel World's "own." She was an ardent knitter and did some tatting as well, buying her supplies in the shop. But she didn't come to the weekly gathering of stitchers, and her cruel tongue kept the Monday Bunch from inviting her to do so.

"Hey, Maddy got the better of him over the Water Street property," said Cherie. She was knitting a big macaw whose bright colors were echoed in the bunch of feathers on the natty green hat she wore. "After all, she's the one who wound up with the deed."

"True, but he—and Joe Mickels, don't forget—bid her up well over what she thought she'd have to pay, didn't they?" said Godwin, the store manager, a young-looking thirty-year-old man with a dulcet voice and very swift fingers. He had been showing off by knitting a leopard, a difficult task because of its random pattern of yellow-centered black spots. As he spoke, he was knitting the fortieth, forty-first, and forty-second stitch in the row of forty-five that made up the long tail of the animal.

"I agree Joe Mickels has to take a share of the blame for the high price it sold for," said shop owner Betsy Devonshire, who wasn't sitting at the table but was working on an order for Silk and Ivory floss over at the checkout desk.

Everyone knew Joe Mickels had long harbored a desire to put up a building in Excelsior with his name over the door. At one time he'd thought to build it on the site of Betsy's building, and his ultimately futile attempts to force her out had led to plenty of bad feelings on both sides. He had recently tried to accomplish his goal when the great big car dealership at the top of Water Street had closed and the property had been divided in half and offered for sale. A whole-foods grocery had promptly bought the southwest end, and after an initial shaking out of half a dozen bidders, three people had contended for the northeastern half.

"It's very satisfying to make your dreams come true," said Valentina, who was driving her contractor crazy because she insisted on supervising every element of the reworking of a house she'd inherited. "So I guess I'm feeling a little bad for Mr. Mickels." She was knitting a beautiful ram, complete with horns.

Joe, Maddy, and Harry had taken up cudgels in a bidding war, all the more ferocious for the big egos of the three participants. All three refused to speak on the record about the struggle, but some local folks knew a few interesting details, and enough of them talked about it that many of the people living around Lake Minnetonka were able to follow with amazement as the bids were raised and raised again. Maddy won at the end, but the dust was yet to settle, and the hard feelings lingered.

And now one of the three final bidders, Harry Whiteside, was dead, murdered in his own home.

"You don't suppose—?" said Valentina, and paused. As the newest member of the group, she wasn't sure how far to go in speculating about people.

"Suppose what?" asked Doris, encouragingly.

Valentina shook her head, but Godwin was braver. "That Joe had something to do with Harry's death?" He looked at Valentina, who nodded, then at Betsy, his expression amused. "Maybe trying to get the bidding reopened?"

"Goddy," said Betsy, a little miffed at his flippancy, "Mr. Whiteside was killed by a burglar he interrupted in his home. That is not a matter for joking."

Connor said, "Anyway, if Joe was out to get the bidding reopened, he'd go after Maddy, not Harry." He was finished with his orange-haired orangutan and was stuffing it from the big heap of finely shredded wood chips on the table.

But Godwin was incorrigible. In his most flamboyant tone and gesture, he said, "We don't *know* that. Maybe he decided first to go after his *rival*, so he'd be less obvious. You all just keep watching. If something happens to Maddy, then you'll *know* I'm right." But he made a face to show he was just kidding.

"Pooh," said Emily, who didn't use strong language.

"Ha, finished!" announced Bershada, tossing down her

knitting needles. The Paddington Bear, complete with blue duffel coat and yellow rain hat, lay in a severely collapsed condition across one of her hands. The bear was about eight inches long and without eyes or the black tip of its nose, and its bottom was open. Bershada reached for the excelsior and began to fill the toy, her beautiful, long fingers moving deftly.

"Awwwww," said Emily as the little bear took shape. "How many does that make?"

"Of critters? An even dozen. This is Paddington number five."

"That's amazing!" said Valentina. "I've made six of these rams and thought I was doing well."

"You *are* doing well," said Bershada. "Compared to that ram, this bear is really easy."

"I've only done three toys," said Doris, "so you both are doing well."

Emily said, "I'm glad you're making the bear's coat and hat part of him, Bershada, because otherwise they'd get lost by the second day." She spoke from experience, having three young girls in her household whose ability to remove and lose accessories from their toys held, she was sure, national speed records.

Emily was working on a toy kitten with "tuxedo" markings: It was mostly black with white on its face, chest, and paws. She had a big plastic sewing needle and was using it to fasten the fourth leg to the creature. On the table in front of her was a pair of green glass cat's-eyes with little metal loops on their backs, waiting to be sewn on.

Doris, sitting next to Emily, frowned, sighed, looked

away and back, then snatched up a linen bookmark with an Easter bunny stitched on it and tossed it over the glass eyes. "Well, they were staring at me," she explained as the others looked at her, surprised then amused.

Doris was less than half finished with a lion, her most ambitious project to date. She was using the directions in Sally Muir and Joanna Osborne's delightful *Knit Your Own Zoo* to make the toy, which would be about ten inches long—not counting the tail. At this point the lion's front left limb and both hind limbs were opened out in front of her, their upper ends suspended on separate knitting needles, waiting for her to get that far. She was working on knitting the right front leg onto the right side of the body. There was no head in sight.

"Are you going to have that finished by tomorrow?" asked Godwin. With a contented little sigh he closed his copy of the book in front of him, *Knit Your Own Zoo*. He didn't need instructions on how to stuff his leopard.

"You just mind your own project," advised Doris cheerfully, her fingers moving in the patterns of knit one, purl one. She was not as fast a knitter as Godwin, but neither was she as slow as her husband, Phil, sitting beside her.

He was knitting the second wing on his bat, consulting the pattern he'd photocopied from his wife's copy of the book, then pausing to count the number of stitches on his needle.

Godwin had found a doorbell device that played music whenever anyone opened the door. It sounded like a toy organ and would play anything programmed into it. Godwin hadn't settled on one tune. Today it was playing "Hail to the Chief" and the knitters looked up to see Maddy O'Leary enter, holding a big brown canvas bag in one hand. She was a large woman with masses of gray hair pulled back into an untidy bun, a habitually downturned mouth, and a habit of wearing sturdy wool suits with long skirts.

She turned toward the source of the music, then glanced at the Band-Aid around one of her fingers: a patriotic one in red, white, and blue.

Phil sniggered, and she whirled back to impale him with a glare.

"Ms. O'Leary," said Betsy to distract her. "What can I do for you?"

"I brought some more toys," she said in a strong, unfriendly voice. She walked to the table and upended the bag carelessly. Its contents landed on the excelsior, scattering it onto everyone else's work. Her contribution consisted of four knit dogs: a border collie, a Scottie, a whippet, and a silly-looking flop-eared mutt; and a bald eagle with glaring eyes and folded wings.

"Hey!" exclaimed Phil, hastily lifting his bat and shaking off the wisps of stuffing.

She scowled at the ugly gray-black creature in his hands. "Good heavens, Galvin, who's going to want to bid on that?" she asked.

"Some strange little child is going to beg and beg her mother to get it for her," asserted Phil with happy confidence.

"Humph, I think not!"

"Well, what did they put the pattern in the book for, if they thought no one would want it?" he asked.

"Humph!" she said again. "Betsy, could you write me a

receipt for these toys?" Maddy was generous but business-like. She kept good records of her donations in order to make proper tax deductions.

"Certainly. I can't believe how many contributions you've made to the auction. More than anyone else, did you know that?"

"It's nothing. Got to do something with my hands to keep them busy."

Chapter Three

THE Knit Your Own series had been popular from the day two years ago Betsy first put *Knit Your Own Dog* out on one of the box shelves that divided the front of her shop from the back. Beside it she had put a knit boxer her boyfriend, Connor, had completed for her—Betsy wasn't an expert knitter, and the pattern had proved more difficult than she anticipated.

But later she had managed to knit her own rooster—she had an inexplicable fondness for chickens and found the pattern in *Knit Your Own Farm*, the latest in the series. The result was a red-feathered rooster with a typical arrogant look in his eye and a comb tipped dashingly to one side (an unintentional error—but she'd seen many a rooster with the same tilted comb). The rooster had brought on a little rush to buy the farm book, which was very gratifying.

But it was last summer that Bershada Reynolds had

come up with the idea of donating toy animals for an auction to raise funds to repair the elderly little brick building in Excelsior's lakefront park, the Commons. The building contained restrooms on one side and a snack bar on the other. The electrical wiring needed replacement, the tile on the snack bar floor was so badly cracked it was impossible to clean properly, and the restrooms needed new fixtures.

The fund-raiser committee was formed in September; by January donations had faded to a trickle, and the amount raised was insufficient.

Bershada was in Crewel World that August looking at a richly colored cross-stitch pattern leaflet dating back to 1983 of Santa unloading his sack under a tree decorated with apples, pears, and oranges—Betsy had found it in the basement when clearing a shelf. The pattern was on a table of half-price items. Bershada decided to buy it and was going over to select the floss she'd need for it when she saw Betsy putting the new knit rooster beside the boxer.

"Now that is a *chicken*!" she said.

"Isn't it nice?" agreed Betsy.

"You know what? That thing would sell for a lot of money. A lot of the animals in those books would sell very well. We could use the money for the Commons's snack bar repair fund."

"Are you suggesting I turn my needlework shop into a toy store?"

"No, of course not. But we could sell them at garage sales or even open a little shop temporarily. No, on second thought, that would probably cost more money than we'd raise. Hmmm—wait, I know, we could do an auction."

"Who could?" asked Betsy.

"We could—we should! We, the committee to repair the snack bar!"

"An auction?" said Betsy doubtfully.

"Sure! That's what we should do!" Bershada's boyfriend's cousin-in-law was an auctioneer, she said, a bright and funny man, and, even better, an exciting person to watch in action.

Betsy had been to a few auctions and knew how a good auctioneer could stir up the audience, persuading them to spend more than they planned on going in.

"What do you propose to auction off?" asked Betsy.

"What I said: these. Handmade stuffed toys," replied Bershada. She picked up the rooster and gestured at the books with it. "Here are dozens of patterns we can use. Plus, I've got some more at home. I've even got a pattern for a knit sock monkey."

"Are you serious?" Betsy asked.

"You bet I am. We've got some very talented knitters here in town."

"Well," Betsy said, "not a great number. If you're going to do a sale, you need a lot of things to sell. Now over here I've got another animal pattern book, called *Mini Knitted Safari*, by Sachiyo Ishii. Incredibly simple patterns, knit flat and then sewn into shape. Beginning knitters, especially children, love them. You could make a lot of them in a very short time."

"Yes, I've seen that book, but they're so small, I don't think they'd raise a lot of money auctioned one by one."

Another customer had come up behind Bershada. "That's a beautiful rooster," she said. "He's got a real rooster attitude." She raised her head, turned her mouth down, and gave an arrogant sniff. Then, laughing, she reached for a copy of *Knit Your Own Farm*. Paging through, she started making happy noises and nodding at the color photos of the animals: cow, pig, horse, goose with goslings, ram. Then she looked at the several pages of pattern that followed each photograph.

"I like these, but the patterns look kind of hard," she said.

Godwin was immediately at her side. "Oh, you can do these, absolutely, Shar," he said. "I'm thinking of starting a class."

"Well, all right, I'll wait for the class." She put the book back.

But Godwin took it down again and held it out to her. "I'll give you a hint you can use right now."

"A hint? What is it?"

"Write out the pattern. You're not an advanced knitter, but I bet you know most of the abbreviations used in knitting patterns. Like here." He opened the book and quickly searched a pattern. "See?" He pointed to a line in a pattern, K2tog. "It means?"

"Um, knit two together?"

"Right. So take a sheet of paper and write in so many words, knit two together. That's what I mean, go through the pattern you want to knit, writing the instructions. Translate those abbreviations. And also, when it simply says R-E-P, meaning repeat, go back and write out the instructions again—and again, as many times as the repeat calls for. It makes it easier to follow the pattern, plus helps get it clear in your head. I've seen your work, and if you use that method you can absolutely do these, even on your own."

"You think so?"

"Absolutely." He handed the book to her.

"And when you finish one of the animals," said Bershada, in imitation of Godwin's confident tone, "I hope you'll consider donating it to the auction."

And that was the start.

In late February, near the end of the run-up to the auction, Irene Potter came into Crewel World with a large cardboard box. Irene had a lifelong addiction to stitching, and some years back she had begun designing her own needlework patterns. She had an unusual imagination, and her pieces often had eerie, overwrought images. The art world began to take notice, and Irene became famous, which she felt explained her eccentric personality. In Irene's opinion, she had an "artistic temperament." That, she said, was why ordinary people didn't understand her work (though she failed to consider that perhaps her problem was that she didn't understand ordinary people).

"I heard about your wonderful fund-raiser," Irene said, her shiny dark eyes keen, and her graying black curls trembling with excitement, "and I just had to make my own little contribution."

She had put the box on the library table in the center of the room and briskly begun tearing off the tape that held it closed. The box was a cube about fourteen inches on a side. As she tore the last of the tape off, its sides fell open to reveal a terrifying dragon in bright greens and deep purples, with splashes of orange, red, and yellow. It seemed to be made mostly of a combination of knit and crochet laid over a wire form. The scales on its back and sides were outsize and lifted at the edges. It had a long, thin neck that sagged between its hunched shoulders and an unusually large head, which had stiff wires for whiskers. The creature was balanced on its kangaroo-like hind legs, which ended in big, sharply humped nails. The wings were tall and wide, of delicate crochet lace stiffened with starch, but the front claws on the small forepaws were out-of-proportion huge—and a short length of red silk floss hanging on one of them suggested a streamer of blood. The eyes were dull and stupid, and instead of lots of sharp teeth, it had rodent incisors, one of them gold. Its tail was very long, and there was a knot tied in the middle of it, as if it were there to remind the creature of something.

All its contradictions, its combinations of materials—wool and cotton yarns, silk and metallic flosses, thin silver wire, even bits of gold and silver foil—made it an intriguing puzzle to look at.

Then recognition set in. "Why, it's the Jabberwock!" Betsy exclaimed.

Irene looked a little shamefaced. "Is that okay?" she asked. "I did start with the old pen and ink drawing from *Through the Looking Glass*, but I thought I made enough changes that I wouldn't break any copyright laws."

Betsy said, "That doesn't matter, I'm sure it's long out of copyright. Anyway, you could say it's—what's the word?—an homage to the Jabberwock. And you say you want to donate this to the auction? Are you sure?"

"Do you think I shouldn't?"

"I think you should do whatever you want. But your work brings very high prices, so this piece will earn far and away more than anything else up for bids. When people hear an Irene Potter work will be in the auction, I'm sure some will come just for a chance to acquire it. To the auction committee, that's a good thing, a very good thing. But you do realize the money will go into the pot being created to repair the Commons's snack bar? This isn't going to be a sale for you."

This seemed an obvious point, but Betsy knew Irene didn't always understand how the real world worked.

But Irene nodded eagerly. "Yes, yes, I understand. That's why I want to donate it. I like that dear little snack bar, but I no longer go into the restrooms." Her small nose wrinkled. "Sometimes the floor is . . . wet."

Betsy nodded. "You're right, the fixtures are leaking. It's extremely generous of you to offer this wonderful work to the auction so they can make repairs." Betsy walked around to the other side of the table, noting that the creature's knotted tail ended in a tiny bit of red glass shaped like a heart. "This is amazing, Irene. Just wait till the auction committee sees it!"

BETSY called Bershada about the dragon, and she came in the next morning to see it. "Oh my goodness," she said, awed, and a little alarmed, touching it on one of its raised front claws.

"People are going to come just to bid on this," she agreed. "It's going to change the size and shape of the event. We'll adjust our advertising, of course, and expect to get people who want this piece."

"I wonder if you're not going to have to change the

venue," said Betsy. They'd planned to have the auction just up West Lake Street from her shop. Once a grocery store, now it was an art gallery that rented space for small events. "I've been to that gallery," said Betsy. "It looks as if maybe fifty people could sit down in there. That's adequate for what you initially expected, but you've been telling me how the number of expected attendees has grown. And now this! What if Irene's offering doubles that?"

"I'm sure it will—and from what we're collecting in toys, we underestimated our original number anyhow. I'm going to cancel our reservation, then go over to talk to Kari Beckel, who is facilities director at Mount Calvary. There's an atrium in their church hall that is spectacular—and if that proves too small, they have a full-size gym."

"Very wise," agreed Betsy.

"We were planning on raising a few thousand dollars, but now I'm thinking we should add a zero to that." She frowned and walked around the table, looking at the dragon from all angles. "I don't know whether we should offer Irene's piece first, to clear the room of the collectors, or hold it till last so maybe they'll also bid on the small pieces."

"I suggest last, because a lot of these toys are beautiful, made with lots of invention and talent."

Bershada turned around, eyes brightening. "Girl, you are right! That rooster of yours is amazing, and whoever gave us the feathered serpent deserves a special round of applause. Irene isn't the only talent in the area. So, sure, I'll recommend we offer Irene's Jabberwock last. I'm getting a real good feeling about this fund-raiser."

Chapter Four

Now the auction was tomorrow. The Monday Bunch decided that Maddy's entrance with her bag of knitted animals marked the end of its special Friday stitching session. They began putting away their needles and yarn, stacking the finished toys at the end of the table—except Doris, who took her unfinished lion home with her, promising to bring it back in the morning.

Bershada stayed after the others to sweep together the scattered excelsior and put it back in its drawstring bag.

"Maddy—Ms. O'Leary," she called, as Maddy was about to depart, "I want to thank you for changing your mind and agreeing to be honored with the other major donors at the auction tomorrow."

"About that," said Maddy, turning and approaching Bershada, "I've changed my mind again. I'd prefer to just sit in the audience with everyone else."

"Oh, but you can't!" said Bershada. "You agreed to sit with the other six people who are the top knitters donating toys!"

"I know, I know. But I just . . . can't. All those people, staring at me. I just can't." Her usual truculent expression was overridden by something like fear.

And suddenly Betsy gained a new insight into Maddy O'Leary, she of the rude tongue and haughty attitude: She was actually shy.

But Bershada persisted. "They won't be looking at you, they'll be watching Max Irwin in action, calling on people to raise their bids." She made an attempt to imitate an auctioneer's chant. "Hey, now here's a ten, a ten dollar, do I hear twelve, say a twelve, say a twelve!" She waved her arms as if pointing at individuals in a crowd and took a few steps back and forth. "Twelve, I've got twelve dollars—sold!" She continued in her usual tone of voice, "No one will be paying any attention to the seven of you, trust me!"

"Then why ask us to sit there?"

"Because we will introduce you at the start—"

"See?" interrupted Maddy.

"But that will take maybe three minutes, spread over seven people. That's what, ten seconds of focus on you? And remember, as I told you long ago, we're giving each of you a ball of yarn and a pair of knitting needles. You don't have to look back at the audience. You can concentrate on your knitting. I told you that, and you said okay, that you'd just sit there and knit."

Bershada fell silent, and Betsy bit her tongue. Maddy kept drawing a breath to say something, then didn't say it, but finally she tossed her head and said in a hard tone, "Very well, you're right, I did say I'd do it. But I'm not happy about it."

"I understand. And thank you. The amazing number of your contributions will go far to make this auction a success."

"Well, if I'd known you were going to make such a fuss, I wouldn't have given you anything." And on that ungracious note, Maddy turned on her heel and left the shop.

"That was well done!" said Betsy. "She's a difficult person, but you handled her beautifully!"

Godwin asked, "Bershada, are you all in a swivet about the auction tomorrow?" He liked finding and resurrecting old-fashioned terms.

"Swivet?"

"You know, nervous."

"Not now, because I've nailed Maddy to that chair at the front of the room."

"That was a great idea, giving those seven honorees balls of yarn and needles to keep their hands busy during the auction," said Betsy. "You and the rest of the committee are doing a fine job. This is going to be a real success."

"I sure hope so. We've been working hard. Thank you, by the way, for donating the yarn, needles, and little canvas bags to hold them in." Bershada had come up with the idea nearly a month ago, giving Betsy the task of calling the honorees to see what kind of yarn they wanted in their bags.

"The bags say CREWEL WORLD in nice big letters, so I'm calling it an advertising expense," said Betsy with a smile.

"Nevertheless, thank you," repeated Bershada. "Now I've got to run. We're setting up the chairs in the atrium today."

After she left, Godwin said, "Whew-ee, I'm glad I didn't get nominated to that committee! Way too much work!"

Chapter Five

BETSY had stayed after closing that Friday. The auction was tomorrow, Saturday, and she had some packing up to do. Over the past few weeks, Betsy had filled two big cardboard boxes with over a hundred knitted animals. She brought them up from the basement to the front of the shop. She had put some of the best ones on display in the shop and was now going around collecting the last of them and putting them with the others in a row in front of the boxes.

The Irene Potter Jabberwock piece had been taken into custody by the auction committee and was never on display in Betsy's shop.

Other stores in town had been collecting toys made of fabric and, in one case, wood. There was a secondary movement afoot for many of the toys' new owners to donate them again to hospitals, day care centers, and charities. Betsy was pleased that Crewel World had outpaced them in donations.

She had just put the last toy, a giraffe, on the table when the door to the shop sounded its music. The door had been left unlocked in anticipation of the arrival of someone from the committee to pick them up. Betsy turned and saw Bershada. With her was a short man of stocky build with a fringe of yellow hair around a bald head. He was wearing white running shoes, pale blue jeans, and a blue blazer over a tan T-shirt, and he was smiling broadly. He looked around the shop with interest, taking in the many spinner racks of floss, the long white cabinet full of needlework books and gadgets, the wall hangings of finished needlework projects, and then returned to Betsy. He was still grinning, prepared to be pleased to meet her.

Bershada said, "Betsy, this is Max Irwin, the auctioneer I've been telling you about."

Betsy put her hand out. "I'm pleased to meet you, Mr. Irwin."

"Max, call me Max," he said, taking her hand in a warm grip. His voice was rough-edged, probably from years of loud and fast talking.

"All right. Max. I hope Bershada has prepared you properly for this auction. It's kind of different from the usual."

Max laughed. "Ma'am, they're all different. No two alike. That's what keeps me going, the variety." He gestured toward Bershada. "This kind lady knows her stuff. She has her eye on the goal and takes dead aim at it. This is going to be a great auction."

Betsy said, "I hope you're right. I guess I'm a little nervous, worried they might end up selling all these beautiful toys for a quarter apiece. People have been working very hard on them."

Bershada said, "Trust Max. That is not going to happen."

"That's right," declared Max, one hand on his chest, elbow out. "Trust me."

"Max wanted an advance look at what we're auctioning off," said Bershada, "so I brought him here."

"All right," said Betsy. She gestured at the toys she'd been picking up, about a dozen of them. They were standing in a row on the library table. "Here are some of the best examples. I've been using them as displays in the shop, both to encourage customers to knit and contribute some, and to sell the books of instruction I have in stock to make them."

Max went to the table and picked up Godwin's leopard. "This is nice, real pretty. I bet it took some talent to make it."

"Yes, it did. My store manager knit it. I'm thinking of bidding on it myself so I can keep it on display next to *Knit Your Own Zoo*, the book he got the pattern from."

Bershada reached around Max to pick up the red rooster. "Oh, I think you should bid on this—it's more of an eye-catcher."

"No, I'm going to knit another one. It'll be easier to talk about it to a customer if I've done two of them."

Max eyed her sideways. "You did this?"

"Yes. I find I have to at least try to work the kinds of patterns I'm selling, so I can answer questions about them. But Godwin's my real expert; he can do just about any kind of needlework."

"Where is this paragon?" asked Max, looking around.

"Gone for the day. He and his partner are going to a concert in Saint Paul, so I let him cut out early."

"Ah," said Max. He picked up a pair of very small penguins. "I don't think these come from the same book as the leopard."

"No, they're from a book called *Mini Knitted Safari*. And there are other books by the same author, too. Quite a few children knitted toys designed by her."

"Maybe we should auction these in lots," he said.

Bershada said, "My son Chaz made a wooden model of the Ark, and I'll finish knitting a figure of Noah tonight. You're right, and there are duplicates of many of these tiny animals, so I'm going to put a group of pairs into one lot with the Ark and Noah."

"Wow, what a great idea!" said Betsy. "Be sure to tell Mount Calvary about that. They might want it for their Sunday school."

"Yes, that's a terrific idea." said Max. "Divide some of the rest of these little bitty ones into lots, so maybe others will get the same idea."

Bershada said to Betsy, "See? I told you he was good!"

Betsy said, "And maybe I can hire Chaz to make me an Ark and sell me the pattern. That should sell more copies of the books—the author has others in addition to that *Safari* one." Betsy was always on the lookout for ways to improve sales.

Chapter Six

MOUNT Calvary Lutheran Church was on the southwest side of Excelsior. The church was relatively new, but not so modern it couldn't be recognized as a church at a glance. It was built in Gothic style, of pale stone, with lots of parking in back and multiple entrances to the large hall.

The atrium was large and beautiful, circular in design, with offices, classrooms, a hallway to the kitchen, and another to the restrooms off it. There were lots of tall windows, and there was a big skylight in its slightly domed ceiling. The floor was light-colored tile, currently covered with padded folding chairs in a crescent pattern, facing a lectern. The lectern was flanked by two pairs of long tables, each pair heaped with toy animals, mostly knit, some crocheted, several made of wood.

On a small, long-legged table by itself was a glass case, and inside it was Irene Potter's strange vision of the Jabberwock. Behind the lectern and tables was a single row of seven folding chairs.

The doors to the hall opened at 1:15 p.m. People filing in for the auction were directed to a desk near the rear of the atrium to sign in and receive a deep yellow cardboard paddle with a bold black number printed on it. Most of the people signing in took a detour to get a closer look at the toys and the dragon before finding their seats.

The auction was scheduled to begin at 2:30 p.m. At 1:30, a musical duo consisting of a husband and wife playing an oboe and a double bass fiddle came in and performed a mix of music as odd as their pairing: some folk, some Renaissance, some original compositions, a couple of Irish jigs. The audience applauded, though more thinly as the hour approached for the auction to begin.

At 2:25 p.m. the duo quit and left the room as a group of two men and five women filed out of one of the hallways near the tables and lectern. The new arrivals were wearing dressy casual clothing—good shirts and blazers for the men, skirts and fancy blouses or sweaters for the women. Maddy O'Leary, in the middle of the row, wore her usual wool suit, this one a purple so dark it was almost black. Each of them carried a small, bright green canvas bag with the CREWEL WORLD logo on it and a pair of bamboo knitting needles poking out the top.

They paused in front of the row of chairs, turned to face the audience, then sat down. The audience, which had fallen silent at their entrance, murmured in bemusement.

Bershada Reynolds came out of the same hallway and stepped up to the lectern. "Ladies and gentlemen," she said, "these seven people"—she half turned and made a wide gesture with one arm—"are responsible for nearly half of the items we are auctioning off here today. In fact, one of them—who does not want me to identify her, thank you, Maddy—knit twenty-six toys all by herself."

The audience burst into applause. Maddy, seated in the middle of the row, kept her head down but blushed furiously.

"Now," continued Bershada, "I would like to introduce you to our auctioneer, Max Irwin."

She got no further.

"Hello, hello, hello, and welcome!" bellowed a man's hoarse voice, and Max came striding out from the same hallway, with his arms wide and a big grin on his face. He was wearing a red T-shirt under a brown blazer, blue jeans, and red high-top canvas shoes. "Wow, what a great turnout!" he continued, stepping behind the lectern. "Must be three hundred people here."

The audience was slow to quiet down, so he slid the on-off button of the microphone back and forth a few times, making it pop, and suddenly his voice was a deafening roar: "Can you hear me now?" The audience yelled in protest, and he leaped back in mock astonishment. He stepped forward and said in a much quieter voice, "I guess so!"

The audience laughed, its attention fully captured.

"Are you ready for a chance to do some good for Excelsior?" he challenged them.

"Yeah!" replied many voices. "Right on!" said one, and "Bring it!" said another.

"Are you ready for some excitement?" he asked, louder.

"Yeah!" came the reply, also louder.

"Wanna have some *fun*?"

"*Yeah, yeah!*" they replied, at top volume now, and somebody whistled.

"Well, all right, let's get down to it. Let's raise a little money! Here are the rules: My assistant, Frankie—Hey, where is Frankie? Frankie? Frankie! Where are you? Come on out here!"

An extremely attractive young woman wearing tight jeans and an oversize red sweater came out from the hallway making such elaborate apologetic gestures to him and the audience that they laughed.

"Where you been?" he demanded.

She glanced at the audience and came to whisper in his ear.

"Oh," he said, immediately mollified. The audience laughed again. "Okay. You ready to get to work?"

She nodded and smiled at the audience.

"Again, here are the rules: She's gonna hand me one toy at a time! If you want it, you hold up your paddle"—he held up a hand, palm forward—"and call out your bid. We're taking bids in dollar amounts only—no fifty-cent raises! There are people around this room—spotters—who will call my attention to your bid! Somebody else wants it more, hold up your paddle and call out a higher number! Highest bidder gets the toy! At the end of the whole shebang, bring your payment to that nice young lady right over there!" He turned sideways to point with both hands at Bershada, who was standing at the far end of the left-hand table. She held up a notepad and pen in one hand and pointed to a gray cash box in front of her. "You pay her, she'll give you the toy!" he continued. "We take cash, checks, and credit or debit cards! Got it? Everybody ready? Then let's have us an *auction*!"

The audience, roused by his words, cheered and waved their paddles.

His assistant moved swiftly to the table on his right and grabbed a toy. It was a gray felt elephant with a cross-stitched red-patterned blanket on its back, its trunk raised gracefully to its forehead.

"Who's got the money, who's got the money, how much, how much, say ten dollar, ten dollar," he chanted rapidly.

A paddle went up. "Five dollars!" shouted the owner, a man with white hair. A tall, thin man with red hair standing in the aisle nearby pointed at him.

"Five dollar, got five dollar, who'll make it ten, make it ten, five dollar, say ten, say ten," chanted Max.

"Ten!" called a woman near the front.

Max instantly pointed at her. "Ho! Ten dollar, make it fifteen, fifteen dollar, fifteen, I got ten, make it fifteen!"

He was talking so rapidly his audience barely caught one word in three or four—those who had never heard auctioneer chanting before looked around, totally baffled. Then, one by one, they realized they didn't have to hear every word, just the numbers. The lower number was the current bid; the higher what he wanted to hear as a raise. The paddles started coming up faster, in greater numbers, and a kind of fever began to grow among members of the audience.

The elephant went for thirty-five dollars, a wooden camel on wheels went for fifty, and a knit pig for seventy-two. The Noah's Ark went for a hundred and twenty-five.

Chapter Seven

IT took Maddy a very few minutes to realize that no one was looking at her; everyone was focused on that fast-talking auction man. She pulled the bamboo knitting needles out of the bag and then the ball of dark blue merino wool. Was it darker than she remembered? No matter, it was just something to keep her hands busy while she and the others sat on display.

Ugh, *display*. What an awful label to put on a human being!

Like that strangely beautiful dragon on display in the glass case over there, gorgeous scales and delicate wings—and stupid face. What must Irene have been thinking? And what a peculiar name on the tag leaning against the case: JABBERWOCK, it read. What did that mean? Maddy had somehow never read *Through the Looking Glass*. *Jabberwock.* Perhaps it was an Asian fry pan talking nonsense?

Her lips quirked just a little in amusement. She was fond of elaborate puns.

But never mind, she was becoming too aware of the audience and the gibberish Mr. Irwin was shouting at them. She swiftly cast on twenty-one stitches. She was going to do the plaited basket stitch. It wasn't hard, but it took concentration. The result would be attractive, looking like the yarn was woven, two threads by two threads.

She started by knitting twice, then skipped the next stitch and put the right-hand needle behind the second stitch, knitting it but not taking it off the needle, instead bringing the right-hand needle around to the front and knitting it, then taking both stitches off. She continued like this until the last stitch, which she knitted, then turned to begin the next row. She purled two. Then, as before, she purled the second stitch behind the left needle, brought the needle around to purl the first stitch, then pulled both off.

The noise Max and his audience were making faded as her concentration increased.

It took a few rows for the pattern to become apparent, but there it was, perfect! She felt energized, and ignoring the racket going on in front of her, she fell to her task, her fingers moving deftly. In a short while she had nearly four inches of knitting completed.

Her hands began to move even more swiftly, and she went from warm satisfaction to pride to something like exultation. She could feel her heart beating rapidly, and her hands moved faster and faster.

The auctioneer's rapid chant and the eager shouts of the bidders, which she had been unable to completely ignore, now seemed only to increase her excitement. Her breath came more rapidly, and her head started to ache. She began to make mistakes in her knitting as her concentration faltered. She took a big breath, trying to calm herself, but it didn't work.

Her fingers closed on the yarn, and her heart seemed about to explode in her chest. The pain in her head was unendurable. This was wrong, something was wrong. She tried to stand, to call for help, but all her joints were stiff, and her tongue would not obey. She fell, and darkness came over her.

Chapter Eight

MAX'S fast chant and the audience's excited response kept everyone's attention from Maddy's distress. Not until she tried to rise and instead fell to the floor did a few notice and exclaim at her.

"What? What?" Max interrupted himself to look around and see her folded in her wool suit in front of her chair. "Hey, what the devil?" He started for her, then turned back to the audience. "Is there a doctor in the house?"

Meanwhile, Bershada ran to her, stooped, and tried to roll her onto her back. But Maddy was rigid, as if having a seizure. She was not breathing. Bershada was about to call for someone to dial 911 when she saw that more than half the audience had cell phones to their ears. And five people were running toward her. She was not surprised to hear three of them say they were doctors, one say she was an ER nurse, and one declare himself an emergency tech. In less than a minute they had Maddy, now gone limp, flat on her back and were beginning CPR. Bershada got out of their way.

In less than eight minutes a police officer and an emergency crew arrived to the accompaniment of sirens. The techs took over the CPR. They fitted an oxygen mask to Maddy's face, scooped her onto a wheeled stretcher, and took her out.

Bershada conferred with Max while the audience talked among themselves. Finally, Max went to the lectern to bring order to the room.

"All right, all right, let's settle down!" he shouted. "Please, come to order! Come to order!" The audience slowly fell silent. "I am reasonably certain Ms. Maddy will be okay, even though she scared us all half to death just now," he said. "Thanks be to the quick action taken by members of this audience to keep her going until help arrived. Let's give them a hand!" He started to clap and was enthusiastically joined by the audience.

Max let it go on until it just started to fade. "Okay!" he shouted. "All right! Now, are we ready to get back to business?"

"Yeah! Yes! Okay! Carry on!" cheered members of the audience, and the rest applauded.

"We were taking bids on this magnificent leopard. Ho, who's got the money, I got forty, forty, forty, how about fifty, I want fifty, how about fifty, I got forty, you gimme fifty, I got forty, forty—"

"Sixty!" shouted the man who hadn't gotten the elephant.

"Here you go, sixty, sixty, I got sixty, gimme eighty—"

"Eighty!" called a woman dressed all in yellow.

"Eighty-five!" shouted the man.

"Ho! Eighty-five, now I got eighty-five, can I get a hundred, can I get—"

"One hundred!" came the call from the back of the room.

"Whoo!" cheered someone.

"One hundred!" shouted Max. "One hundred, a hundred, a hundred, now looking for a hundred and fifty, one hundred fifty, got a hundred, looking for one hundred fifty—"

"A hundred and fifty!" cried the woman in yellow.

"Yes!" cheered someone.

"One fifty, got one fifty, got one fifty, do I hear two? Two hundred, two hundred, one seventy-five, I got one fifty, one fifty, can I have one seventy five, one seventy five? One fifty, one fifty, lookin' for one seventy-five, one seventy-five."

But he looked in vain. "Can I get one sixty, one sixty, one sixty, I got one fifty, got one fifty, got one fifty, looking for one sixty, one sixty. All in, all done? One fifty, all done?"

"Two hundred!" called the man in the back of the room.

"Two fifty!" the woman in yellow responded instantly.

"Yowser!" shouted someone—the same someone who'd cheered before. It sounded suspiciously like Godwin, sitting in the row facing the audience with the other champion knitters.

"Yo! Two fifty, two fifty, I got two fifty, how about three, do I hear three, three hundred, two fifty, two fifty, two fifty, do I hear two seventy-five, two seventy-five, I got two fifty, two fifty, lookin' for two seventy-five, two fifty, two fifty—" There was a brief pause. "Two fifty, all done, all in? Two fifty, I got two fifty. All in, all done? Sold! Two hundred and fifty dollars! Paddle number forty-seven. Thank you, ladies and gentlemen!"

The audience applauded. Bershada made a note.

Max's assistant picked up the knit fruit bat, saw what it was, and dropped it, pulling her hands up and back in disgust.

"No, no!" called someone. "Let's see it!"

"Yeah, bring it!"

"What is it?" asked someone else.

"Lemme see," ordered Max, and his assistant very gingerly picked it up by one wing, her face reflecting her reluctance.

"Hey, lookit this!" Max shouted, holding it up. He adjusted his grip so each hand was holding a wing and it was spread wide.

"Ewwwww!" went half the audience. The other half laughed, and someone called, "One dollar!"

"Two dollars!" said someone else.

"Seven dollars!" said a third, and they were off. With Max urging them on, Phil's fruit bat sold for seventy-five dollars.

The auction, back in full swing, continued for another hour. At the end, Irene Potter's amazing dragon was brought forward.

"Five hundred!" shouted someone before Max could say anything, and the bidding built swiftly from there until the creature finally topped out at five thousand seven hundred dollars.

Chapter Nine

"DEAD?" murmured Betsy. "Oh, but she can't be! They did CPR right away, and the emergency people got here quickly—she can't be dead!"

Betsy was standing in the parking lot beside her car. Jill had seen her, waved to get her attention, and now was standing close to her, talking in a low voice.

"She was dead on the gurney," said Jill. "You know how nowadays they can bring the freshly dead back to life, at least for a little while—well, not in this case. There was no obvious cause, so they'll do an autopsy."

"I thought it was a stroke."

"Did you, Doctor Devonshire?"

Betsy blushed and shrugged. "Just a layman's opinion."

"Probably as good as mine."

A voice called, harsh and alarmed, "Hey! Hey, anyone!" Jill and Betsy whirled to look toward the church hall, where Max was standing shouting at them. "Hey! Is there a doctor still around?"

"What's the matter?" called Jill, starting for him, Betsy on her heels.

"We got a man sick in here!"

Jill went through the door into the hall. Betsy stopped to ask, "Who is it? What do you mean, sick?"

"Sick to his stomach, big headache. He's sitting on the floor. I don't know who it is. He was helping pick up after the auction."

Betsy put her fingers to her lips. Connor had volunteered to stay and help put things away.

A woman, white-haired, thin, short, put her hands on Betsy's shoulders. "Excuse me, let me by, I'm a doctor." She had been one of those who had rushed to help Maddy.

Betsy hastily stepped into the hall. "Sorry," she said, "sorry."

Without replying, the woman hurried by her.

Betsy followed, half afraid of what she was going to discover. To her dismay, it *was* Connor, sitting bent forward on the floor in front of the row of chairs where the honorees had been placed. His face was red, distorted by pain. Jill and another woman were standing nearby, and the woman doctor was kneeling beside him, with one arm around his shoulders and the other taking his pulse. There was a towel across his knees, another under his feet.

As Betsy watched, he picked up the towel from his lap and wiped his face with it. She ran to him. "What's the matter? What happened?" she asked.

"Dunno," said Connor, forcing the words out. "I was

folding the chairs," he gestured to his right, where half the row had been folded and leaned against the wall. "Saw someone's knitting . . ." He stopped to retch, then wiped his mouth with the towel. "God, my head!"

Betsy looked around and saw the knitting, about seven inches of plaited basket weave stitch in dark blue. She recognized the yarn; it was Maddy's. She picked it up. Maddy had been about halfway across a row. The last two or three rows were a mess, hardly recognizable as a pattern.

"Look at this, Jill," she said, holding out the knitting. "I think Maddy did have a stroke."

"Maybe, maybe," said Jill, who was still focused on Connor and the doctor.

Betsy picked up the ball and wound the yarn onto it, following the unspooled yarn to the bag under a chair, and stuffed the ball and knitting into it. The fingers of her right hand felt odd, and she rubbed them with her thumb. "Oof," she said. Her heart was beating fast. "Oof," she said again, and put her hand to her forehead, which had begun to ache.

Connor said, "I was winding the yarn back on the ball, which had rolled away, and all of a sudden I got this headache."

"Jill," said Betsy, dropping Maddy's bag. "Jill!"

Jill started at the sound of her friend's voice. "What is it?" she said. "Oh my gosh, oh my gosh. Here, Betsy, come with me."

She helped Betsy get to her feet and hustled her off to the restroom, so she could wash her hands. Then she had Betsy wash them again. And again.

"Wow," said Betsy. "Wow." She splashed cold water on

her face, which was very pink, and dried it and her hands with paper towels. Her hands felt normal, but her pulse still seemed a bit rapid.

"What happened?" asked Jill. "What were you doing when you started feeling like this?"

"All I did was pick up Maddy's knitting and wrap loose yarn around the ball and put it in the bag. Then my fingers started tingling and my heart started beating a hundred miles an hour."

"Did you touch anything else? Drink something?"

"Nuh-uh. Wow. Whew! But I'm feeling better now. How's Connor? Can we get back to Connor?"

"Sure, let's do that."

When they came out of the restroom, they saw Connor, over his objections, being walked out to an emergency vehicle by the doctor. "I'm all right," he kept saying, "See? I'm feeling much better now."

But his face was still red, and he was walking with a stiff gait unlike his usual smooth one.

"Wait a minute," called Jill, and she ran to the bright green canvas bag into which Betsy had pushed Maddy's needlework. She picked it up carefully by its string handle. She brought it to the doctor, hanging it over her fingers, and said, "Maddy is dead, Connor is sick, and Betsy had a bad reaction, all because the three of them handled the contents of this bag. Give it to someone who can tell us what the problem with it is."

Chapter Ten

CONNOR was treated and released the same day. "I haven't been taken that sick for a long time," he said, as he got into Betsy's car. "Do they know what did it to me?"

"No, not yet," said Betsy. "But they're pretty sure it's the yarn she was knitting with."

"The yarn? That's odd. Didn't you give the same yarn to everyone?"

"No, Bershada and I asked each one of the knitters what kind they wanted. Maddy's the only one who picked the dark blue merino. Maybe I'd better pull the rest of that yarn until we find out what's wrong with it."

"Do you think it could be the needles instead of the yarn?" Connor asked.

"Nnno," she drawled, thinking. "Everyone got the same size bamboo needles from the same box. Besides, it was the yarn you and I were handling, not the needles."

Connor nodded. "That's true. So yes, you should pull the merino."

THE following Monday, the Bunch was in session, and the participants spent a few minutes talking about Maddy's strange passing. Betsy, as crack amateur sleuth, was asked for an opinion, but she said she didn't know what to think. Phil suggested it was a sudden allergy to wool brought on by all that knitting Maddy had done in aid of the auction, but his theory was voted down. No one else had any ideas, so the members dropped the subject and began working on needlework projects—any kind but knitting, as they'd all had their fill and more in the last few weeks.

Fulsome congratulations went around to all those who contributed: to Godwin, for the amazing price his knit leopard had brought; and again to Godwin, for winning a place among the honorees who had knit the most toys; to Betsy for contributing time, effort, and material to the auction; but most of all to Bershada, whose idea it was, and who ran the committee organized to pull it off.

Betsy said modestly she hadn't done all that much, Godwin smiled and allowed that the leopard had come out rather well, but Bershada just sat and raked in the accolades, secure in the knowledge that these people didn't know the half of it.

Just then the door chime broke into "I Want to Be Happy" and Jill came in. She was not a frequent attendee of the Monday Bunch anymore, with three young children and a part-time job at the police department (administrative assistant to the chief, a job she shared with another woman). She had her stitching with her and was brimming with grim news.

"What is it?" demanded Godwin before she had even said a word.

"The preliminary autopsy report on Maddy is back. It appears she was poisoned with nicotine."

Everyone at the table stared at her in surprise.

"Nicotine?" said Emily. "You mean she smoked herself to death?"

"No, nicotine was found on the yarn she was knitting with at the auction."

"Ick," said Emily. "I hate the smell of cigarettes. But how did it get from the yarn into her stomach?"

"It didn't go into her stomach. It went through her fingers into her bloodstream. You can absorb nicotine through the skin. When she handled the yarn while knitting, she absorbed a fatal dose."

"Then how come people who smoke cigarettes don't die from it getting on their fingers?" asked Phil. He looked around the table. "I smoked for over twenty years, and so did just about everyone I knew back in the day. Many's the time we stayed up all night, playing cards, talking, drinking beer, and smoking like chimneys. Didn't kill any of us. Not right then, I mean. Lung cancer might've got one or two of us, but I don't know, I haven't seen many of them in a long time." He sighed and looked a little sad about that.

Jill said, "I guess the paper wrapping protected your skin. Besides, tobacco leaves aren't pure nicotine, it takes a special laboratory process to extract the nicotine."

Betsy said, "You mean, nicotine all by itself is a poison?"

"That's right," replied Jill. "Someone poured pure liquid nicotine over the ball of yarn in Maddy's bag, and by handling it, she absorbed a lethal amount through the skin of her hands. It doesn't take much. It's an ingredient in insecticides; a squirt or two will kill a whole nest of yellow jackets. I know, I've done it."

"If liquid nicotine is so dangerous, why can you buy bottles of it in those e-cigarette stores?" asked Alice, a senior woman with a deep voice and rather a lot of chin. She was crocheting a fluffy blue prayer shawl for her church.

Godwin asked, surprised, "How do you know about bottles of nicotine?"

"There was a news segment about it back around Christmas. The bottles come in different sizes and different strengths. And they said even one small bottle can kill a child who drinks it—they come in tempting delicious flavors, apparently. I was quite appalled."

But Phil said, "I think those bottles aren't pure nicotine, they're diluted. And at least the smokers are not getting all that tar and other things you find in tobacco leaf. E-cigarettes are a lot safer than the real thing."

"No, they're not!" said Alice, surprised. "It's the nicotine that causes lung cancer."

"No, it's the tar," retorted Phil, equally surprised.

"I think it's the formaldehyde," volunteered Godwin.

"Formaldehyde!" said Doris. "In cigarettes?"

"Absolutely," said Godwin.

"What, do they embalm the tobacco leaves before they chop them into cigarettes?"

Godwin leaned sideways, laughing. "That's good, Dorie!"

"Surely you're joking; there isn't any formaldehyde in cigarettes," said Emily.

"Oh, there are all kinds of chemicals in cigarettes," said Godwin. "Nitrogen oxide, benzopyrene, hydrogen cyanide, and ammonia are just a few, besides formaldehyde."

Jill, meanwhile, had sat down at the table and brought out a project: a cross-stitched inspirational motto ornamented with a big, elaborate feather. It read, "She took a Leap of FAITH and grew her Wings on the way down." Done all in shades of blue, Jill had bought it in Betsy's shop as a kit.

"Has Joe Mickels stopped in to talk to you, Betsy?" she asked.

"Joe? Why on earth would he want to talk to me?"

"Didn't you hear what I said? The poison that killed poor Maddy was nicotine."

"What has that got to do with Joe Mickels?"

"Right around Christmas he bought a little chain of e-cigarette stores."

Betsy stared at her. "He did?"

Godwin said, "Why didn't we hear about it?"

Valentina said, "I heard he'd gotten into e-cigarettes, that he'd bought a store that sells them."

"Where did you hear that?" asked Jill.

"At the Leipold's store. Somebody was smoking one in there, said he'd bought the outfit to do it with at Joe's new store in Uptown." Uptown was an artsy neighborhood of Minneapolis famous for its night clubs, sophisticated shops, and ethnic restaurants.

"Oh my God," said Doris.

"But he wouldn't—he just wouldn't!" said Emily.

But Betsy was remembering some years back, when she and Jill stood in Joe's Excelsior office while he ranted viciously about another murdered woman, saying that if he'd known then what he knew now, he would have killed her himself. She looked at Jill, wondering if she was remembering that, too. But Jill had her deadpan cop face on, so Betsy couldn't tell what she was thinking.

"Wait a minute," said Phil. "I've looked at those bottles of nicotine they sell, and like Alice said, they all smell like candy or flowers, plus they look thick, like syrup. How could Maddy use yarn that smelled like strawberries and stuck to her fingers?"

"There!" said Emily. "See? There!"

"Why are you so hot to defend Joe Mickels?" asked Godwin. "He is not a nice man."

"He is a sad man. I think he's lonesome and doesn't know what to do about it."

"My goodness, Emily," said Alice. "Where on earth did you get an idea like that?"

"I saw him the other day—he didn't see me—just sitting in his car, and his face was sad, so sad. I almost went over to him, but he drove away. Honest, he was sad!"

"When was this?" Jill asked.

Emily thought briefly. "I'm not sure. Maybe a week ago? Or longer?"

"Before Harry Whiteside was murdered? Or after?"

Emily thought some more. "Before. I'm sure it was before."

"Maybe it was around the time he found out that Maddy

won the bidding war for that property on Water Street," suggested Godwin.

"I hope so," said Betsy. "Much better that he was sad, not angry."

There was a thoughtful silence.

Chapter Eleven

"WELL, well, well," murmured Detective Sergeant Mike Malloy, looking over a photocopy of a single document laid in the center of his small desk in a back room of the Excelsior Police Department. He spoke to himself—the desk pushed up against his was unoccupied. Elton Marsh, the second investigator in the department, was taking a day off to attend a school concert his youngest daughter had a solo part in.

The document was a record of the sale of three e-cigarette stores to one Joseph Alan Mickels on receipt of "one dollar and other good and valuable considerations." Malloy had run across that phrasing before; it virtually always meant more money.

Malloy wasn't interested in how much more money; he was interested in the fact of the e-cigarettes. His fellow investigator was a smoker, and it had taken an order from the chief to get him to take a smoker's break outside the building. The problem now was, he was a heavy smoker and was frequently gone during the working day for five to ten minutes at a time. In Malloy's never humble opinion, he had just about gone from full-time to part-time employment and ought to be given a commensurate cut in pay.

Apparently the chief thought so, too, because the instant e-cigarettes appeared on the market, Elton had been persuaded to transfer his addiction to them and began smoking at his desk again. He and Malloy exchanged research on them, and Malloy was forced to admit that e-cigarettes were not a source of the tar that instigated lung cancer, and that what a "vaper" exhaled was merely scented water vapor.

"That's why we call it 'vaping,'" Elton had said smugly.

The only concession Malloy had managed to get from Elton was a switch from scented nicotine to the unscented variety. Filling the office with the smell of wintergreen or oranges was distracting and unprofessional, in Malloy's never, *ever* humble opinion.

Maddy O'Leary had been killed by nicotine. It had been absorbed through the skin on the palms and fingers of her hands—shocking to learn that nicotine could be absorbed through the skin. It could be absorbed quickly, too, judging by the way Connor Sullivan had gotten so doggone sick just from handling the yarn while helping clean up after the auction.

Nicotine is never a natural ingredient in yarn. So someone put it there. Who? And when? And why?

When investigating crimes against a person, Malloy knew you began with the victim. Why would someone have wanted Maddy O'Leary dead? She was a wealthy businesswoman, somewhere in her fifties—accounts differed as to her age. She was tall, five seven and a half, gray haired, with a robust build—one sixty-eight, the ME reported. She had been widowed after a brief marriage, had no children, no near relatives in the area.

Several people he'd talked to indicated she'd had a strong A-type personality that included a quick temper. She was the widow of a wealthy attorney and had immersed herself in business and become very successful at it.

Maddy's success came from her skill in real estate. She always appeared to know what the competition was up to and took quick action to counter them. She had a reputation for sharp business dealings but hadn't broken any laws—or at least was too sharp to be caught doing something illegal. She was not a drunk or a doper. Once a year she took a two-week vacation, but nobody knew where she went. Seven years ago she had left her Methodist church and formally become a Baptist. She was very generous toward her church and various charities, a surprising discovery few knew of, as she never spoke of it to anyone.

And she liked to knit. That last bit of information came from Betsy Devonshire, who said she had donated more knitted toys to that fatal auction event than anyone else. Who would have thought?

People were complicated. That's why Malloy preferred the kind of crime committed by professional—or at least semi-amateur—criminals. There, motives were clear and simple. Plus, it was relatively easy to convince a pro to confess or at least drop a dime on the perp. These amateurs lied when they didn't have to, or couldn't get their facts straight when they were trying to be truthful, or refused to learn the rules of the game. Malloy strayed from his train of thought. Funny how the expression "drop a dime"—to make a phone call offering a solid clue about the perpetrator of a crime—was still around, when public phones, which once charged a dime to make a call, now charged fifty cents if you could find one at all.

But back to the subject at hand. Who hated Maddy O'Leary enough to think up that ridiculous—and successful—plan to kill her?

Because it *was* ridiculous! Pouring a poison on knitting yarn so she'd absorb it through her skin! Why not just take a hunting rifle and ambush her from behind a tree, or use a handgun and shoot her from your car as she walked down the street? Or, like the unfortunate Harry Whiteside, lay in wait in his house to knock him on the head?

Say, could there be a connection between the two murders? O'Leary and Whiteside were bidding against each other—and Joe Mickels—for that property on Water Street. And Malloy's fellow investigators in Wayzata thought that maybe the mess in the Whiteside house wasn't what you'd expect a burglar to leave. It was more like vandalism; there was anger, even hatred, in the destruction inside that house.

Also, O'Leary hadn't paid off on her bid yet—she'd just won the war. Did her company inherit the right to buy the property? Or an heir? Or did the bidding reopen as a result of her death? Or, perhaps, was the property offered to the last person standing in the bidding war: Joe Mickels?

Mickels, notorious for his violent temper; Mickels, the recent purchaser of three e-cigarette stores. Hmmm . . .

Malloy reached for his phone.

Chapter Twelve

BETSY was in her shop sighing over a bill that had come in, because it seemed to be charging her a whole lot of money for items she hadn't ordered—nor had they been delivered. Godwin was standing beside her making angry sounds.

"They did this once before, remember?" said Godwin. "There's another shop named Crewel World, in Iowa, and this vendor sent them an order we had made and billed us for it. This time they sent us a bill for some things they ordered. It's funny how they don't know that IA and MN are two different states."

"Maybe they think we're a chain, like McDonald's."

"Even so, if the Excelsior McDonald's orders a truckload of buns, I don't think the Hopkins McDonald's wants to pay for it. Give me that bill, I'll go call them."

"Thank you."

He was well into his tirade at the hapless accounts

manager and so didn't pay any attention to the door's "Hello, Dolly!" announcement of someone coming in.

Betsy looked up and saw it was Joe Mickels. His normal blustering demeanor was gone; he appeared uncomfortable and diffident. She had been wondering if he would dare stop in to talk to her. Apparently he did dare, but he didn't like it. Given their unhappy history, his attitude wasn't surprising.

Betsy put on her blandest expression and said, "Good afternoon, Mr. Mickels. How may I help you?"

He took a deep breath and walked to her desk, a solid chunk of a man, but not above five foot five, with a pigeon breast, a proud beak of a nose, nineteenth-century sideburns, and bushy eyebrows nearly hiding sharp blue eyes. Yet still she was struck by how much of a facade this bold front now appeared. Normally, he was strength and aggression to the bone.

"Good afternoon," he croaked quietly, then cleared his throat and tried again. "Good afternoon!" he barked assertively.

"Is there something I can do for you?" she asked.

"I hope so," he said, and it was a confession. "Sergeant Michael Malloy has been talking to me—almost accusing me."

"Of what, Mr. Mickels?" She was not surprised that Malloy had gotten around to Joe.

"You know, I think, that I own three e-cigarette stores."

"Yes, I had heard that."

"And you know Ms. O'Leary was poisoned to death with nicotine."

"Yes, I had heard that, too."

He drew a deep, angry breath through that nose. "Well?" he demanded.

"Well, what, Mr. Mickels?" She was having trouble hiding her smile.

And he realized that she was enjoying this. He turned on his heel and started for the door. Then, just as she began to regret baiting him, he thought better of it and turned back.

They said, simultaneously, "I'm sorry."

And they both grimaced.

She said, "Obviously you are here to ask me to get Mike Malloy off your back, either by providing you with an unbreakable alibi or by proving someone else guilty."

"Yes," he said, nodding, relieved. "I'm prepared to pay any expenses you may incur."

"That's generous of you. But please be aware that this . . . talent I have for discovering the truth behind a crime is just that: a search for the truth. If I agree to look into the case, it's not going to be entirely on your behalf. I'm not going to be out to clear you but to find out who murdered Maddy O'Leary."

"Sergeant Malloy thinks I also murdered Harry Whiteside. Will you investigate that, too?"

"I wondered if he'd roll that into the case, too," said Betsy. "He probably thinks it was an attempt to reopen the bidding on the Water Street property."

"Exactly," said Joe, nodding once, sharply. "It's not possible to do that, but it's an easy conclusion. I think he's not the only one thinking that's the case."

"I know he's not the only one," said Betsy. "I've heard it stated baldly right here in my shop."

Joe snorted. "I had better instruct my attorney to file for a change of venue as soon as I'm arrested!"

"Maybe it won't come to that," said Betsy. "Maybe Mike will find out what really happened, if it wasn't you. Maybe he'll discover Maddy and Harry are two different cases with two different murderers. They were each done in a different way, as if two different minds were at work on them."

"Do you think that's likely?" asked Joe.

"I think it's a valid theory. Harry was attacked in his home, his skull was fractured, and his house was burglarized. Maddy's knitting yarn was soaked in a poison she absorbed through her fingers, possibly by someone thinking her death might be ruled natural. That's two different mind-sets, don't you think?"

Joe thought about it. "That means two different murderers, which would mean two different motives."

"On the other hand, they were both into property—design, construction, rental."

But Joe had landed hard on her first theory. "Think about it. They moved in two different areas of that world. Maddy was into housing, Harry was into commercial and industrial buildings. There was some overlap, of course, but that's a lot of difference."

"So why did they both try to buy the Excelsior property?"

"Because they both planned to put retail on the ground floor and residential above. O'Leary was going to emphasize the retail end, Whiteside the residential. Me, I was going to have stores on the ground floor, business offices on the second, residential above that." He looked around the shop. "It's a common plan, business on the ground floor, residences above. What you've done here is like that. I'm just taking it a step further."

Actually, all Betsy had done was continue the setup she inherited from her sister: a two-story building with three apartments on the second floor—one lived in by herself—and three stores on the ground floor—one her own needlework shop. Even the other two, a used-book store called ISBNs (pronounced "Iz-bins"), the other a deli whose name had remained Sol's through several owners, were in place when she came to Excelsior.

"Is it possible there's a fourth bidder waiting in the wings?" asked Betsy. "Someone who thought it necessary to get rid of Maddy and Harry but thinks he or she can outbid you?"

"I hadn't thought of that," said Joe, surprised.

"Maybe you should. Also, has anything threatening or dangerous happened to you recently? Something you might feel was a close call? Maybe the murderer is thinking he'll get rid of all three of you."

"No, of course not!" The thick eyebrows came down and gathered over his nose like thunderclouds over a mountain. "I don't like where you're going."

"Where I'm going is to look at alternatives to the theory that you murdered two people in order to gain ownership of a piece of property."

"And your theory is that there is a fourth person after the property who is willing to kill Harry, Maddy, *and me* to get it?" He snorted again. "Preposterous!"

"What's your theory?" Betsy shot back.

"I don't have a theory. That's why I'm here. You have a talent for helping people who've been falsely accused of a crime. I came here to hire you to work for me, proving to the satisfaction of the police—or a jury if it comes to that—that I have not murdered anyone. But if all you can offer is some ridiculous story of a fourth person who wants that Water Street property, then I withdraw my offer."

"Well, that's your choice," said Betsy with a good show of indifference.

Defeated, Joe turned and started for the door.

"Wait!" called Betsy.

He stopped and slowly turned back. And there again was that sad and baffled look.

"I spoke rashly just now. You must know you are a . . . difficult person for me to relate to, given all we've been through. But I don't think you are a murderer. I don't know if I can be of any real help to you. I'm willing to try. But you can't hire me. I don't take money for my efforts to clear people who've been mistakenly accused."

Joe stood silent for a long thirty seconds. Then he said, "All right. Go ahead with it." After a just-noticeable pause, he added, "Thank you."

Again he turned to the door.

Betsy called again, "Wait a minute. Maybe we should get right to it. Mike Malloy must have more than motive to be looking at you. For example, maybe you don't have a solid alibi for one or both murders?"

He said, "I don't think they know when nicotine was put on that yarn Maddy was using when she died. It could've been weeks ago."

"No, the window of opportunity is more or less a week. I didn't announce that champion knitters were picking their own yarn. And I didn't have the yarn and needles put into marked bags until near the auction."

"Still, you're talking about a week or so. I don't know how anyone could cover every minute of a whole week with alibis. I know I can't."

"Fair enough. What about the night Harry Whiteside was killed?"

"The night he was killed I went to a dinner meeting with a man I thought to hire to survey some land I bought up in Cass County. But he turned out to be a flake; he believes in extrasensory perception guiding his surveying. He told me he was in the process of moving from Chicago to Duluth, and now he's canceled his phone service, so I can't get hold of him. And he won't be getting in touch with me; I told him I wasn't going to hire him."

Betsy pursed her lips then said, "That's too bad."

"You think?" he growled. "If this was going to be easy I wouldn't have come to you." He turned away and reached for the door, but before opening it, he looked back at her and said, "You have no idea how hard it was for me to come in here." He left before she could think of a reply.

"ARE you serious?" demanded Godwin. "You are going to help that, that, that—?"

"I'm going to try. We've both known him for a long time. Years. He doesn't play nice, he's greedy, and he's bad tempered." She smiled. "Once, something set him off in front of me and he shouted words I haven't heard for a long time—from back when I dated a U.S. Navy bosun's mate."

The smile faded. "But I don't think Joe's a criminal, and I doubt he'd ever kill someone, especially in that sneaky way Maddy was killed. That's not his style at all."

"Yes, but from what you just said, that skull bashing poor Harry Whiteside got does sound a whole lot like him."

"Well . . . okay. Trashing someone's house sounds even more like him. If Harry walked in on him vandalizing the house . . . But think of this: Would he murder someone and then trash his house?"

"What, you think Harry's house was trashed *after* he was killed?"

Betsy suddenly realized she was thinking of the terrific mess left right here in her shop by the person who murdered her sister—and the fact that it was done after her murder. "I don't know that, either, not for sure. In fact, I don't know what was taken from his house." She frowned at her disorganized thinking. "Anyway, he has an alibi for Harry Whiteside's murder."

"He does?"

"Well, sort of. He was having dinner and a talk with someone he was thinking of hiring. But the man seems to have disappeared."

"In other words, no, he doesn't have an alibi for Harry's murder."

"No, he *sort of* has an alibi for Harry's murder. Plus, Joe Mickels must be eighty years old. Can you really see him trashing somebody's house and capping his efforts by beating the owner to death?"

"Well, okay, that's a good point. But what about Maddy's murder?"

"No, no alibi. He pointed out very sensibly that since

there's no firm day and time when the nicotine was put onto the yarn, any alibi he offers would be at best . . . spotty."

"But he has a motive for both murders."

"Well, yes, he does."

"And you agreed to help this man?"

Betsy sighed. "Yes, I did."

Chapter Thirteen

Like many Baptist churches, Maddy's church—First Baptist of Minnetonka—was a modest white clapboard with a small steeple surmounted by a plain iron cross at the front of the roof. The windows, four on a side, had pointed arches, but the glass was plain gray. The small parking lot was crowded, and the street in front of the church was full of cars. Connor pulled into a space a block away, and he and Betsy walked back. It was raining, not hard but in that earnest, straight-down way that probably meant it was going to do it all day. There was no wind, no thunder and lightning.

"It's a *Schnurlregen*," said Connor, holding his big black umbrella so they could both huddle under it.

"What is?" asked Betsy.

"This kind of rain. Salzburg, Austria, is famous for this determined kind of heavy drizzle."

"*Schnurlregen*," said Betsy. "Very descriptive."

Betsy and Connor stopped inside the church to pull off identical raincoats. Under them, they were dressed alike in navy blue suits and white shirts—well, all right, he wore a shirt, she wore a blouse. He had a dark green tie; she had a modest white ruffle. At first they took a pew near the back of the church. A piano was playing a hymn very softly.

Despite all the cars and the smallness of the church, the pale oak pews were full but not packed. Connor nudged Betsy and nodded at the severely plain coffin up near the front. It rested on a wheeled bier and had a single bouquet of roses so dark a red they were nearly black.

After a few seconds Betsy realized the coffin was not wood but a heavy grade of tan cardboard. That's right, she thought, Maddy was going from here to a crematorium. It looked as if there was an aimless, widespread pattern of scribbles on the coffin—and it looked as if the man standing in front of the coffin was scribbling some more on it. Betsy was shocked—then she realized he was signing the coffin, the same way someone might sign a cast on a broken leg. Say, what a lovely idea! She stood and went forward. About to search her purse for a pen, she saw a cluster of Sharpie pens gathered around the bouquet to facilitate the writing.

She picked up a Sharpie. *I am grateful you brought your nimble fingers into my life*, she wrote. *God bless you. Betsy Devonshire.*

Connor took the pen from her. *You are at last in a place where there is nothing to try your patience*, he wrote, which Betsy thought was an impertinence, though it made her smile. She noticed he did not sign it.

They went back to their places. Betsy, unfamiliar with

Baptist churches, looked around. Plain off-white walls, no stained glass, no contrasting color anywhere. Up front was a vestigial altar with a bouquet of white lilies and a large black Bible on it. To the right was the upright piano whose notes they'd heard upon coming in. The pianist was a middle-aged woman with dark curling hair and an impressive bosom. She wore a long-sleeved gray knit dress with a black-on-white polka-dot scarf. Now she was playing a gentle version of "Nearer, My God, to Thee," and as Betsy tried to remember the words to it, she rolled it into another hymn Betsy did not recognize.

At ten thirty on the dot, the pastor, a rotund man with thinning dark hair and a pleasant face, came in from one side and took his place at the lectern on the left. He was wearing a charcoal black suit, white shirt, and dark maroon tie. A square of maroon silk handkerchief was peeking from his suit coat pocket.

"Good morning," he said. The piano player noticed his presence, stopped playing, and put her hands into her lap. "Good morning," he said again.

"Good morning," replied the congregation solidly.

"Welcome to a House of God, to a place of worship and praise. We have come here this morning to thank God that He led Maddy O'Leary to us, to praise God for her life, and to glorify God that she is now living in the perpetual sunlight of His eternal kingdom. Maddy was a faithful member of this church for nine years, a good Christian woman. But I suspect few of us really knew her. She kept herself to herself, and her charities, while many, were mostly anonymous. How many of you knew that our new piano was a gift from her?"

There was a murmur of surprise.

"Or that half the cost of our new roof came from her?"

More murmuring, louder.

"Maddy O'Leary was a God-fearing, intelligent, hard-working . . ." He paused for effect. "Difficult woman, who loved her fellow man, preferably at a distance."

There was surprised, agreeing laughter. "Amen," called someone.

"But she loved God and praised Him for sending His only begotten Son to us, to teach us how to live, to die for us, and to open the gates of heaven for us." He was getting into his preaching voice now, and electricity began to trickle into the room. "Let us praise Him!"

After a heartfelt invocation, he led them in singing "Face to Face with Christ, My Savior," a hymn Betsy was not familiar with. Connor, she noticed, seemed to know it. Or maybe, since he was holding an open hymnal, he could read music. He was always surprising her with a display of some skill or other she hadn't known he had.

When the pastor called on the congregation to speak about Maddy, only one person rose: Chaz Reynolds. Betsy hadn't realized he was there. He wore a dark brown suit with a dark brown shirt and black tie, and he went to the lectern with a deeply grave expression on his handsome face.

Betsy sat up straighter as he took hold with both hands and looked out at the congregation. "I don't think any of you know me," he began, "so I'm grateful you gave me this opportunity to speak. I had to come. I'm not even a Baptist, I'm a Lutheran. But I couldn't stay away!

"I worked for Maddy O'Leary for seven years. She took me on as a kind of office boy, taught me step-by-step how to collect rents, how to do basic repairs to kitchens and bathrooms, how to interview prospective tenants, how to evict tenants. I learned to keep records, fill out tax forms, make reports, do all the things necessary to keep her business running smoothly. She shouted at me—a lot—and praised me—not to my face, but to others. She raised my pay at least every year, upgraded my benefits, set me up with an investment program, and matched whatever I put into it. She gave me responsibilities and dared me not to live up to them. She made me a better man, faster than I thought possible." His voice was thickening and slowing. He stopped to swallow. "I loved her, though I never dared to tell her that. So I hope she can hear me tell her now." He looked upward. "I love you, Miss Maddy, and I miss you every day."

He tore himself away and stumbled back to his pew in front. Bershada was there, and she put an arm around his shoulders.

The pianist played a few bars, and the congregation broke into "Sweet, Sweet Spirit."

The pastor preached and offered more prayers, more hymns were sung, then he offered a blessing and said, "Because Ms. O'Leary is going from here to be cremated, and her ashes strewn in an undisclosed place, we ask that all who can please stay here for a luncheon prepared by the Ladies' Society. There will be a fifteen-minute break, then we will reconvene in the church basement. The stairs are forward and to your right, or if you want a breath of fresh air, there is another entrance around the east side toward the back. I hope to see all of you there."

Four people—two obviously from a funeral home—came to wheel the casket out while one more hymn was sung, and Betsy was reduced to tears, as always, by "Amazing Grace."

Chaz and his mother left without talking to anyone. Chaz was so obviously in distress that no one remarked harshly on his departure.

Many of the congregation chose to go outside into the open air, where, *Schnurlregen* be damned, it had stopped raining and sunlight was trying to break through the clouds. They stood around speaking in amazement of a fellow church member they only thought they knew.

The pastor joined the group. "You know, I didn't tell the whole story during the service," he said. "Ms. O'Leary helped build my discretionary fund to new heights so when members came to me with a financial emergency I would be better able to help them." He looked around the group. "Without naming any names, there are a number of you who needed your rent money or a mortgage payment made, or a month's worth of groceries, or a tooth cap replaced, or a plumbing bill paid that I was able to handle, thanks to Maddy."

An indignant man said, "Pastor, why in, uh, the heck didn't you say something about that a year or two ago? It would have been nice to know, y'know? So we could have thanked her while she was alive."

"Yes, it would have been nice and done her reputation a lot of good. But Ms. O'Leary gave me strict instructions not to say anything to anyone. I suspect it was because she didn't want to start a stampede of mendicants in her direction."

"Kind of sad she thought so poorly of us," remarked a woman.

"Well, now, think about it, Marcy," said another woman. "Suppose you knew there was a member of our church who was rich and very free and generous with her money. You recently had a big bump of a mortgage payment, didn't you? It hurt you, making that payment; you asked me to help you pray over it. Would you at least have thought of approaching her? Especially if you knew she had helped others?"

"No, of course not. Well, okay, maybe." Marcy laughed. "So all right, I might've joined the line with my hand out."

Her friend drew up her shoulders and confessed, "Me, too."

The group began to join the others going around the side of the little church toward the basement entrance.

"Is it true you don't know where her ashes are being strewn?" Betsy asked the pastor.

"She didn't want to tell anyone."

"Such a secretive woman!" said a man disapprovingly. "There's no reason for all that secrecy!"

"Does anyone know?" asked Betsy.

"I can give you the name of the funeral home," the pastor said. "I think they might know. But I'm sure they have been instructed not to give out that information."

"Thank you, Pastor," Betsy said. Shy, shy to the very end, she thought.

The luncheon was very like every church dinner Betsy had ever attended. The menu was fried and baked chicken, cole slaw, potato salad, baked beans with strips of bacon on top, dinner rolls, two kinds of Jell-O salad, and sheets of carrot cake studded with chopped nuts and little pieces of carrot and topped with cream cheese icing. Lemonade, milk, and coffee to drink. The meal was served buffet style; middle-aged women with hairnets handed out plates, silverware, and thick, soft paper napkins, and they brought out more food as needed.

The pastor offered a short blessing as the double line formed at the head of the long tables.

"Wow," said Betsy on the way home. "People sure are shocked at how they only thought they knew Maddy. Turns out her death is a serious loss to her church community. I wonder if that's so in other places."

"Didn't you say Bershada told you how Maddy would give her a check to cash so she could pass the money on anonymously to various charities? I suspect a lot of communities are going to be sad that Maddy is gone without ever knowing who she was."

As they drove up Highway 7, and nearly home, Connor asked, "Is there any reason you want to know where her ashes might be scattered?"

"I'm willing to ask anybody anything. There's got to be a key question in all this that will point me toward an answer. Who hated Harry strongly enough to physically attack him? Who was willing to play that sneaky, deadly trick on Maddy? Could it possibly be the same person? I don't really want to know where Maddy's ashes are going to end up. But I do want to know who she picked to do the scattering."

"I should think that information would be in her will," said Connor.

"No, wills sometimes are not even read until well after the funeral. They are mostly about the distribution of the decedent's property. Funeral arrangements generally have to be made before that. A 'living will' could have those instructions, I think. Or some kind of similar document." She frowned. "I should find out, because I need to ask someone to handle my instructions."

"What do you want that someone to do?" he asked.

"At present, you are that someone," she said. "And I want an Episcopalian church funeral, preceded by a wake at a funeral home. I keep meaning to find out if there's a space available next to the grave of my sister and her husband here in Excelsior, because if there is, I want to be put there. If not, cremate me and pour my ashes into Minnehaha Creek while a CD plays Bill Staines singing"—and she began to croon—"River, take me along, in your sunshine, sing me a song, ever moving, and winding and free; you rollin' old river, you changin' old river, let's you and me, river, run down to the sea.' Because the creek runs into the Mississippi, and it runs into the Gulf of Mexico."

She sat back with a sigh of contentment, thinking about little pebbles of bone carrying her spirit into the place all life began, the ocean.

HAVING delved all she could into Maddy's life, Betsy decided to switch direction and try to find out something about Harry Whiteside. She knew very little about him. She'd read the newspaper accounts, but in her experience, newspapers didn't always have complete or accurate information. She'd heard the gossip about the three-way struggle to buy the big property on Water Street. But a lot of gossip could be described as exaggerated and unsympathetic speculation, and in any case, it made two-dimensional caricatures of its subjects. The word *triangulate* appeared at the front of her mind. She needed another source, so maybe she could triangulate and from three flawed angles find information she could trust. So where else to look?

She turned to Whiteside's obituary in the *Star Tribune*. That at least would be a compassionate summary of his life.

There, as elsewhere, she learned that he was sixty-seven, the father of three children, all boys, all grown and married, with children of their own—and that he had two ex-wives. The children were all by his first wife. He had an MBA from the College (now University) of St. Thomas. He was the founder and CEO of Whiteside Design, Incorporated, the fourth-largest designer and builder of commercial property in the state.

He was to be interred in Lakeview Cemetery—where the elite were buried—on a date yet to be announced. Memorials were to be sent to the University of Minnesota.

The tone of the obituary was staid and respectful, without flowery or sorrowful prose. She wondered who had written it.

Now she felt prepared to talk to someone who knew Harry Whiteside personally. One of his children or ex-wives would be best to start. Bershada, who helped his second wife move out, could probably help her connect with the ex-wife. But Bershada was in Arkansas for the marriage of her youngest daughter and had apparently shut off her cell phone. Nor was she reading her e-mail. Both decisions were understandable; Bershada had talked several times about the "Bridezilla" her daughter Leeza had become, and about her overbearing and even bizarre behavior as the wedding date approached. Doubtless Bershada had her hands full with her large and sometimes volatile family's issues.

Then she remembered Phil's remark that Harry's downfall would be bankruptcy, not murder. What did Phil know about Harry?

She called him. Pleased to be consulted, he said, "I got a friend, he's a contractor. He says ol' Harry's a manipulator. He can be—excuse me, he used to be—your best friend when he was looking to hire you for a job he had pending. Saw you in a restaurant, he'd pay your tab. Out on the town, he'd buy you a drink—hell, two drinks. A real hail-fellow-well-met. See? Then you signed the contract and all of a sudden he was mad at everything you did. It wasn't good enough, it wasn't fast enough, you weren't working hard enough, he was losing money and it was your fault. He'd grind you down till you agreed to give him a discount. Once the job was done, he'd grudge that maybe you did all right, and in a few weeks he was fine with you, happy with the work you did, and if your paths crossed again, he'd shake your hand and offer to introduce you to someone he thought may be useful to you."

"What awful behavior!" said Betsy. "Do you think maybe he was bipolar? How did he stay in business behaving like that?"

"According to what I heard, when he was being nice, his deals were more than fair, and in the end he paid the amended amount in full and on time—which is not always the case with these big-time builders. Any contractor who could develop a tin ear to Harry's rants could make a living off him. But if enough people got tired of his methods, his business could suffer."

"This is wonderful information—thank you!"

"Hey, remember, this is all what they call hearsay. On the other hand, it's not just from my friend but a couple of his friends, too—during a late-night poker game when we were all half in the bag. Or is it still hearsay when it's from three drunk people?"

Betsy chuckled. "I think so. Still, this is very useful. You don't happen to know anything about his wives and children, do you?"

"'Wives'? What was he, a polygamist?"

"No, they were in succession; he married his second wife after divorcing his first one." She stopped short. "You know, I actually don't know if that's true. Maybe she died?"

"Sorry, I don't know, either."

"Well, do you know anything about his children? All I have is that there are three boys, all grown and married."

"'Fraid not. I guess that's what comes of him living on the other side of the lake. Like I told you, he owned a big architectural design company, and he had property all over the state. So this would be just another notch cut in the handle of his pistol."

Betsy said, "I wonder what will happen to it. I mean, who will come into possession?"

"If he left a will, you can find out."

"I can?"

"Sure, once it's filed, you can read it. Wills are public information."

"That's good to know. Where would I go to find it?"

"Now that I don't know. Call City Hall in Wayzata."

"Thanks, I will. You've been a great resource on this, and I'm grateful."

"You're welcome."

But the will hadn't been filed yet. So Betsy decided to run a Google search on Harry's sons. She went back to the obituary and found their names: Hamilton, Howard, and Hector. Whiteside surely wasn't a common surname. Or was it? Out of curiosity, she did another search and discovered about one person in twenty-five thousand is surnamed Whiteside. With that in mind, she searched the three sons by their first and last names and found links to three men named Hamilton Whiteside, two named Hector Whiteside, and five named Howard Whiteside. Five were businessmen, one was a builder, one was a hog farmer, one was an architect, and one was a college professor, but only four were of the right age to be Harry Whiteside's sons. One was a very old man and another perhaps of an age to be Harry's younger brother. None lived in Minnesota—was that a clue?

One of the Hamiltons and both the Hectors had contact information, and Betsy sent a brief e-mail to them, asking each if he was Harry Whiteside's son.

Now all she could do in that direction was wait, so she turned her attention back to Maddy O'Leary. Maddy was a longtime resident of Excelsior. Her life, like that of almost everyone in town, had been thoroughly sieved. Maddy, she knew, had begun her adult life as a legal secretary in a Minneapolis law firm specializing in real estate. She took classes and became a paralegal and a few years later caused a minor scandal when she married a senior partner in the firm—

who died after three months. Betsy held that thought out in front of her mind for a short while. What did her husband die of? She didn't know, but it couldn't have been something violent, or that fact would be prominent. Maddy wasn't left pregnant and never remarried.

Though her brief marriage left her well-off, she stayed with the law firm for a few years more, then began to buy distressed and/or repossessed properties, hiring people to rehab them, then selling some, keeping and renting others. Over time she moved from single-occupancy homes to duplexes and fourplexes and then to apartment buildings. As her holdings became more numerous and complex, she quit the law firm to focus on them. Gossip had it that nowadays some renters moved out when she took over a building because she was a harsh landlord, but she was never the subject of a successful tenant's lawsuit. When she sold a rental property, it was usually at a profit because of the upgrades she'd done. But a not inconsiderable part was because her tenants tended to be orderly. Betsy, who had twice suffered with difficult tenants, had often promised herself that she would ask Maddy her secret. Was it because she intensely interviewed prospective renters in order to screen out potential problems? If so, what did she ask them? How would she make that kind of interview legal? Or was her manner of supervising her properties such that she overawed her tenants? Betsy had never learned the art of overawing.

Or was it something else, something Betsy could emulate?

But Maddy had been abrupt to the point of rudeness to everyone, and Betsy had found herself shying away from asking her questions. Not that there was a lack of opportunity. Maddy bought a lot of yarn and other stitching materials in Betsy's shop. If she wanted something, she tended to buy it at once, only rarely waiting for a sale. Despite the amount of yarn and other items she purchased, she never asked for special consideration, such as a discount for buying in quantity. On the other hand, she was quick to return a product she found faulty or inappropriate for its intended use. Betsy was equally quick to make reimbursements, though she was careful not to overcompensate. As far as possible, she had wanted to keep both Maddy's custom and her respect.

She could remember only one time Maddy came into her shop in such good humor that Betsy dared to banter with her. It was the day Maddy had won the bidding war on the Water Street property.

"Hello, Betsy!" she had boomed in her loud voice, her eyes sparkling and her long skirts snapping in the speed of her stride.

"Well, something's made you cheerful this afternoon," Betsy had responded, surprised.

"I took down two people who were giving me grief," Maddy had said.

"Looks like they never laid a glove on you," Betsy had dared to say.

"Oh, metaphorically, I'm all over bruises," she had said, coming down to almost her usual brusque tone. "But unlike them, I'll be more than fine. I want three more skeins of that green Appleton wool I bought in here last week."

That was the only time she had been anything but abrupt. Too bad it was so shortly before her death; Betsy would have liked to look behind that shield to see what

Maddy was really like. And now it was particularly sad to learn there was another, softer, side to the woman. It appeared she gave generously but worked always in the background, not just at her church but in the toy auction. She knit more toys for it than any other person. But she had objected strenuously to Bershada's insistence that she sit in a place of honor for doing so.

I believe I was right, she was shy, thought Betsy now. Maddy hated being singled out, even for praise.

Betsy wondered what kind of childhood she had had.

But first, and more importantly, she wanted to find out if that gruff exterior and overweening ambition had created an enemy so angry that he—or she—had resorted to murder.

Chapter Fourteen

IT was a slow time in the shop. Godwin had gone across the street to have lunch with Rafael in their condo. Betsy was at the big checkout desk writing checks for suppliers—and sighing over the numbers—when the door announced its opening with a bright chorus of "Anchors Aweigh." She looked up to see Detective Sergeant Mike Malloy coming in. Backward.

Actually, he had turned around to stare in bemusement at the door frame. He held the door open until the tune finished. Then he closed it and turned to see Betsy looking bemused at him.

"You don't know that melody?" she asked.

"Of course I do. Doesn't everybody? But you are going to get very tired of it after a few dozen repeats," he predicted.

"I won't have time to get tired of it. Godwin changes the music at least once a week. He's working his way down a very long list of titles."

Malloy looked back again at the door. "That's the Navy Hymn, isn't it," he said.

"No, the Navy Hymn is 'Eternal Father, Strong to Save.' What you just heard is a traditional Navy drinking song."

He looked at her. "You sure?"

She offered a snappy salute. "Ex–Navy WAVE here. I know at least two verses of 'Eternal Father.' I even know the countermelody to 'Anchors Aweigh.'" She would have sung it to him, but he didn't look interested. Instead, she asked, "How may I help you, Mike?"

"I'm here about the Maddy O'Leary case."

"I'll be glad to help any way I can."

He smiled his thin smile and came forward, a slim man of average height with a densely freckled face. His hair was a shade of tan, which happens to some redheads as they age. His light blue eyes were tired.

"I made a fresh pot of coffee less than half an hour ago," she said.

"Yes, thanks. Black."

"Have a seat." She gestured at the library table in the center of the room.

When she came out of the back, carrying two mugs, one of coffee and the other of an herbal tea, he was seated near the far end of one long side. On the table in front of him was a notepad with sewn-in pages and a fat ballpoint pen.

She put his coffee beside the notepad, put her own tea in front of a chair across from him, and sat down.

"Where do we begin?" she asked.

"Whose idea was this auction at Mount Calvary?"

"It was Bershada Reynolds's idea. I can't believe you don't already know that."

He nodded, but whether in agreement or not, she couldn't tell. "Who supplied the yarn for those little canvas bags?"

"I did. And the bags themselves, too." Surely he must have known that already, too. *Aha*, she thought, he's asking questions he knows the answers to in order to see how I tell the truth. Or don't. But that must be from habit; he knows me, and he knows I don't lie. She looked at him and smiled.

"What?" he said.

"Nothing," she replied. "Just recognizing your style of interrogation."

"This isn't an interrogation, it's an interview. I interrogate suspects, I interview witnesses."

"Noted, thanks. Next question."

"How did you select the yarn that went into the bags?"

"Bershada told me who the people were, and I asked them what kind of yarn they wanted."

"How far in advance of the auction did you pull the yarn?"

"About ten or twelve days."

"Was the yarn from your stock?"

"Yes. One person came in to look at what I had, and two people told me directly what they would like. Goddy, of course, picked his own yarn."

"Which way did Ms. O'Leary go?"

"She asked me if I had dark blue merino wool. I did, so I turned the skein into a ball—"

"What? Why?"

She turned away in her chair. "Those are skeins," she said, pointing to a basket full of fat ovals of yarn cinched in the middle by a broad paper wrapper. "It's how yarn comes, in skeins. I have a device that will turn a skein into a ball. It's easier to knit from a ball."

"So why don't they come already in balls?"

"Because balls roll away, and they unwind as they roll."

He wrote that down, paused, brightened, and said, "I remember how in old movies a man would sit with yarn kind of wrapped or draped around his wrists while a woman pulled it off in a single strand to make a ball." He held his hands about two feet apart, palms facing in.

Betsy nodded. "That's the traditional method. You can also drape it around the back of a chair, but my device is much faster. It depends on what the knitter is after, a quick ball of yarn or a chance to sit and talk with someone. Interestingly, it was also used as a safe kind of courtship. The man and woman could talk at length, but they couldn't get up to anything while his hands were engaged like that. Plus she got a ball of yarn with which to begin to knit him a pair of argyle socks."

"That's kind of nice," said Mike, nodding thoughtfully, and Betsy recalled he had two daughters of dating age. One of them was a knitter.

But the task of writing checks prodded, so she pushed forward. "What else do you want to know?"

"Where were the bags kept after you put the yarn in them?"

"I have a storage room in the basement."

"Is it locked?"

"No, but the front and back doors to this building are, as is the door to the basement."

"Who has the keys?"

"I have keys, my tenants have keys, Connor has keys, Godwin has keys. Only Godwin and I have the keys to the front and back door of the shop. We lend a key to the shop's front door to an employee who is coming in early, but only that one key. And we take it back when we come in. All the locks are dead bolts."

Mike, writing swiftly, nodded, then paused. "Your tenants have keys to the basement?"

Betsy nodded. "A washing machine and dryer are down there."

"Would they lend their keys to a friend?"

"Maybe. I ask them not to when I give them the keys, but you know how people are. The Pearsons, who have the front apartment, have a big family who drop by a lot, so it's likely their keys have been temporarily loaned out. It's even possible they've made copies for them." She frowned. "I should ask them about that."

"So getting at the bags of yarn might have been inconvenient for a non-tenant or non-employee, but not impossible."

"I would prefer difficult and complicated to inconvenient. But yes, not impossible."

"Did you see any evidence of tampering when you took the bags of yarn over to Mount Calvary?"

"I didn't take them over. Bershada came with another woman, and they took them out of the basement. Have you talked to her?"

"Not about that. When did the transfer take place?"

"The Wednesday before the Saturday auction."

"Did you see the bags in the basement at any time before that?"

"Probably. I mean I went down to the basement a few times between putting them down there and Bershada taking them away. I think I would have noticed if they'd been moved around or some were missing."

"Were they on a row on a shelf, or kept in a box, or what?"

"In a double row on a shelf. It was deep enough so the bags could line up two by two."

"But plainly visible to anyone going into that room," Mike said.

"Or just standing in the door, yes."

"Was Ms. O'Leary's yarn in the front row?"

Betsy thought. "I'm sorry, I don't remember. Godwin and I put the yarn and knitting needles in the bags and took them down."

"You didn't pack each bag yourself?"

"No. I had made a list of who got which ball of yarn. Goddy took the list, loaded the bags, and I took them downstairs. It didn't take long, but I remember waiting till after closing that day, so he wouldn't be thrown off stride by having to wait on a customer."

"Do you know of anyone involved in the auction who smokes e-cigarettes?"

Betsy shook her head. "No."

Mike sighed, made a note, sighed again, and closed his notebook. "Okay, thank you."

"I take it you're trying to clear Joe Mickels?"

"No, I'm trying to clear everyone else so I can arrest him." He stood, looked into her shocked eyes, and said with a straight face, "If you believe that, you're not half the sleuth I've taken you for."

Relieved, she laughed. "And sometimes I need to remind myself you're twice the investigator I used to take you for."

"SEE, I told you he's not the sharpest hook in the tackle box!" said Godwin.

"He was kidding, Goddy! Kidding! He's out to find the person who killed Maddy. Right now he thinks it might be Joe. So do you, remember?"

"Yeah, well, he hasn't had your experience with Joe, so what does he know?"

"He knows plenty—and he's had the training to see it properly. Plus, he has the backing of a very large set of scientific testing methods we have no access to. Let him do his thing."

"Yeah, okay, maybe you're right. But we'll do our thing, too, right?"

"Of course."

"So where do we go next, *kemo sabe*?"

"I want to talk to people who knew Mr. Whiteside and Ms. O'Leary."

"Looking for what they were like?"

"Looking for who hated them."

Chapter Fifteen

LATER that day, Betsy wondered again what would happen to the property on Water Street. She called her attorney, Jim Penberthy, to ask.

"Real estate, especially commercial real estate, is not my area of expertise," he said. "I think the property belongs to Ms. O'Leary's estate. But let me check and I'll call you back."

Betsy returned to the struggle to assign her part-timers slots that met her needs and the desires of her employees. One never wanted to work on Wednesdays, another wanted to work only half days, and the third wanted to continue working even though she was two weeks overdue in her pregnancy.

So it was a relief to take a break when the phone rang. But it wasn't Penberthy. It was Bershada.

"Welcome home!" Betsy said. "How was the wedding?"

"Don't ask. And now Chaz is hanging around my house

making me crazy. I finally sent him to the store, but he'll be back in a few minutes. Will you please take him off my hands for a couple of hours? He would be wild to talk about Maddy with you, if you'd care to ask him."

"Yes, I'd like that very much. I was going to ask him to talk to me about her, if he would. What would be a good time?"

"Well, what are you doing this evening? Could your menu possibly stretch to a third person? Be warned, he eats like a horse."

"I think we're having beef stew. I'll call Connor and ask him and call you back."

Connor said he'd make biscuits to stretch the stew and prepare something with Jell-O to fill in the cracks. "Do you want me to make like a hoop and roll away after dinner?" he asked.

"No, please don't. You have a good ear for things; you might pick up something I miss." Betsy called Bershada back to say yes, and she said, "He's right here, talk to him."

In a few seconds a very pleasant man's voice came on the line. "Hello? Mom told me about you, but I don't think I've ever met you."

"Not formally," said Betsy, "but I saw you at Maddy's funeral and was impressed, plus I've often heard good things about you. Are you available to talk this evening? We'll feed you supper."

After a brief, surprised pause, he said, "Well, sure! Okay! What time?"

"About six thirty?"

"Okay. Thanks."

"Now, can I talk with your mother again?"

"Sure." His voice faded as he talked away from the phone. "Mom, she wants to talk to you some more."

In a few seconds Bershada came back on. "What is it?" she asked.

"You said you helped Harry Whiteside's second wife pack her clothes when she left him."

"Yes, I did."

"Were you and she friends?"

"Yes, she volunteered at libraries all over the nine counties that make up the Twin Cities, and the first time she came to Excelsior, we struck up a friendship. I didn't pry too much, and she liked that. But we talked about everything else. She was especially good with children, which was my area of expertise at the Excelsior library. She started coming regularly, and every time we'd wind up talking nineteen to the dozen, at work, over lunch, even sometimes over dinner. She was a kind woman, with a silly sense of humor the children loved."

"Did she talk about her husband?"

"Not at first. If I asked her about him, she'd say, 'Oh, he's so busy with work, I've almost forgotten what he looks like.' Or, 'I'm glad I've got my volunteer work. Harry doesn't want me to work for pay, and I'd go crazy just sitting at home, especially now all the boys are gone.'"

"So how did you find out she wanted to leave him?"

"She came to work with a bruise that went from just above her left eye nearly to her jawline. She'd tried to cover it up with makeup, but it wasn't just black and blue, it was swollen. I marched her into the ladies' room and ordered her to tell me what happened. She tried to say she'd fallen, but I could tell she was lying, and she started to cry. He didn't often hit her, but when he did, he'd do it where the bruise didn't show. And he was always telling her she was worthless and stupid—all the things that that kind of man does to his wife. She absolutely refused to make a police report, I think because she was afraid he might kill her. She said she'd been secretly saving money and had just barely enough for a bus ticket to Columbus, Georgia, where her sister lived. But this hit on her face was absolutely the last straw. I drove her home and helped her pack and took her to the station and sat with her until her bus was called. She wrote me a few weeks later, saying Harry had found out where she was and called, but her brother-in-law told him that if he came down there, he'd introduce him to his backhoe in the east forty and nobody would ever see him again."

Bershada chuckled and said to Betsy, "He must have sounded very convincing, because Harry didn't even come down to contest the divorce."

"Do you still correspond with her?"

"We did for about eighteen months, then she wrote she was getting married and moving to Costa Rica, and that's the last I heard from her."

It was just about closing time. Betsy was running the cash register and Godwin was cleaning the toilet when the phone rang.

"Crewel World, this is Betsy, how may I help you?" she said into the receiver.

"Betsy, this is Jim Penberthy. I was right about the Water Street property. The estate has possession of it—or rather the option to buy it. They can either proceed with the purchase, or they can offer the option to interested parties. But the original owner no longer has any ownership in it."

"Well, that's interesting. Thanks, Jim." So that at least removed one motive for Joe. Killing Maddy and Harry didn't give him the right to buy the Water Street property. It did, however, give him the opportunity, which he'd lost when Maddy won it in the original auction if her executor decided to put it out for bids.

CHAZ arrived about five minutes early at the downstairs entrance. Betsy opened the door to her apartment to wait for him.

He was as she remembered him, a little above medium height, slim, his face a masculine echo of his handsome mother's, and as dark complexioned. His hair was cropped short. He wore a dark red wool shirt under a light tan leather jacket, close-fitting jeans, and moccasins. An interesting touch was his pair of gold-rimmed spectacles—he hadn't worn glasses at the funeral or in the shop. They gleamed in the staircase lights, hiding his eyes.

"Ms. Devonshire?" he asked as he came up the last few steps into the broad hallway outside her door. His voice was the pleasant tenor she remembered from the funeral, unaccented.

"Yes, and thank you for agreeing to come."

"No problem."

She stepped back, gesturing for him to come inside.

Chapter Sixteen

CHAZ paused in the entrance hallway to the Devonshire apartment. It was small, with a narrow door that was very probably a coat closet. A nice warm smell of beef stew, the kind with a mix of vegetables, was in the air. Beyond the closet door on his left was a galley kitchen, and in the kitchen stood a tall white man with graying hair, his two hands working in a big bowl. Facing Chaz was Betsy, a short, plumpish, middle-aged blonde with penetrating blue eyes. She was wearing a long blue skirt the color of her eyes and a pale ivory sweater in a complicated weave. She was smiling—she had a nice smile—and had her hand out, so he took it.

"Hello, Chaz," she said in a warm, pleasant voice. "I'm glad you could come."

"Hi, Betsy," he replied. "Offer to feed me, and I'll follow you anywhere."

She chuckled. "This way."

She turned and led him straight ahead to a wide, low-ceilinged living room. She let him pause for a few seconds to take his jacket off and look around the room.

The walls were painted a quiet mauve, and the carpet was a very pale cream, which Chaz thought daring. These people must rarely have visitors, especially children, over. On the wall to the right was a triple set of windows covered with drapes that were two shades darker than the carpet. Under the window was one of those cat beds that looked lined with sheepskin, and in the bed was a very large cat with tan and gray spots on its head and down its back. It regarded him with cool yellow eyes. A second cat bed, this one dark brown, was unoccupied.

Betsy came back from hanging up his jacket. "Would you care to sit down?" she asked. She went to stand beside a couch upholstered in narrow stripes of mauve, olive green, and cream with too many hand-stitched pillows on it. But it looked comfortable—and was, once he moved two pillows aside. *Why are women so nuts about pillows?* he wondered. "Thank you," he said. "This is a really nice place." Because apart from the pillows, it was.

"Thank you," Betsy said.

The tall man, who looked somewhere in middle age but was very fit, came into the living room from the other end of the kitchen. "Hello," he said, and Chaz stood up.

"Connor, this is Charles Reynolds, Bershada's son."

"Call me Chaz," Chaz said.

"Chaz," repeated Connor. "I'm Connor Sullivan. Nice to meet you." He came forward, and the two shook hands. "Dinner will be ready in about fifteen minutes."

"Great." Chaz sat back down. Betsy sat in the comfortable

chair positioned ninety degrees to the couch, and Connor sat at the other end of the couch.

Betsy's chair was an olive green wingback chair, low to the floor so it suited her petite stature. Behind the chair was a silver lamp with a flexible neck curved to look over the shoulder of someone sitting in it, and beside it was a small wooden folding frame holding a bag made of napless carpet. He'd seen those carried by his mother's stitching friends.

She sat back and said, "I think you may have important information to share with me. Your mother explained how I'm involved in trying to solve Maddy's murder?"

Her blunt question, coming in this comfortable place, struck him to the heart. Would he never even begin to heal? "Yes. I hope I can tell you something useful. But where do I begin?"

"I think by just talking about her. Her death hit you hard, I know. I'm so sorry that Maddy was taken like that, with no warning. But it's helpful that you agreed to talk with me about her. You probably knew her better than anyone. What was she like?"

"Well, like Pastor Woodruff said, she was a difficult person," he said, reluctantly admitting to an obvious fault, "especially at first. But she was totally amazing once you got to know her. She was strong and smart, and she taught me more about business than all my college courses put together."

"How long did you work for her?" asked Betsy, reaching sideways into that carpet bag, pulling out a long and narrow notepad. Where had he seen a pad like that? Oh, right, in a newspaper reporter's hand. Saves half a second when you don't have to come back across a wide notebook when taking notes. Interesting that she had figured that out, too. She opened the pad, pulled loose a pencil stuck crosswise into its middle, and scribbled something on an upper corner of the page—probably the date, or his name. Or both.

"Seven years, or close to it. I started out collecting rents and trying to talk tenants into using automatic withdrawal to pay rent. Our tenants are good people, most of them, just trying to get by or even move up a little. But sometimes . . . disorganized."

"Are you acting on behalf of Maddy's estate?"

Did she know this was an ardent desire of his, to remain involved in Maddy's business? Wait, she couldn't know. He said, "No, but I've got an appointment with her lawyer tomorrow. I thought it was about going over the books with him. Do you think—?"

"Think what?"

"That they'll let me continue to work with her properties?"

"I don't know. Would you want to do that?"

"I sure would. I really got to like the work. There was always something interesting going on, problems to solve, tenants and plumbers and glaziers and all to deal with, money to be collected, repairs to be made. She even taught me how to bypass locks some tenants would put on themselves. Plus—" He had to stop. How to explain?

Betsy said, "Plus it's a way of keeping her alive. I did the same thing with my shop. It was my sister's, and when she was murdered, it was a comfort to me to keep it going."

"You really do understand! Thank you!"

"You're welcome. How familiar are you with the way her business was run?"

He sank back. "Only with the rental stuff. She had all kinds of properties: houses, stores, apartment buildings, even a lumberyard." He shrugged. "And, of course, she was a real estate agent, too. I didn't know how big-time until I saw she was going after the Water Street property. That thing is going to cost millions to buy and build. Millions."

"Was she overextending herself to try for it?"

"Oh, I think she must've been, yes. Or, no. Well, maybe." He laughed at himself. "I really don't know. I thought I knew her business affairs pretty well, but I probably didn't."

"Was she secretive?"

He twisted his shoulders in discomfort. "Not exactly. People thought she was . . . blunt. And of course she was. She'd say right out what she thought about things, if she was willing to talk about them at all. If she didn't want to talk, she wouldn't say anything. Like, when I first started to work for her, I thought she owned a couple of houses and an apartment building on the north side of Minneapolis. Then I found out she owned a couple of houses in Uptown. And a store. Then more houses in south Minneapolis, a small lumberyard in Golden Valley—and a start-up construction company up halfway to Duluth. Whenever she widened my responsibilities, I'd find out she owned more property. The latest was I found she had this plan to build a multipurpose building in Excelsior. She never hinted at something, she'd just spring it on me." He shrugged, smiling wryly. "I think she liked to surprise me."

Betsy was busy writing all of this down. Then she looked up from her pad to ask Chaz another question. "She usually struck me as angry or impatient. Was she like that with you?"

"Oh yes," Chaz said. "That was her at her core. I think she was born mad." He grinned. "I got used to it. She barked a lot, but she never bit me."

"And she paid you well."

"Yes, she did. She even bragged about me, in her own way. 'At least Chaz doesn't shout at tenants for being late,' she'd say to a building manager she was about to fire. 'He's a chameleon, he knows how to get along with anyone, even me,' she'd say to someone asking how I kept on working for her."

"How do you know she said those things about you if she never said them to your face?"

"Sometimes she'd leave the door to her office open just a little bit. She never praised me to my face, but she did that eavesdropping-enabler thing enough times that I began to realize it was intentional."

His nose twitched. Was that the lovely smell of biscuits baking?

Betsy nodded, made a note, and said, "Now to the hard part: Did anyone you know truly hate her?"

Chaz laughed. "Oh God, yes. People she evicted would write terrible things about her on their Facebook accounts, or in anonymous letters, or even in spray paint on walls or the doors of their former houses or apartment buildings. People she outdid on business deals, too. Well, the business people didn't resort to spray paint. They'd sue. I think she kept one of her attorneys on speed dial."

"Did any of these people threaten her life?"

"Frequently." He smiled, remembering.

"How serious were these threats?"

"They were mostly just venting. Maddy didn't take them

seriously. Except some of the people who threatened to sue. She got right on those cases. Only one actually came to court while I worked for her, and she won that case." He snapped his fingers. "Like that."

"Did she ever sue anyone?"

Chaz nodded. "A couple of times, mostly small claims cases. One big one, but it got dismissed."

"Against anyone we know?"

Chaz looked uncomfortable. "Harry Whiteside," he admitted. "I think she was in the right, but Harry had a big-time law firm on his side, so she never had a chance. But at least she fought him to a draw."

"Now, let's turn my question around. Who was Maddy angry with? Was there anyone she hated?"

Chaz leaned back into the couch and fell silent. Betsy bit her tongue, and Connor, after a glance at her, followed suit.

"Oh God," sighed Chaz. "Harry came to Maddy's office a few days before he was killed. Now, he'd come before, just a few times, like less than once a year. I think there was bad blood between them going way back. Years before I came to work for her. I'm not sure what started it, or when, but whenever they communicated with each other, they tried to do it by letter or e-mail. If it was necessary for them to meet face-to-face, the temperature in the room would drop about thirty degrees when he walked in, and then the mercury would start to rise until they both came to a boil. Then the shouting would start. And a funny thing, she would meet him in the outer office where I could overhear at least the first part of their conversation. Maybe she wanted him to be aware there was an eyewitness."

"What would they argue about?"

"Deals they were making. She'd find a property she liked and then discover he was the one selling it. Or vice versa. Or she'd bid on a project and find herself dealing with him somehow, like maybe he was financing another part of the build, or bidding against her. She was always sure he was rooking her somehow, and he was sure she was doing the same. He'd swear to God that one day she'd regret ever knowing him, and she'd say that he was the one who'd be sorry, and when he left she'd sit in her office knitting ninety miles an hour until she cooled off."

"And this last time was different?"

He nodded. "It was like he was the one who won the bidding war. He was smirking and, and . . . well, it's hard to describe. He was standing like a winner. No, worse than that, like he was standing over her dead body and glad to be there."

"Do you think he'd found some kind of weakness in the deal?"

He sighed lightly. "Well . . . no, I don't think so. Oh, I don't know! Like he beat her in some other area. Yeah, like that."

"So this bidding war they got into wasn't just about acquiring the property."

"No, it was about 'doing' the other." He grimaced.

"Was she expecting him to come in that day?"

"Yeah, I think so. She didn't act surprised to see him. But the look in his eye—and the look in hers—made me break out in a sweat watching them, scared they'd lose it and she'd grab my laptop and smack him upside his head, or he'd knock her down. But neither one of them ever took that swing."

"What did he say that was different?"

"He said, 'Have you had your windows replaced yet?'"

"Had there been some windows broken in her properties?"

"Not that I knew of. But there must've been, because that's when I got scared she was going to pop him one."

"Does she have properties you're not aware of?"

Chaz stared at her, and suddenly she laughed. "Like you would know about some building you don't know about."

He nodded, grinning. "Yeah, like that." The grin faded. "On the other hand, if there was damage somewhere, I should've known. That was one of my jobs, arranging repairs. Or even doing them. I'm pretty good at replacing windows. Plumbing, not so much."

"So what do you think?"

"I think you're right, there's a piece of property I don't know about, that nobody is supposed to know about, but Harry found out. And it's damaged; someone broke some windows."

Connor asked, "Is it possible that Harry broke the windows?"

Chaz drew breath in through his teeth. "I hadn't thought of that! But no. I think she was so damn angry—surprised into anger—because he found out about this secret property."

Betsy frowned. "What kind of property could she own that she wanted kept secret?"

Chaz shrugged. "Beats me."

"Did he say where this property was? In the Twin Cities area?"

"No." Chaz shrugged. "But . . . I got the feeling it was out somewhere, maybe up north. Vacation property, maybe. Up at the lake."

Connor said, "Which lake?"

Betsy said, "In Minnesota, everyone who owns a cabin on one of our ten thousand lakes calls it 'the lake.' As in, 'We're going up to the lake this weekend.' The lake is never mentioned by name. Maybe to discourage drop-in visitors who'd want a free stay."

Connor laughed. "Very clever."

"*Row*," came a sound that could have been from a cat, except it was deep.

Chaz, looked around, startled, then saw the owner of the second cat bed, a Siamese, emerging from a back room. So it had been a cat's voice, after all. The cat, whose "points"—face, ears, legs, tail—were very dark, came to stand in front of Chaz. "*Arow*," it said again, more of a statement than an inquiry.

"That's Thai," said Betsy. "With a T-H. If you want to pet him, hold out your hand. He'll come and sniff your fingers, which is permission to stroke the top of his head."

"Huh," said Chaz, but he leaned forward experimentally, arm extended, fingers out.

The cat came near, lifted his small head, and sniffed, then presented his forehead. Chaz obediently stroked it a few times. The cat, satisfied, walked away toward the kitchen.

"What would have happened if I hadn't held out my hand?" Chaz wondered aloud.

Connor said, "He would have walked away—but a few minutes later he would have landed on your shoulders from behind the couch, just to see how high you'd jump and how loud you'd shout. He has a wicked sense of humor."

Chaz laughed. "I guess I should be grateful it's not that other cat who has a sense of humor."

"Indeed," said Connor, also laughing. "She currently weighs twenty pounds." He glanced at Betsy and said, "May I ask Chaz something?"

"Of course," Betsy said, looking a little surprised.

He turned back to Chaz. "This may seem like an odd question, but when you heard that Maddy had been murdered, whose name immediately jumped into your mind as the possible murderer?"

He said at once, "Harry Whiteside," then raised both hands, his gesture of frustration. "But of course he was already dead. Someone murdered him before he could murder her."

"Why did you think of Mr. Whiteside?" asked Betsy.

"Mostly because of that Water Street property. I remember he said, 'At least I made you pay more than you wanted, maybe more than it's worth.' Which might be true, I think he could have afforded the higher price better than she could. Still, he backed down first."

Betsy said, "So did Joe Mickels. Did you think of him, too, as a possible murderer?"

"No, not right away. He and Maddy had no relationship I knew of until this Water Street thing, but . . ."

"But what, Chaz?"

"Well, I'm sure Maddy was stretching herself pretty thin on this Water Street property. She had taken out mortgages on some of her buildings so she could keep up with the bidding, and she was angry about that. And that last confrontation, that was *serious*."

"Her behavior must have been disturbing. Did you ever think about quitting your job?"

"Yes, off and on. But never for long. She was honest—I know, I know, but she was. She wasn't out to cheat anyone, she just wanted a fair chance. She was the most . . . straightforward person I've ever known. She knew what she wanted and went for it." As he spoke, his tone grew warmer. "And she was interesting. She was complicated. She knew lots of things about lots of things. That sounds like Trivial Pursuit, doesn't it? But deeper than that, not trivia. Things like history, science, and art." His voice softened further. "She was a thinker. She challenged me to think, and I liked that." His throat filled, and it became hard for him to talk. He swallowed and tried to suck it up. "I loved working for her."

"That's wonderful, and it was brave of you to stand up among a gathering of strangers and say you loved her." Betsy made a note on her pad and asked, "How did Joe Mickels fit into the bidding war?"

"Well, I heard Mr. Mickels wanted that property, that he was a fanatic about it. But I'd also heard he was kind of a miser, so I think he was mad that the two of them kept bidding the price up. I'm pretty sure he knew Maddy and Harry were enemies—you couldn't get anywhere near them without learning that—but he didn't take sides or interfere between them that I knew of. He didn't egg them on." He stopped short, and added, "It would have been stupid to egg them on, as it would have just raised the price even more."

"Was he angry at them?"

Chaz nodded. "I think so—no, Maddy told me he was. He thought they were unbusinesslike, she said. Taking it personal, when this was a business deal—though it was personal with her, too. Maddy told me Joe had wanted a big building with his name on it for a long time. Years."

"That's true," said Betsy. "He tried to force me out of this building—he was my landlord back then and wanted everyone out so he could tear it down and put up the Mickels Building." She sighed. "I think all three of them were taking it personally, though perhaps not for the same reasons.

"You talked about her being angry. Was she capable of violence? Physical violence? Did you ever see her strike someone?"

"No, absolutely not. When she got really angry, it was mostly at herself, for losing her temper or making a mistake in managing or selling or flipping a property. She'd stomp around her office, and sometimes she'd throw something hard enough to break it, but it was her own something, and not just a stapler or a wastebasket. She might smash a valuable clock or vase, or she'd rip up a document, or, once, a nice wall calendar, the kind that comes from a museum, and then have to buy a replacement, and that would make her even madder. So then she'd sit down and knit. I was surprised at the way she'd knit, too, almost like she was mad at the yarn." He smiled and shook his head. "Knitting was her act of violence."

Connor said, "Maybe that's another reason she didn't want to be honored as the person who contributed the most knitted toys. It was a reminder of how often she was angry."

Betsy looked admiringly at him for his perceptive comment, and Chaz nodded over and over. He said, "Yes, that makes sense. On the other hand, I wonder if maybe she didn't see herself that way, not as an angry person, just as a person coping with a lot of stupid people and events."

Betsy smiled, made a note, and underlined it.

Then something in the kitchen dinged, and Connor said, "The biscuits are done. Let's eat."

Chapter Seventeen

AFTER Chaz left, Connor said, "Well, what do you think?"

Betsy said, "I think he's a fine, intelligent young man who knows his own mind. Interesting how close he felt to Maddy. You saw how he's deeply grieved by her death."

"Do you think you have a better understanding of Maddy now?"

"I think so. Chaz is obviously biased, in that he liked and admired her, but he seems to have a good understanding of her difficult personality. What do you think?"

"I think she was a deeply flawed person," said Connor. "Problems with anger, first and most obviously, but also plagued by ambition and lack of empathy."

"I'm not so sure about the lack of empathy. She was exceptionally generous to various charities—you saw how she knitted more toys for that auction than anyone else. But I agree she was unhappy. Do you think she would have been happier if she'd had a better grasp on her anger issues or been better able to empathize with her business rivals?" asked Betsy.

"Maybe. But she wouldn't have been as successful in business. There's an element of ruthlessness in people who are successful, in any field. Don't you think?"

Betsy nodded. "Yes, I think that's true. Ambition has to sit in the driver's seat if a person's going to get good at something. Like you and ships, or me and my little shop." Emily was right: Betsy could sell it and never have to work again, but she remained determined to make it pay.

"You love your shop, but I think it's sleuthing that drives you," amended Connor. "But what do you think is sitting in Chaz's driver's seat?"

She looked at the closed door to the apartment, through which Chaz had exited a few minutes ago.

"I'm not sure."

GODWIN was feeling down. He and Rafael had gone out on his day off for an early spring game of golf, and while he hadn't lost his putting skills over the winter, his drive was yards shorter than usual. Now the two were cleaning and polishing their clubs in the kitchen of their condo.

Perhaps to distract him, Rafael asked, "Has Betsy been keeping you up to date on her investigation into the murders of Harry Whiteside and Maddy O'Leary?"

"She is trying to prove that Joe Mickels had nothing to do with them."

"And you believe Joe Mickels is guilty?"

"Yes. Yes, I do."

"Does she really believe he isn't guilty?"

"I don't know. It's hard to think so. I mean, he's such a terrible man!"

"So maybe what she'll prove is that he *is* guilty."

Godwin nodded as he rubbed hard at a grass stain in the grooves of his driver. It had turned out that way once before. "I'd like that." He put down the head of the club he'd inspected and sighed sadly at it. "I don't see what I'm doing differently in my driving," he complained to his partner.

"I noticed you were behind your usual distance," replied Rafael, putting his driver away and pulling out his chipping club. "But your stroke didn't seem any different."

"Yes, and my aim was good, the ball went right up the middle of the fairway—ah, mostly—but it was twenty, twenty-five yards shorter than usual."

Rafael stopped inspecting his club to look at his companion. "You are placing your feet correctly, so the ball is nearer your left foot?"

"Yes." Godwin wrapped his hands around the top of his driver, putting the club end on the floor next to an imaginary ball, feet apart, elbows straight, head down, knees slightly bent. He waggled his hands a little, preparing to lift the club.

"Ah, I see!" exclaimed Rafael.

"What? What am I doing wrong?"

Rafael moved to stand close behind Godwin and wrapped his arms around him, grasping Godwin's hands. He very slightly twisted Godwin's left hand clockwise. "There," he said. "Now, when you bring your arms back, and bend the wrists, you will find more power available on the down stroke from your left hand." But he did not step back.

"Is there something else?" asked Godwin.

Rafael said, his voice roughened, "I love you so very much, *mi gorrión*," which is Spanish for sparrow, his nickname for Godwin.

"Well, I love you, too, you know that." Godwin wriggled just a little, but still Rafael did not release him.

"I want you to marry me," said Rafael softly.

The wriggling stopped. "I—I—Do you mean that?"

"I do, with all my heart. Will you?"

"Oh, Rafael! Oh, my dear! Oh yes!" He twisted violently in Rafael's arms, so he could turn and face him. The golf club fell to the floor. "Oh, yes, yes, yes!" He was crying with joy and threw his arms around him. "Oh my God, I'm so very happy!"

"Then I am happy, too, *mi gorrión*. So very happy, too."

GODWIN, of course, wanted to plan the whole wedding out at once. Large or small (large), outdoors or in (in because it might rain), what each of them would wear (a black tuxedo for Rafael, a white one for Godwin), when (next June), how many to invite (hundreds, everyone they knew!), what to serve at the reception—

Here Rafael called a halt. "It is getting late, and you have filled my head to its capacity. I want to go on the Internet and see how that Davisson auction is doing, then do some more research on English coins. Or is the correct word *coinage*?"

"How can you talk about coins when we haven't decided on beef or chicken?"

"It doesn't matter. We could serve hamburgers, or shrimp salad, it doesn't matter. What matters is that we exchange rings and tell each other 'I do.' So which is it, coins or coinage?"

"Why are you asking me?"

"You have been speaking English longer than I have."

"So? Numismatists speak their own language. My second language is needlecraft."

Rafael laughed. "Well said, my dear. Now you also must find something to do that will unwind you enough for sleep. What will it be?"

"I don't know, all I can think about is— Wait, yes, I do. I've been neglecting my counted cross-stitch for knitting, so I think I'll get out that little bookmark I didn't finish in time last year." Godwin often stitched bookmarks as Christmas and birthday presents, working them between bigger projects all year long.

"That's better," said Rafael. And he went off to his office.

Though he did not display it, Rafael was elated over Godwin's acceptance of his proposal. He had begun to think such a wonderful thing as a lifetime partner was never to be his. Afraid his excitement would overwhelm him as it had Godwin, he determinedly set the subject aside and opened the locked cabinet where his collections—he had several—lay.

A numismatist is interested in money. Not as a medium of exchange, but as objects of beauty, markers of history, and items with a value outside—usually over—their face value. Rafael was a coin collector. Like most collectors, he had more than one interest, but he had focused hardest on one corner of the vast world of coins; in his case, medieval English hammered silver coins. Starting casually, but more ardently as time passed, he bought an Edward the Third here, a Richard the Lionheart there, a Henry the First, a Henry the Sixth, an Edward the Second. Eventually, he had a set that ran down six centuries, pausing at every reign, beginning in 1066 with the accession of William the Conqueror and ending in 1603 with the death of Elizabeth the First. The monarchs after her he considered less interesting.

Well, except Victoria, a remarkable woman who, like Elizabeth, gave her name to an era. He had a beautiful uncirculated crown coin from Victoria's reign, which he kept separate from the others, both because of the centuries-long gap between her and Elizabeth and because it was a "milled" coin, not a hammered one.

But now, having gone to coin shows at which the Minnesota coin dealer Lief Davisson had a booth, and seeing Davisson's remarkable offerings of British coins, both before and after the centuries covered in his own collection, he was thinking of expanding. He noted that if he went back just a few kings, from the Conqueror to his predecessor Harold the Second, then to Edward the Confessor, then to Harthacnut, then to Harold Harefoot, then Cnut, who became king in 1016; then forward beyond Elizabeth the First to the present queen, he would have a thousand years of English coins, a lovely round number.

To a collector, the hunt is even more engaging than the collection. Finishing a collection is satisfying, but it can be almost a letdown, too, and generally leads to the start of another, or at least endless upgrades of the individual coins. Here was a chance to build on a collection he had seemingly finished.

Toward his new goal, Rafael had signed on to an online auction Davisson was holding, hoping to win a good-looking Cnut he had on offer—and a superior Edward the Confessor. He booted up and went to the auction site.

There were excellent pictures of the many coins in the current auction, as well as the years they were minted (if known) and where. He scrolled down past the ancients to the medieval.

There he found coins dating back to before England was united into a single kingdom in the tenth century, back when kings had names like Sigehere and Egbert, and whose portraits were sometimes hard to identify as human. Reaching at last to England as a kingdom, Rafael found no one had raised his bid on the Edward. There was a Harold the Second being offered, but the portrait wasn't very good—Rafael insisted on good portraits—and besides, the price was already beyond what he was willing to pay.

Harold was king for less than a year before he was defeated at the Battle of Hastings in 1066, seriously altering the course of English history. Harold was a Scandinavian, and William the Conqueror, French—sort of. William was Duke of Normandy, a dukedom so named because it was settled by Northmen, or Vikings. So in a way, England ended up with Scandinavian rulers anyway, though by the eleventh century all of Normandy had become thoroughly French.

There was also a James the First, Elizabeth the First's successor, being auctioned. Among his few achievements,

James had introduced the custom of milled coins—made by a machine rather than struck by a hammer one by one, the blank round held on the die by a nervous apprentice. Just as you could tell a blacksmith by his burn scars, you could tell a medieval coiner by his crooked fingers.

Rafael found the coin uninspiring, perhaps in part because he found the king himself uninspiring. Okay, James had summoned the committee that wrote the King James Bible. But he also was responsible for the torture of witches and had a number of embarrassing personal defects.

Still, if Rafael wanted to complete the expansion, he was going to have to get a James the First. And then Charles the First, Cromwell (ugh!), Charles the Second, James the Second, William and Mary, Anne, George the First, Second, Third, and Fourth, William the Fourth, Victoria, Edward the Seventh, George the Fifth, Edward the Eighth, George the Sixth, then the current queen, Elizabeth the Second, the longest reigning monarch in English history. That admirable woman would put a nice finish to the collection. Eighteen coins—but all more common than the medieval ones, and getting more and more common as they approached the twentieth century.

Godwin had once asked Rafael how he kept track of all those kings and queens, and Rafael proudly recited a Victorian schoolboy's mnemonic rhyme that listed them from William the Conqueror to Victoria:

Willie, Willie, Harry, Stee—
Harry, Dick, John, Harry three,
One, two, three Neds, Richard two,
Harry four, five, six, then who?

Edward four, five, Dick the Bad,
Harries twain, Ned the Lad,
Mary, Bessie, James the Vain,
Charlie, Charlie, James again,
Bill and Mary, Anna Gloria,
Four Georges, William, then Victoria.

Then all he had to remember was Edward, George, Edward, George, and Elizabeth. But Rafael could not have told, for a million dollars, why he, a Spaniard by birth and an American by adoption, was so fascinated by British history.

Chapter Eighteen

THE next morning, up in her apartment, Betsy found a reply to one of her e-mails. It was from a Howard Whiteside.

Hello, Ms. Devonshire, it began. *I am Harry Whiteside's oldest son. I am in Wayzata to make final arrangements of his estate, and to oversee the police investigation of my father's murder. I am the executor of his will. Are you a police detective? Your name is not familiar to me. Is this an interview we can conduct by e-mail? Or Skype? Or even old-fashioned telephone?*

But he did not give his phone number, so she e-mailed him back.

Hello, Mr. Whiteside, she typed. *I understand how busy you must be, and how sad an occasion this is for you, so thank you for your prompt reply. I am not associated with the police but an independent business owner who occasionally does private criminal investigations. I have been asked to look into a pair of murders that happened within a few days of each other in the area around*

Lake Minnetonka. One of them was your father's. It is possible that two different people are responsible but also possible that they are the work of a single individual. I would take it as a great personal favor if you would care to talk with me, however briefly.

She concluded by offering details about the shop she owned and giving the hours it was open and its phone number. She re-read the e-mail a couple of times, corrected a typo, and clicked Send.

When she went down to the shop fifteen minutes later, the phone was ringing.

"Crewel World, Betsy speaking, how may I help you?" she answered.

"Seriously? Cruel World?" demanded a man's voice, a light tenor with a little pleasant sand in it.

"Yessir. Perhaps you have the wrong number?"

"Are you Betsy Devonshire?" he asked.

"Yes, I am. Are you Howard Whiteside?"

"Yes. But Cruel World?"

"Oh my gosh, I didn't put the shop's name in my e-mail! It's crewel, C-R-E-W-E-L. It's a kind of needlework."

"Ah, I see. And you're also a private eye."

"No, I don't have a PI license."

A little sarcastically, "Oh, so you like to mix a little crime into your knitting."

"Sometimes. Reluctantly. It's a wild-card talent I often wish I didn't have. Murder is a very unhappy event."

"You got that right. Things are upside down around here, and I'm having all kinds of problems dealing with not just my father's business affairs but the fact that he was . . . murdered."

"It's an incredibly painful thing to have happen, I know.

My sister was murdered. The unfairness of it, the mess of trying to wind things up, the unexpectedness of it making your own life complicated—it's hard, very hard. I'm sorry this has happened to you."

There was a little pause, while he estimated the accuracy of that statement. Then, "So why are you poking your oar in?"

"Because someone has asked me to. As I said, it's something I have a talent for."

"I wish the local cops did. They're like from a comic book."

"Real cops are rarely from a comic book. I take it you're not happy with the official investigation?"

"I am not!"

"Why is that?"

"They all know who did this. They just lack the guts to go and arrest him!"

"Which 'him' are you talking about?"

"That jerkface from over your way: Joe Mickels."

"What makes you think that the police are ignoring evidence pointing to Mr. Mickels?"

"He had a motive, didn't he? He's rich, isn't he? He's not under arrest, is he? That triplet of facts speaks for itself."

"Maybe he's not under arrest because there's not enough evidence to make the case. Do you know of anyone else who was in opposition to your father? Because of something he might have done, or said?"

"No, of course not! My father was an honest businessman, well respected in his community."

"I see," said Betsy, and even as she spoke she could tell her doubts rang clear.

There was an icy pause. Then Howard Whiteside surprised her by saying, "All right, what I said is not exactly true. My father was a successful businessman, and successful businessmen have to step on toes now and then to make a buck. But I've been taught it's worse than rude to say something mean about someone who recently died. Plus, he's my father. Double-plus, who can I trust not to repeat anything I may say?"

"I understand, truly I do. All I can do is say that I'm trustworthy. I could give you some names of people to ask about me—but you don't know them any more than you know me."

"And so here we are, Mexican standoff—right?"

"All right," Betsy said, but doubtfully, because she was pretty sure that wasn't the definition of a Mexican standoff.

"Somebody's at the door. I'll call you back later." *Kuh-lick.*

GODWIN was late. She wasn't too worried; sometimes he didn't show up quite on time—and he was always willing to stay a little late to compensate. When he finally came in this morning, he was grinning so broadly she began to be nervous for his mouth.

"Are you all right?" she asked.

"Yes, oh yes, I'm all right, I'm more than all right, I promised myself I wouldn't say anything until you asked, thank you for asking, I'm engaged!"

"Engaged? You mean to be married?" She was smiling herself.

Godwin was nodding over and over, short little nods, bob, bob, bob. He came and took her hands in his. "Isn't it wonderful? He asked me last night, just popped the question out of thin air! I couldn't believe it, I can't believe it, my face hurts from smiling, but I can't stop it, I'm engaged to the most wonderful man in the world!" He was dancing a kind of jig. His face was pink, his eyes shining. He had buttoned his shirt wrong. He'd missed a spot shaving.

She pulled him in for an embrace. "I'm so happy for you!" she said.

"We're going to be married in June next year, an indoor wedding. Will you be my matron of honor?"

"Hey, Goddy, are you sure?" Betsy looked flustered. "I mean . . . me? I'm not gay."

"Of course you. You're my best friend—except for Rafael, of course. And you're such a level head, maybe you can keep me from turning the wedding into a three-ring circus. I mean, I started planning last night, and I think Rafael is already scared. It's okay that you're not gay, nobody's perfect. Except Rafael, of course."

Moved to tears, Betsy hugged Godwin again. "Then of course I accept. I'm honored. You're the sweetest man I know. Except for Connor, of course."

He laughed, delighted, and did his famous "Singin' in the Rain" dance step, arms holding an invisible umbrella out in front of him, around the library table.

"I didn't get an e-mail about this, Goddy," she said when he'd made two circuits and stopped to breathe. "Who else have you told?"

"No one, I wanted you to be the first. Except Rafael told

his family last night. Or was it already early this morning there when it was last night here?"

"I'm sure they will be very pleased for him," said Betsy.

That dashed cold water on Godwin's ebullience. "Well . . . probably not. I'm pretty sure they've been holding on to the last shreds of hope that he would marry—not me, of course—and produce a son to carry on the family name. He's the only male of his generation, and they really do not want the name to die. They can trace their line back six hundred years, you know. And there are knights and earls and dukes and even a king or two in their lineage, I think. He doesn't care, he hardly talks about it, but it's terribly important to them."

"Oh dear."

"Do you know his grandmother actually suggested he marry a woman and keep a boyfriend on the side?"

Betsy nodded. "I think he mentioned that once, a long time ago."

"And she's the reasonable one."

"Oh *dear*! Maybe he shouldn't have said anything until after the wedding."

"I told him that, but he's got this honor thing going—can you imagine, honor among a family group like that?—and said it was the right thing to do."

"Well, it's his family, perhaps he knows best."

"We can only hope."

Apart from intermittent sighs and giggles on Godwin's part, the day went as usual. Howard Whiteside did not call back.

* * *

CONNOR and Betsy were preparing for supper. He was building a very elaborate omelet around a pair of pork chops, and she was setting the table. They were anticipating a quiet evening at home, so she put out the wineglasses.

"So Mr. Whiteside never called back," Connor called out from the galley kitchen.

"Well, he didn't say he'd call back today," she replied, inserting a napkin in an embroidered fabric napkin ring.

After they sat down, they used up the wine making first elaborate and then increasingly silly toasts to Godwin and Rafael and their amazing (probably) wedding.

They were just wrapping up dinner when the phone rang. Connor took the last of his wine in a single gulp ("And to their all-girl band," he said) and went to answer it.

"Hello?" he said, and after a pause, "Yes. Just a minute." He turned to Betsy, who was gathering up the dishes, and said, "It's for you. Hector Whiteside."

"You mean Howard," she said, coming to take the receiver from him.

"He says Hector."

"Hello?" she said into the receiver.

"Hello, Ms. Devonshire. Am I interrupting anything?"

The voice sounded different than Howard's, deeper, with a slight drawl. "Who is this?" she asked.

"I'm Heck Whiteside, Howard's brother."

"Oh, are you in town, too?"

"No, Howie called me. We agreed I might be the better one to talk to you. I'm flying out tonight, to Minneapolis."

"Just to talk to me? We're talking now, saving you a trip."

"I prefer face-to-face whenever possible. And I need to come anyway. Ham will fly in day after tomorrow."

"Ham? Oh, Hamilton."

"Yeah, cute nicknames we ended up with, Howie, Ham, Heck. Our parents obviously weren't thinking clearly when they named us."

Betsy chuckled politely, not sure whether the complaint was sincere. "I'd like to meet with one or all of you, if that's possible."

"It's possible, maybe. But I'm not sure if we can be of any help. We're not exactly a close family. Plus, I'm not sure Ham will go for this. But I'm with you; I think it might be a good idea."

"HAM, Heck, Howie," said Connor later from his side of the bed. "What a collection of names! How can parents do that to their children?"

"I don't know. Some of them aren't thinking of nicknames—I mean, Hamilton is a great American name, Hector a famous ancient Greek hero, Howard—Howard, hmmm, I don't know any famous Howards."

"There's Thomas Howard, a man famous in fifteenth-century England. His niece was Catherine Howard, who married Henry VIII, although that didn't turn out so well."

Betsy chuckled. "And on thinking further, there's Howard Hughes, Howard Hawks, and Ron Howard, from television and the movies. Or maybe Howie's named after a grandfather, or uncle. He's the oldest, so that's not unlikely. And then his parents went with that custom of giving each of their kids a name starting with the same letter of the alphabet."

"I see that none of the brothers live in Minnesota. What kind of information from them could be useful? What can they know about their father's business dealings?"

She said, "I want to know what kind of person Harry Whiteside was. I'm looking for the kind of personality that creates enemies. These three have probably known Harry Whiteside longer than anyone. I'm hoping they're perceptive and willing to be honest with me."

"Two—count 'em, two—big requests of this trio. I wish you luck."

"Thank you." And despite being excited at the prospect of really digging into Harry Whiteside's personality, Betsy quickly drifted off to sleep.

Chapter Nineteen

❖❖❖

"EVERYTHING is closed in London today," Connor remarked over breakfast Friday morning.

"What for, spring break?" Betsy replied, dipping into her Rice Krispies topped with canned peach slices.

"No, because it's Good Friday."

"I thought England was no longer a Christian country," she said, surprised.

"As long as the Church of England is the state religion and the queen is Defender of the Faith, schools and many stores close on Good Friday, Holy Saturday, and Easter Sunday."

"Wow," said Betsy, after a moment, because for all that America was a Christian country, stores were open the entire Easter weekend, at least in part.

"You're a Christian," he said.

"Is that a hint?" she asked, smiling.

"The weather report this morning is for unseasonably warm weather under clear skies."

"If we were to close Crewel World for religious reasons, we should go to church."

"I intend to, from twelve to three. The morning is for walking from Minnehaha Falls to the Mississippi and back again."

"I'm going to redesign the front window with Godwin to reflect summer patterns, and design the ad for the Big Bang July Sale. We've got to do something to recoup the bad sales we've suffered the past four months."

The first three months of any year at Crewel World were slow, but this year, for some reason, sales had been alarmingly poor. And despite the two good days of fourteen so far in April, they hadn't fully rebounded from the slump. Politicians had been insisting the economy was recovering, but evidence of it in Betsy's shop had been lagging. The fall and winter hadn't been too bad, but once Christmas was over, the bottom—while not exactly falling out—had been steadily drifting downward.

Easter was late this year, falling on April 16. Easter marked the start of spring, which generally brought in advance a noticeable uptick in sales. But that wasn't happening. Where was everyone? Had all of Betsy's customers moved south? It had been a hard winter, after all.

No, customers had been coming in, but fewer in number, and they just weren't spending as usual. Mrs. Hardy, for example, hadn't bought the materials for another pattern that would need expensive finishing.

When Betsy went down to open the store, she found Godwin impatiently waiting. "What's up?" she asked.

"Two things. First—" He held out his left hand. His

ring finger was newly graced with a fat gold ring set with a large, red cabochon stone.

"Oh my goodness!" said Betsy.

"I can't afford anything like this to give him for an engagement ring," he said a little sadly. Then he brightened. "Still . . . It's a real ruby!"

"It's beautiful, congratulations!" She took his left hand and looked more closely at it, a massive chunk of gold, elaborately worked in an antique design, and a startlingly large stone red as fresh blood. "Gosh, Goddy, I bet your hand will get tired carrying that thing around."

He smirked. "I'll have to start eating my Wheaties every morning."

"So, what's the other thing?"

"I've got a couple of ideas for the window."

"Good, let's get opened up and you can share them with me."

They turned on the lights, made an urn of coffee—Crewel World offered a free cup of coffee to any customer—and put on the electric kettle so there would be hot water for anyone who preferred tea. They put the start-up cash in the drawer, turned on the computer, and tuned the Bose radio to a soft jazz station. They did a walk-through to make sure the shelves were stocked and in order and dusted. Then, since the kettle hadn't started to sing, each pulled a Diet Pepsi from the little refrigerator in the back and sat down.

"So what's your idea?" asked Betsy. He had two, actually. One of them was a Fourth of July theme: "Skyrockets of happiness! Explosive bargains! Shooting star designers! Like that."

Betsy nodded. Little wonder Godwin had chosen something exuberant. "I like it, but we'll have to come up with another idea for after the Fourth."

"Well, yes, that's right. But that leads to my second idea. So we'll keep the Fourth and then have something else so the summer window doesn't start to look tired. I'm thinking we could call it Summer Under the Stars? Showcasing our best and most popular designers."

"Now that I like, it's a follow-on!" said Betsy. "Okay, let's start pulling patterns for the Fourth. There's that red, white, and blue butterfly, the eyeglasses case kit that's a flag, the patriotic Jim Shore angel, the E Pluribus Unum eagle."

"There's that sampler that says 'O Beautiful for Spacious Skies,'" said Godwin. "That needs to go in the window for sure. It's really pretty."

"And so for the Summer group, let's use Lizzie Kate's Sweet Summer booklet," said Betsy. "And keeping up the star theme, there's Flag of Stars from Bent Creek." That one was a simplified American flag made of red, white, and blue stars.

"Ooooh, good, we can feature that in the newsletter when we announce the Summer Under the Stars sale."

When Connor came in a little before noon, he found them at the long table scattered with patterns and models and notebooks covered with sketches. Betsy looked up to see he was smiling. "A nice walk?" she asked.

"A pretty walk and too early for mosquitoes," he said. "Now, can you abandon all this and come to church with me?"

"I would, but I can't. Mrs. Phillips called, and she wants to place a special order for a canvas."

"Goddy can take the order."

"Mrs. Phillips doesn't like Goddy," said Betsy, casting a compassionate look at Godwin, who raised his hands in a what-can-you-do gesture.

"You could tell her you won't serve her until she changes her attitude," said Connor.

"And end up like that bakery that refused to bake a wedding cake for a couple they disagreed with? Not a chance," said Betsy.

"Ah so," said Connor. "Sorry, fellow," he said to Godwin and, "See you later," to Betsy, and he went out. Mrs. Phillips was nearly eighty, hard to please, and chronically tardy. After she had finished placing her order, Betsy, fasting, spent the third hour in Excelsior's Trinity Church listening to readings and music until the lay reader declared, "It is finished."

GOOD Friday in the Christian religion memorializes a shocking, painful, sorrowful, "precious" event. But it's an event, something happening to make a big change in the world. "Sorrowing, sighing, bleeding, dying," predicts one of the Three Kings at Christmas.

Connor, usually not able to keep a Christian calendar while at sea, nevertheless often found himself during those years inquiring of God if He please could see Himself taking care of Captain Connor, his crew, and his ship when the seas were high, the sky dark, and the wind a massive, roiling presence. "O God, Thy sea is so great and my boat is so small," he often pointed out.

So now in safe harbor for good, he was glad of a church nearby where he could offer thanks for the fact that he had never been shipwrecked, or taken by pirates, or cheated by owners.

He and Betsy sat patiently through the reminder of the terrible three hours that Jesus had endured on the cross, and they came away mildly downhearted at the end.

He was glad that Betsy, this strong, warm comfort of his later years, would join him for part of it.

Of course, there was another big event coming, the polar opposite of Good Friday: Easter Sunday. But first, of course, there was Holy Saturday, a day the Christian world sat with its pensive head down, sorrowing, waiting. It's possibly the longest day of the religion for believers.

BETSY closed on time Saturday afternoon and shared a light supper with Connor. Then they shortened the wait for Sunday by setting off for Saint Mark's Episcopal Cathedral near downtown Minneapolis around seven ten, arriving just at seven forty to find parking already at a premium. It was a clear, chilly evening.

The church was unlit, but there were people, lots of people, gathered inside. And more coming.

It was dark out, or as dark as a big city gets at night. And dark inside. The big stained glass windows were barely visible shapes in the brick walls of the cathedral, the saints depicted indecipherable. Betsy and Connor found seats about halfway up the center aisle. An usher waiting at the door had given them, like everyone else, a slim, unlit taper with a cardboard collar and a bulletin with the order of the service printed in it, which they could not read in the dark.

At eight, a hush of garments was heard at the back, and heads turned as the congregation tried to make out who was gathering there and not coming forward. Then a click and a gout of yellow flame rose out of a pale stone about twice the size of a football, a stone that hadn't been there in the middle of the floor before. By its light people could be seen, perhaps a dozen of them, in ecclesiastical robes. One of them lit a long, fat candle at the flame and then from it, smaller candles young people in white albs were holding.

The acolytes came forward to light the tapers of the people in the back pew, who in turn lit the tapers of the people in front of them, who handed the flame forward until everyone had a lit candle, two hundred and more dots of yellow filling the nave with very soft, warm light.

Meanwhile, the Dean of the Cathedral was reciting, in a carrying voice, prayers about Christ passing from the darkness of death into the light. When everyone had a lit taper, a deacon raised the big candle and called, "The Light of Christ!" and the congregation, now reading from the bulletin by the light of the tapers, responded, "Thanks be to God!"

The group of priests, deacons, and acolytes at the west door started forward and up past the choir to the altar. As they processed, a member of the choir floated, a capella, something exotic and mournful in Latin. Gregorian chant, thought Connor, half closing his eyes in pleasure.

The hymn ended, and, having reached the altar, the

Dean turned to the congregation and proclaimed, "This is the night when Christ vanquished hell, broke the chains of death, and rose triumphant from the grave!"

Then a woman from the congregation made her way to the lectern on the left side and turned on a small reading lamp. She read from Genesis about Adam and Eve in the Garden. She was followed by three more lectors, all men, who read about Abraham, ordered and then stopped from sacrificing his son Isaac; then about the Jews crossing the Red Sea out of slavery in Egypt; and last, about Ezekiel telling of God turning from anger to bless his people.

The readings weren't long, but by the end Connor noticed his taper was becoming short, and he saw Betsy adjusting the collar on hers down to the very bottom.

The last reader was still making his way back to his pew when every light in the church came on, the organ blasted a mighty chord, and the Dean shouted above the uproar, "Alleluia, Christ is risen!"

The reader staggered in surprise, then laughed at himself and joined with everyone shouting in reply, "The Lord is risen indeed! Alleluia!"

And, accompanied by the organ, the choir broke into "Glory to God in the Highest."

Betsy's was not the quietest voice giving the reply, and Connor looked a little sideways at her. But she merely grinned back at him and blew out her taper, so he blew out his.

The candles on the altar were lit during all this, and there followed an Episcopal High Church Eucharist service, without a sermon, and with lots of familiar joyful and triumphant hymns. By ten o'clock it was over, and the altar crew stood at the door to shake the hands of the congregation as they left. Betsy noticed several women in large and elaborate hats. She turned to Connor. "I wish I had consulted with Cherie about an Easter bonnet for me."

"Please do next time," he replied. "I'd like to see you in one."

"You have to promise not to laugh."

"Oh, well, in that case, never mind."

They shook half a dozen hands and went out into the chilly night's nippy breeze to find Betsy's Buick. She wove it expertly through the crowd of departing vehicles, and they started up I-394 for home.While driving, Betsy remarked, "I've always felt a little sorry for people who celebrate Easter without suffering through Good Friday. You really need the contrast to get all the flavor."

"You wish they would just stay home and eat a marshmallow bunny instead?"

"No, it would be unkind to wish that. For a long while I was a Christmas and Easter Christian, myself. But it's much more thrilling to glory at someone rising from the grave when you first grieve at His dying."

"Kind of like celebrating spring without first suffering winter," agreed Connor.

"And Mardi Gras loses some of its meaning if you don't follow it with Lent."

"Well . . ." said Connor, "that's doing it backward. First the joy, then the repentance."

"I wonder if that's how the person who murdered Harry

Whiteside feels. Bang, slash, steal, wreck, then Harry walks in and the intruder smashes him on the head, in an exhilarating whirlwind of rage. But in his cooler moments the next day . . ."

"I hope so," said Connor grimly. "I truly hope so."

Chapter Twenty

ONE of the rewards of going to the Easter Vigil service on Saturday night is that you can sleep late on Easter Sunday while still feeling virtuous. Connor and Betsy read and stitched through what was left of the morning, ate a debauched lunch of hard-boiled eggs and jelly beans, then spent the afternoon with Jill and Lars and their three young children. Lots of talk, a couple of silly board games, a walk along the lakeshore with Bjorn the big black Newfoundland, and a nap for the children. Dinner with them was ham, sweet potatoes, and Brussels sprouts, with creamed corn only for the adults and children who ate at least one brussels sprout (Einar was caught feeding his to Bjorn the dog and so was disqualified). Then they all watched *Easter Parade*, starring Fred Astaire and Judy Garland. Erik and Emma Beth thought the best part was Judy Garland walking down the street making a really horrible face.

* * *

On Monday, Bershada came into Crewel World with Alice. Both carried stitchery bags, ready for the weekly Monday Bunch meeting.

Bershada was speaking. "Girl, you would not believe the talking-to my aunt Sadie gave my daughter a month before the wedding! Backed her up against the wall! Put her finger right up to her nose and said"—here Bershada's voice changed to a thin old black woman's Southern drawl—"'Ef you don' straighten up an' fly right, child, ain't nobody comin' to this wedding, 'cause I'll call Pastor Rivers an' tell him it's *off*!'" Bershada laughed. "And she could have done it, too, because my daughter had moved the wedding from her own church to Aunt Sadie's church because her own church was 'too small, and not fancy enough.'" Bershada had assumed a high, breathy voice with a nasty undertone to it when quoting her daughter. Then she broke again into laughter.

"Her own church is beautiful. Small, yes, but beautiful. I grew up in that church—so did she. The pastor married her father and me. He baptized her, and loves her like a daughter. But the church was too small for my daughter's big fat wedding."

Bershada threw a hand up in the air. "Children! Betsy, you are so lucky you didn't have children! They break your heart!"

Betsy smiled. There were days when she was sure Bershada was right, but today wasn't one of them, not after she had spent a blissful Sunday afternoon and evening in the company of the three Larson youngsters, who were sunny and charming the whole time. "In a week or two, you'll change your mind," she said.

"Humph," snorted Bershada, going to the library table. Alice trailed behind, her face sad. An elderly widow, she had lost her only child many years ago to a heart ailment.

Betsy said, "Bershada, I want to tell you that you have a remarkable son. I was so impressed with him at Maddy's funeral. And he was extremely helpful to me over supper the other night. I'm so glad you sent him to me."

Bershada sat down and pulled out her counted cross-stitch project of two kittens frolicking on a stack of books. "Yes, he's turning out to be my pride and joy. And I suppose in a month or two I'll forgive my daughter for her antics."

Alice said to Betsy in her deep voice, "So you are getting involved. On whose behalf?"

"Joe Mickels."

Alice blinked three times at Betsy, her mouth open in surprise. "Joe Mickels? Why, is he offering you half his kingdom?"

"No." Betsy smiled, taking a seat at the table. "What would I do with half a kingdom? What would half a queen look like?"

"Amateur night at the Gay Nineties?" suggested Godwin. The Gay Nineties was a downtown Minneapolis nightclub that offered a female impersonator competition once a month.

Betsy looked at him, laughing. "Hush, baby, we're trying to talk."

He sniffed and went back to pinning up some new needlepoint canvases on the set of hinged fabric "doors" hanging on a wall.

Alice said, "I assume Joe came to you because he feels he's a suspect in Maddy's death."

"And in Harry's."

"What, both of them?" said Alice.

"Mike Malloy thinks the two might be related."

"Ah, because of the property bidding war on Water Street."

"That's right."

Bershada said, "I should think Joe would be too busy coming up with a defense for when Mike arrests him to complain about his methods."

Betsy nodded, leaning sideways to pull out her current project: a counted cross-stitch pattern of nine young trees stitched in black and dark gray on white Aida fabric. She'd found the project for sale for two dollars in Leipold's eccentric shop on Water Street. The pattern, floss, and fabric were in a plastic bag, but without the original packaging, so there was no title or designer's name. One tree was finished, one was about half done, and one had just the back stitching. The rest was blank fabric. Stark and graceful, it was lovely. Mrs. Leipold said, "I hope you can finish it—and I hope you'll bring it back here when you do, because I'd like to buy it from you." Mrs. Leipold had a good eye for beauty but was not a stitcher.

Betsy bought it because she agreed it was beautiful, and she was working on it because, since the placement of Xs to indicate leaves was pretty much random, any mistakes she made were invisible. Usually counted cross-stitch made her tense; here she could relax.

Alice, preparing to continue her project of crocheting a prayer shawl for her church, arranged her yarn in her fingers and said, "I keep remembering what Emily said about seeing Joe just sitting in his car looking sad."

Betsy said, "You know, I think I saw that same sadness on his face when we talked. He's a hard man, but he seems pretty sure he's going to be arrested. And that may be making him sad."

"He shouldn't be sad, he should be scared," said Bershada. "Suppose he didn't murder Harry and Maddy. If someone else murdered both of them, then he may be next in line."

The thoughtful little silence that followed that statement was interrupted by the door's announcement of someone's entrance. Today Godwin had set it to play a chorus of "Mairzy Doats," which made Alice chuckle, since she remembered the silly song from her youth.

They all looked to see Jill Cross Larson come in. A tall, sturdy, beautiful woman with ash-blond hair and a Gibson Girl face, Jill worked in an admin capacity at the police department, where her husband was a sergeant. So they all were especially pleased to see her, because maybe she had news of the investigation.

"Good afternoon, everyone," she said after a pause, surprised at their intense interest in her arrival. Then she came to the table and sat down.

"What news?" demanded Godwin.

"About what?" she asked.

"The investigation into Maddy's murder, of course. Is Mike going to arrest Joe?"

"I don't think so, not right now." Everyone could see Jill was avoiding eye contact, uncomfortable with the topic.

"Do you know something we're not supposed to know?" asked Alice in her blunt way.

"No, of course not."

But as others arrived—Phil and Doris, Emily, Cherie, Valentina, Connor—they also asked. Jill, sensibly aware they hadn't already heard her uncomfortable reply, simply repeated it.

When the last arrival took his seat, Godwin said, "Let's all agree not to talk about Joe Mickels today."

"No, don't shut down the talk," objected Jill. "I just won't have anything to contribute."

"Why not?" asked Emily, pausing in the act of threading her needle. Unconsciously echoing Alice, she asked, "Do you know something we shouldn't find out?"

"No," said Jill. "But I have an 'in' with the police, so I shouldn't say something that might be misconstrued."

Betsy remembered a time when Jill had carelessly said something to her that broke a police department confidence and got them both in trouble as a result. Doubtless Jill remembered it, too.

To distract them from the topic, Jill said, "On the other hand, I'm dying to hear Goddy tell us why he is wearing a vulgarly large ring on the third finger of his left hand." Of course she already knew; Betsy had told her at the Easter Sunday dinner.

Godwin, delighted that someone had asked about his ring, came to the table to flash it at everyone. "I'm engaged!" he cried, rapturously. "Rafael asked, and he gave me this ring. It's a family heirloom!"

"Wonderful!" "Excellent!" "Congratulations!" "Brilliant!" "Good for the both of you!" went around the table.

"When's the happy event?" asked Alice.

"June. We haven't picked a site yet; all we know is that it won't be a church wedding and it will be indoors—I do not want to stand shivering in a downpour while we exchange vows and the cake gets washed away."

"That practically guarantees it will be a gorgeous day," said Doris, and the others agreed, laughing.

"You're all invited. We'll be sending a save-the-date postcard, of course. Meanwhile we're on the search for a venue we both like and will reserve the date for us." He pressed the back of his gold-heavy hand to his forehead. "So many details, so little time!" he sighed and went back to pinning up needlepoint canvases.

Doris said, "Goddy, you were such a help to me planning my wedding. Please let me help you plan yours in any way I can."

Godwin looked thoughtfully at her. His "help" for her wedding had been to make it bigger, less modest. Might hers, therefore, be to tone his down?

Betsy watched his face parade those thoughts across it.

"I think that's a lovely thing for you to do, Doris," she said. "I suspect Rafael might think so, too."

Amusement broke out on Godwin's face. "Oh, Betsy, you are so right! You should have seen Rafael's face when I talked about releasing a hundred doves dyed lavender! And so, Doris, I accept your offer. Let's you and me get together some evening soon."

"Just let me know when," Doris said, pleased.

"Isn't Goddy just the nicest person?" said Emily. "I'm so happy for him." She turned in her chair and smiled at him. He winked at her.

Then Betsy changed the subject. "Emily, did the refinance of your house go through?"

"Yes, it did. We decided to keep the mortgage payments the same size, but the house will be paid for six years sooner. We're so pleased!"

More congratulations passed around the table.

Betsy said quietly, "Bershada, I'd like to talk with you privately after this meeting, all right?"

Bershada said, "Of course."

Cherie asked, "Is your daughter safely away on her honeymoon, Bershada?"

"Yes, the long nightmare is over, thank God."

"Is she the last one?" asked Doris.

"The last daughter. There's still that one son. I'm holding on to hope that he'll find someone soon."

"Don't be too eager," advised Cherie, "you may not like the bride he picks, and daughter-in-law problems are particularly painful, because they last for years and years."

"Hmmm," said Bershada, who was currently suffering from a son-in-law problem.

Phil said, "Betsy, are you still convinced that Joe Mickels didn't murder Maddy?"

"I'm not 'convinced' of anything, except that this is Monday and you are sitting at this table," she said.

Doris reached over and pinched her husband on his ear. "Ouch!" he said.

"Yes, he's really here," she said. She looked at Betsy. "Shall I reach over and pinch you?"

"If you do, I'll reach over and pinch Jill, and who knows where that will lead?" teased Betsy.

Cherie said, "Let the blood sports begin!"

After the laughter, everyone settled into his or her projects for a while.

Valentina asked, "Does anyone know what will happen to the Water Street property now that Maddy is dead?"

Blank looks all around. Betsy held her tongue, but the others began to guess.

Alice said, "I think the fair thing to do is to open the bidding again. Start over."

Doris said, "No, I think they'll hand the deed to the second-highest bidder. That was Joe Mickels, wasn't it?"

"No, I heard Joe came in third; the second-highest bidder was Harry," said Alice.

"So then, since he's dead, too," said Phil, "Joe gets it."

"No, it should go to Harry's son—the one who's come to Wayzata to take over his father's business," said Cherie.

Godwin said from across the room, "Ask Betsy, she knows."

They all looked at Betsy. "Well, as a matter of fact, I did ask Jim Penberthy about it."

"What'd he say?" demanded Valentina. "Which one of us is right?"

"None of you. The right to buy the property belongs to Maddy's estate. The executor of her will can decide to pay the amount bid by Maddy for it, or he—or she, I don't know who it is—can put the option up for sale."

"What's the son's name?" asked Alice.

"What son? Maddy had a son?" said Valentina.

"No, I mean Harry Whiteside's son, the one come to town to clear up his father's affairs."

Phil said, "I'm not sure. Howard, I think."

"He's very upset with the investigation," said Connor. "Thinks there's a cover-up."

"A cover-up? In favor of who?" asked Phil. "Harry was the richest man in Wayzata, if not the county. On whose behalf would the cops do a cover-up?"

Godwin said, "Joe Mickels, of course. I bet Howard's angry because the cops haven't arrested Joe."

"Is Joe richer than Harry?" asked Connor.

"I don't know," said Betsy. "I don't think anyone but Joe knows how rich he is. He doesn't want it known. And I don't know how rich Harry was, for that matter."

"But Joe wouldn't carry any weight in Wayzata, would he?" asked Phil. "His home ground is over here, in Excelsior."

Betsy said, "He has an office in Excelsior, which is his official mailing address. I suspect he has other offices elsewhere."

"Why does he keep all these secrets?" asked Emily.

"I don't know that they're secrets," said Betsy. "He just doesn't advertise his wealth. People with a lot of money can be targets. If he needs to show the power of his wealth to gain something, he'll show it. But otherwise, he prefers to run quiet."

"Sort of like you," said Emily.

"Me?" Betsy stared at her.

"Sure. You have a lot of money, but you don't let it show."

"Emily, I am not rich!" Depending on how you defined rich, this was true.

"Sure you are. People say you could give this shop to Godwin for free and never have to work a day in your life ever again."

Godwin said, in perfect imitation of Betsy, "*Me?*"

"Sure, you. Who else would Betsy give it to?"

"Connor, of course," he said.

Connor said, "No, I'm done working for a living. I've got a fully funded pension and some modest investments that provide me rent, food, and the occasional new pair of shoes. I especially don't need to be sole proprietor of a small business that has recently decided to stay open late on Mondays."

Betsy said lightly, "Before we start a quarrel over who wants my business least, may I ask Emily who on earth told her these things?"

Emily blushed and looked down at her needlework. She mumbled, "I don't want to say."

There fell an uncomfortable silence, as several members of the group held the same opinion as Emily about Betsy's wealth but had never been rude enough to say so to her face.

Connor said, "Speaking of money, tell us, Bershada, how much money did the auction take in?"

"Our goal was twenty-five thousand dollars, and we raised thirty-six," said Bershada, chin lifted, eyes shining.

"Oooh, that's smashing!" cheered Godwin.

"Good for you!" agreed Cherie, and the others chimed in with congratulations.

Jill asked Betsy, "When is that Barbara Eyre trunk show going to come in?"

"I'm not sure. It got held up when the show was at Orts Galore in Cincinnati and a flood damaged the shop—and about a third of the canvases. Ms. Eyre is trying to restore some of them and add new ones to the collection. We're hoping to see it in about a month."

Cherie said, "I've heard you people use the word 'orts' before. What's an ort?"

"When you finish stitching with a length of floss," said Bershada. "The little end you snip off is an ort."

Emily said, "I collect mine in transparent Christmas ornaments. They look pretty on our tree, and remind me of finished projects."

The stitchers moved on to other topics and broke up around three thirty.

Bershada gave Betsy a few minutes to put her stitching away. Then she said, "What do you want to ask me about?"

"Maddy. How well did you know her?" Betsy picked up her long reporter's notebook.

Eyeing the notebook, Bershada said, "Not really well. I don't think anyone but Chaz knew her well. But I have—did know her for about seven years, maybe eight. Helen Fasciana started a book club, and Maddy was the third person to sign on. She had some excellent suggestions for what we should read, and she had interesting insights into the books, too. She was a very intelligent woman. But, she didn't like it when someone disagreed with her. We were all relieved when she dropped out after her first year."

"But you reconnected," suggested Betsy.

"Yes, we had become friends—of a sort. I wanted to stay in touch because of Chaz—he sometimes forms attachments to people who can hurt him. But I liked her for myself, too, because she had attitude, and I find people with attitude interesting. She wasn't cruel or dishonest. In fact, she was kind, in a sort of angry way. Always giving money to causes, usually anonymously. For example, the library—she'd write a check for a hundred dollars to me, tell me to cash it and give the money to them and not tell them where it came from. 'Here, take this,' she'd say, shoving a check at me. 'Give it to Trinity's food shelf.' Or, she'd say, 'Here, cash this, and give it to Temple Israel, they're raising money to send some young adults to Jerusalem.'" Bershada shrugged. "I think she didn't want to be thanked. Strange, strange lady."

"I got the impression that she was shy, that day she brought that last box of knit toys in here," said Betsy. "She didn't want people to look at her, put her forward, give her any attention. That's why she objected to your plan to put her in front of the auction room."

Bershada thought about that, then nodded. "It could be you're right. Does that put us any closer to finding her murderer?"

"Not really."

"You know, now you've put the word *shy* into my head, maybe another word for her is *defensive*. But I never heard her complain that someone was being cruel or unfair to her or that someone was angry with her—not murderously angry. Chaz says lots of people were angry with her for business reasons, and that Harry Whiteside was a particular thorn in her side. But is that a reason to kill her? She had no family, so there wasn't someone thinking he or she could inherit her money if only she'd die. Is any of this helpful?"

Betsy sighed. "Not in the way I was hoping."

Chapter Twenty-one

IT took some arranging, but Hector Whiteside agreed to meet Betsy for lunch at Sol's the next day. The morning brought a rash of problems. The credit card reader worked only half the time, a customer brought in a painted canvas she'd obviously started and then pulled the stitches out and now she wanted a refund, two part timers called to say they couldn't work next week. Betsy left with a little sigh of relief. The delicatessen was next door to Crewel World, and Betsy went over a bit early so she could watch for him.

A few minutes after twelve a man in his early thirties came in. He was not quite six feet tall, stocky, with curly brown hair just barely covering a bald spot, a pleasant expression on his large, dark-eyed face, and a comfortable way of walking that indicated strength. This was a man who did not spend his workday at a desk. He was wearing a navy blue pullover and dress slacks. The collar of a light blue shirt grazed the sweater at its neck.

Betsy raised her hand, and he smiled affably and came to where she sat at the little table, one of three in the room. The chairs at the table had round wooden seats and wire legs and backs, a charming old-fashioned style, but Betsy wondered if the chair would hold his weight when he dropped onto it.

It did, and without protest. "Hello," the man said. "I'm Heck Whiteside, from Dallas." He did have a mild Texas accent.

"I'm Betsy Devonshire. I'm glad to meet you." She held out her hand, and he took it rather gingerly in his big, calloused one.

"I was shocked and sorry to hear about your father," she said.

"Thank you. But there's more than that with you, right?" he added. "You're interested in how it happened to him."

"And by whom, yes, you're right. I'm at the start of an investigation into your father's murder—into two murders, actually."

He studied her closely, leaning toward her, his mouth pulled a little sideways. Then he came to a conclusion. "You actually think you can find out who murdered my father."

"I think I can. I have done this sort of thing before."

"That's good. So, you have a license, a PI license?"

"No."

His eyes widened in surprise, then his whole face clenched, eyebrows pulling together and mouth pursed. "You're some kind of a goddamned amateur?"

"That's right. Didn't your brother tell you?"

He sat back, but his expression remained angry. "No."

"Nevertheless, I have solved several murders."

"How?" It was a demand.

"I don't understand the question." Was he looking for anecdotes?

"What are your methods? Do you kidnap a suspect and refuse to knit a sweater for him until he confesses?" Now he was teasing her, and not in a nice way.

Betsy held back the angry retort she wanted to make—she had come to this meeting already aggravated. But instead she took a breath and waited for her overheated blood to simmer down. Then she said, "I have been doing this for a number of years, and I have had the support of several current and former police investigators. I do not use force or deception or any illegal method. What I mostly do is talk to people. I look for motive and opportunity. Because I am not a professional, people tend to take me lightly and so give away more than they realize when I talk with them."

"What have I given away?" He was still annoyed but also clearly curious.

"Mostly that you are very angry about your father's death. That is both sad and understandable."

"Only mostly?" he said, eyebrows raised.

"Anger might—might—make you leap to conclusions. You and your brother want a fast, easy solution to this. Since it hasn't come, you and he both think the investigators are incompetent. I think that's why you agreed to talk with me, and why you are so disappointed to find that I'm an amateur, and worse, that I own a sweet little needlework shop. But I'm telling you that perhaps there is more to me than you think, and more to the situation with your father than you would like. Your anger and impatience won't change the facts."

"What are the facts?"

"I don't know all of them, or even most of them. But I want to find out. And I've been asked to find out."

"Who asked you?"

"Why do you want to know?"

"Ha, I bet it's that Mickels person."

"And if it is?"

Again he sat back, convinced and assured, smirking. "Then I won't talk to you. I think he killed my father, and now I think he's convinced you to help him get away with it."

"I think you'll regret that decision."

He leaned forward again and said softly, "I think I won't."

"Very well," said Betsy. She looked around and saw the current Sol—in Betsy's time there had been two previous owners of Sol's Deli, none authentically named Sol—behind the meat and cheese counter. He was looking at her. She called, "I'd like a tuna sandwich on whole wheat, small chips, and a big spear of kosher dill, to go." She looked at Heck. "You?"

And yet again that studying look. "All right," he said, his nod accepting her unspoken offer to pay. "I'll have a chicken on rye." He looked over at Sol and repeated his order, louder. "Chicken on rye! Lettuce and tomato! Mayo! Soup of the day!" He grinned at Betsy. "For here!"

Betsy paid for her meal and his and went back to her shop, her mood not improved by the encounter.

"Uh-oh," said Godwin on seeing her enter. Today the door was playing "With Her Head Tucked Underneath Her

Arm," and she grimaced instead of laughing at the music.
"Not a good interview, I take it," he said.

"No, he's too angry to see I'm trying to help." She went to the library table and dumped her white sack on it. "Rats." She went into the back room to make herself a cup of black English tea, refilled the electric teakettle, and when she came back was surprised to see Heck Whiteside standing at the table.

"I'm not apologizing," he announced stiffly. "But hey, maybe I can tell you something useful and you can pass it on to someone competent." He smiled, recalling to her that affable look she'd noted when he first came into Sol's, though now she could recognize the snark behind it. "I'm not a badass," he continued. "I'm just angry. I've got things to do at home, but I can't leave till this is over."

He held up a white paper bag, a copy of the one in front of Betsy on the table. "Okay?" he asked.

"All right," she said, and gestured at a chair opposite the one she was about to sit in.

But before he could seat himself, she turned toward her store manager and said, "Godwin, this is Hector Whiteside, the youngest son of Harry Whiteside. Heck, this is my store manager, Godwin DuLac."

Godwin said neutrally and without moving, "How do you do?"

Hector replied in an echo of Godwin's tone, "How do you do?" and sat down.

"Mr. Whiteside," said Betsy, "would you like a cup of coffee or tea?"

"No, thank you," he replied, pulling a bottle of cranberry juice from his paper bag.

"Goddy, could you go back to the counted cross-stitch section and straighten out the Thanksgiving and Easter patterns?" Two customers from out of town had taken a special joy in finding patterns they hadn't seen before—and pulling them out of the slanted cabinets for closer looks, and dropping the ones they voted against on the floor. Or worse, stuffing them back into the slots any which way, out of order or even upside down. In the end, they hadn't bought enough to make up what it would cost Betsy in Godwin's wages to put them right again.

Betsy could have stayed after closing and done it herself, but she wanted to talk with Hector now, while he had come willingly to her—and she wanted to reassure him that no one would eavesdrop.

"What made you change your mind?" she asked Hector, opening her lunch bag.

He unwrapped a fat sandwich that dribbled shredded lettuce. "I decided to stop letting my anger run my mouth." He pulled a big, squat cardboard cup from his bag, lifted the white plastic lid, and released a gout of steam that smelled of ham and beans.

She pulled out her own sandwich and snack-size bag of chips. The sandwich was wrapped in translucent paper, the spear of pickle visible, laid diagonally on the bread.

"So, where do we start?" he asked, putting the sandwich down on his unfolded napkin and opening the glass bottle of juice.

"Tell me about your father. What was he like as a father? Were you close?"

"Depends on what you mean by close. He wasn't an absentee father."

"Well, did he take you to work with him when you got old enough?"

"Oh, hell, yes. Put all of us to work while we were still kids, gave us a little plastic bucket and had us picking up nails. He started in construction, was a foreman when I was in middle school. As we got older, we were treated like the rest of the help. He played some mean tricks, threatened to fire us three times a week—but never gave us that relief. By the time I started high school I could read a blueprint as well as anyone on the job, including him. All of us could, the three brothers. I liked it, Ham hated it, Howard started making his own blueprints in junior high. Howard's a designer and contractor, has his own company in Pennsylvania building warehouses and big-box stores. Dad tried to hire him to design the building right here in this town he was out to buy, but Howard turned him down."

"How did you find out about his plans?"

"Howard called me to warn me Dad wanted someone to help him with a building. I was primed to say no, but he never called."

"Were you disappointed?"

Heck thought about that briefly. "Kinda. Like the girl who doesn't want to go to the party but is sad she wasn't invited. Except I think I was more relieved. Dad always was a shouter, even to us as grown-ups."

"He must have been pretty confident he was going to win that bid if he contacted Howard ahead of time."

"He always thought he'd win—and he usually did. Dad was brilliant at acquiring property and making a profit on a build, but he was hell on wheels to work with. He used to knock me down when I made a mistake on the job, even after I was as tall as him. As soon as I graduated from college I moved to Texas, and this is the first time I've been back in Minnesota since then."

"You didn't come home for Christmas or Thanksgiving?"

"No. My wife included him on our Christmas newsletter list, but that was about it."

"Was he a crook?"

He grimaced at her plain speaking but then shook his head. "I don't think so. I'm sure he skated close to the line, and if he did cross it, I don't think it was deliberate. He was pretty sure people were out to 'do him,' as he put it, so he'd get mad, or excited, and push back, sometimes sneaky, sometimes hard, sometimes first. But his—and my—line of work is tough. It's not a place for the meek of the earth."

"How is your business doing?"

He paused to slurp a noisy spoonful of soup. "Okay. We're okay. Not that an infusion of cash wouldn't come in handy right now." He shrugged and admitted, "Damn handy."

"I suppose the lead investigator in Wayzata has checked your alibi?"

He put down his plastic soup spoon so firmly the handle cracked. "What kind of a question is that?"

"Come on, Heck, it's a question anyone with an IQ number above room temperature would ask. You could use the money, and you were not on loving terms with your father."

He said, just a little too casually, "So you actually think I flew up here one afternoon, murdered my father, and flew back the next morning."

"It's possible. Did you?"

"Hell, no!" He picked up his spoon, saw it was broken,

and put it down again. He said in an exasperated voice, as if he'd already said it several times before—as doubtless he had, to the Wayzata investigators—"I was, and am, working on a job, converting a high school building into condominiums. I talked with my foreman, an electrician, a plumber, and an interior designer, all of them on the day and into the evening that my father was murdered, went home to my wife, then first thing the next day I fired the plumber. Okay?"

Betsy, smiling, nodded. "Sounds good to me. Especially the plumber."

"Why the plumber?"

"Because he isn't a friend and so is not likely to lie for you."

The affable look settled again on his face. He nodded once. "Yeah, I see what you mean. And you're right, he was royally pissed."

"Who else was—to borrow your phrase—'royally pissed' at your father?"

"I don't know. I hadn't talked to Dad for three or four years, not a real conversation."

"You said your wife sent him a Christmas letter every year. Did he send one to you?"

"No. A card, yes, one of those commercially printed ones with a photograph of him smoking a cigar while seated in a big leather chair. Even his signature was printed. Two years in a row, the same card. They're cheaper if you order five hundred of them."

Betsy nodded. "Yes, I know. I order and send them to the suppliers and designers I like, and my most loyal mail-order customers."

Heck nodded. "We used to do something like that, but it got expensive, so we quit."

Betsy said, "Would your brother Howard perhaps know who had recently been caught up in some shenanigans or manipulations by your father?"

Hector thought about that while he ate his sandwich. Then he nodded. "Maybe, maybe." He gave her a wry smile. "We brothers don't talk to one another very much, either."

"Is Hamilton coming to Minnesota?"

"Yes, but I'm not sure when he's arriving."

"If Hamilton hated construction, what did he go into?"

"He first became a real estate agent down in Florida. The turnover down there is pretty brisk, you know."

"Yes?"

"They call it God's waiting room for a reason."

"Oh. Yes, I suppose that's right."

"Then after he married he went back to college and became a lawyer. He specializes in construction litigation."

"I'm not sure what a construction litigation lawyer does."

"You hire him after you move into your new building and the roof leaks or the windows fall out or the furnace sets your place on fire. He'll sue the builder for you." He raised his eyebrows significantly.

"So he, more than Howard, might know if your father had been subject to litigation that left him or a client angry."

"Maybe. Like I said, I don't know."

"Could you tell him and Howard that I'd like to talk to them? And that I don't bite?"

He chuckled, picked up the cardboard cup and drank a big mouthful of his soup. "Yes, I will do that."

"Do you smoke?"

He looked down at himself. "Why, do I smell like it?"

"No, but maybe you use e-cigarettes."

He nodded. "I've thought about trying them. But it was too hard to quit the real thing, and I suspect it would be just as hard to get out from under the vapor."

"How long had your father smoked cigars?"

"For as long as I can remember."

"How about Ham, or Howard?"

"I don't think so. No cigarettes, either, as far as I know. What's this interest in smoking?"

"I'm just poking around. I never know when an innocent question will give me a solid lead." Betsy had no reason to tell him she'd reconnected with a hospital pharmacist named Luci Zahray whose nickname was the Poison Lady. Luci had told her that boiling just three cigarettes in a small pot could extract enough nicotine to kill the average adult.

Chapter Twenty-two

❖❖❖

DORIS sat at the dining room table in Rafael and Godwin's attractive condo overlooking Lake Minnetonka. Daylight savings time had been instituted, so instead of darkness, there was a deepening sunset washing over the lake. The view from the windows was to the north and east, so the sun was out of sight, but the colors were muted pastels with a bright flash here and there as a ray of sun caught a wave.

"The first thing you want to do is pick a venue," said Doris.

"No," said Rafael, "the first thing we must decide is how much we can afford to spend."

"If it were up to you alone," said Godwin, "we'd have a quick little ceremony down at the courthouse in Minneapolis and dine afterward at Subway."

"Actually, you are not far wrong," acknowledged Rafael.

"But if it were up to you, we'd have a destination wedding in Paris and a honeymoon in Barbados."

"Oooooh, Barbados," sighed Godwin. "But not Paris. Even your French is not up to their standards, and we'd waste too much time trying to get what we wanted—and end up in some dingy café full of cigarette smoke and cheap wine fumes."

"Are same-sex marriages legal in France?" asked Doris.

Godwin blinked. "You know, I have no idea."

"Yes, they are," said Rafael. "But I don't want to get married in France. Too close to Spain, and my family might choose to come and spoil things."

"You're right, you're right, you're absolutely right!" said Godwin with a shudder. "Nowhere in Europe, then." He looked at Doris expectantly.

"I suggest, since you want all of us to come, you plan on a wedding right here in Minnesota. You've already decided against a church wedding, so next you need to think about whether you want something formal, like in a ballroom setting, or something kitschy and fun like a resort, or something casual like a barbeque, or something truly unique and maybe a little edgy." Doris looked from one face to the other.

"Not edgy," said Godwin, and Rafael nodded. "I see lots of tables in a big room with a high ceiling and tall windows, dark blue tablecloths and silver candles and filmy blue curtains hanging from the ceiling—you know, looped up, with fairy lights inside them. Live music. Buffet dinner with at least three entrees for two hundred guests."

Rafael said, "I see forty guests at two long tables, white

tablecloths with little bouquets of flowers up and down them, and a little table for just the two of us, waiters serving game hens and a really nice cabernet wine."

Doris wrote all this down. "This is not going to be easy, is it?" she remarked dryly. "But you're talking reception. What about the ceremony? Do you know who should perform it?"

"It would be a hoot to get a rabbi, wouldn't it?" said Godwin. "Then I'd get to stamp on a glass at the end."

Doris said, "Be serious."

"All right, sorry. I don't know any judges, Raff, do you?"

"Well, one is a member of the coin club. His name is Franklin Noel. Do you remember him?"

Godwin thought. He'd been to a couple of meetings, trying to share Rafael's interest in numismatics. "What does he look like?"

Rafael pondered this, trying to pick his words carefully. "Tall, thin, very pale complexion, delicate bones in his face, an air of refinement. Wears a bow tie, and on him it looks good."

"Oh yes, I remember him! He'd be gorgeous presiding, don't you think? He's so classy, though, we'd better have a classy wedding."

"Would you mind a 'classy' wedding?" asked Rafael.

"I think it would be adorable!" He turned to Doris. "Write that down. A classy wedding, tuxedos all around. And Judge Noel presiding. He'll be perfect!"

"What if he says no?" asked Doris.

"Oh." Godwin looked crushed briefly, then brightened. "Then let's do it at a farm, in a barn, and have a hoedown reception!"

An hour later Doris went home. She had sixteen pages of notes and not one thing decided.

"I'm not strong enough to do this," she said to Phil. "Herding cats is nothing to those two, especially Goddy."

MALLOY'S questions about how someone might gain access to the yarn that poisoned Maddy had made Betsy think. It wasn't just that some people had keys to her basement—who among them might have wanted Maddy dead? Plus, this person must have had access to nicotine. Did anyone she know meet all three conditions?

No.

Therefore, it was much more likely that the yarn was poisoned at Mount Calvary.

"Really?" said Connor when she shared this conclusion with him. "Maybe there's someone with a key you don't know about. Or, maybe there's someone with a motive you don't know about."

"Well . . . yes, that's true. I suppose I'm doing a sketchy investigation right now, looking for the obvious, hoping to get lucky and short-circuit a complex, lengthy investigation."

He nodded. They were sitting in the living room, having turned off the latest episode of something they'd been watching, finding the series had wandered into silly, stupid, even obscene territory. Their conversation was desultory, as each was focused on a needlework project.

Connor asked, "Do you still think Joe Mickels didn't commit the murders? Or should I say murder, as I suppose it's possible he only poisoned Maddy."

"I think that if I find out he murdered one of them, then he'll have murdered both of them. From what Jill told me of what Lars told her—third hand, I know—the house was trashed by an angry person, and Maddy was killed with nicotine. Joe has a terrible temper and owns stores that sell nicotine products."

"A 'perfect storm' for an investigator," said Connor.

"Maybe if I can establish a very narrow window for when the yarn could have been tampered with, and Joe can establish an alibi for that time, we'll be in good shape to bring it to Mike." She put her stitching down to think. "First, I have to find out if anyone's missing a key to the basement, or thinks it might have been copied, or will admit she (both of Betsy's current tenants were women) left the basement door unlocked."

"And that fact was somehow advertised," said Connor wryly.

"Well . . . yes, I guess so. But one thing at a time." She checked her watch. It was not quite 8 p.m. "I'll go ask right now."

She was back forty minutes later. "I'm going to have to come up with a different form of security!" she griped. "There are at least six keys missing, two of them basement keys. Whenever one of them loses a key, she goes next door and borrows the other's and makes a copy. Bad enough they're doing it with the basement keys, but three of them are to the back door! Now I have to have the whole place rekeyed. What's the matter with these people? Why didn't they come to me?"

"How old are they?" asked Connor, though he knew the answer.

"I'm not sure. Kit's probably twenty-four or twenty-five, and her husband's the same. Jenna's even younger, maybe twenty-two."

"In today's world, they are practically children, and so they act like it."

After a moment's reflection, she said, "You know, you're right. What were you doing at Kit's age?"

"At twenty-four? I was just promoted to second mate on a freighter operating in the Mediterranean. I'd been at sea for six years."

"Six—? Then when did you go to college?"

"At the same time, off and on. I got my degree mostly through correspondence courses. I think I spent less than a year actually on campus. I believe I've mentioned all the spare time a sailor has at sea. No lassies, no pub crawls, no rugby or football—pardon me, soccer—no bright city lights. So you have to do something to keep your brain from turning to pudding."

"And we think getting a degree via Internet courses is the newest thing."

"There is nothing new under the sun, *machree*."

THE next morning, Friday, down in the shop, Betsy called Kari Beckel at Mount Calvary, found she was on vacation, and so asked for Helen Bursar—who had an amazingly appropriate name. "I'd like to come and see you, today if possible," she said. "It's about Maddy O'Leary's death at the auction."

Helen, who with Kari ran the business side of the church, said, "I'm sorry, Ms. Devonshire, but I've got meetings scheduled all day today and into the evening."

"Could I buy you lunch?"

"Well, my brief lunch engagement was just canceled, so yes. But could you bring it here? I've only got half an hour, twelve thirty to one."

"Salad okay if it has chicken on top?"

"Fine. And thank you."

Helen Bursar's office was off the big round atrium that was the center of the church hall, behind the greeter's desk. Betsy carried an insulated bag just about big enough for two plates of Asian chicken salad in peanut sauce with crispy noodles on the side, and she'd brought a liter bottle of diet ginger ale as well.

In anticipation of her coming, Helen had cleared half her desk and pulled an armchair up to it. She was a small, thin woman with thick, dark, curly hair, pale skin, and hazel-green eyes. She was wearing a pale green wool dress with a silver brooch and dangly silver earrings, each with a violet iris on it.

"So nice to meet you, Ms. Devonshire," she said, standing and coming around her desk to hold out her hand. "Sergeant Larson has said nice things about you."

That's right, thought Betsy. Lars was a member of Mount Calvary Lutheran, though his wife, Jill, went to Trinity Episcopalian. "I'm glad to hear that," said Betsy. "You have an amazing musical program here, and such a beautiful church hall."

"Thank you," she said. "Now, won't you sit down and tell me why you need to talk with me?"

Betsy unzipped the insulated bag and brought out the covered plates. A delicious odor wafted from them. From her large purse, she brought out the ginger ale. "I hope you have cups or glasses. I forgot to bring them," she said.

Helen had coffee mugs on her credenza and, surprisingly, real silverware. "Those plastic forks are just not adequate, I find," she said. "So I borrowed these from our kitchen."

In another minute they were tasting the thin slices of chicken breast and crunchy greens. "This is good!" said Helen.

"I like the Wok," said Betsy. "Their food is delicious. Now, to business. You know Maddy O'Leary died right here in your atrium the Saturday of the auction. It turns out that someone poured pure nicotine onto the ball of knitting yarn that was in her bag. None of the other six knitters' yarn was poisoned, and each bag was marked with the user's name, so whoever did this was very likely after her.

"The yarn was poisoned long enough ahead of time that it had dried, so she didn't notice anything wrong with it. It's possible that the poison was put on it while the bags were stored in the basement of my shop, but there were several conditions necessary for that to happen. I am thinking it much more likely to have happened here."

Helen nodded while nibbling on a crisp noodle. "Sergeant Malloy was here yesterday. He seems to be thinking along the same lines you are."

"Where were the bags kept here at the church?"

Helen gestured toward the door to her office. "Here in the hall, right next door to me—it's a room where janitorial supplies are kept. We put the bags in there so they'd be handy on the day of the auction."

"Is that door kept locked?"

"Yes, always."

"Who has the key?"

"Our maintenance man has one, I have one, Kari has a master key that unlocks every door at Mount Calvary, Pastor Royale has another master key . . ." She paused, then nodded. "That's all." She gave a little start. "Oh, wait, that door was left unlocked from the day of the Lenten music performance, because we weren't sure when Ms. Reynolds was going to bring those bags over. And so of course it was still unlocked the day of the auction so the bags could be brought out for the seven people who'd be using them. That was such a clever idea, having those winning toy makers knitting up front during the auction."

"The door to the church hall wasn't locked when I came. Is it always unlocked?"

"During regular office hours, it is. Or when there are special events held here, like the Thursday before the auction. And we had a reception after the performance here in the hall."

"Did a lot of people come to that?"

"There were close to three hundred people in attendance."

Betsy said despairingly, "I don't suppose you kept a list of the people who bought tickets to the program."

"No, but while we don't have cameras in the church, we do in the atrium. Three of them."

Betsy's heart perked up. "Could I look at the videos?"

"I'm afraid not. Sergeant Malloy took them away with him."

"Did he look at them while he—and you—were here?"

"He started looking at one, just to see how clear the picture was. He said they were pretty good."

"Did they show anyone going into the room where the bags of yarn were being kept?"

"I didn't see that—but we only watched a few minutes of the video footage."

"Did you recognize anyone?"

"I sure did. A lot of the people who came are members of Mount Calvary."

"Do you know Joe Mickels?"

Helen thought about that for a few seconds. "He's not a member, is he?"

"I don't think so. But his appearance is distinctive: short, stout, white hair, big old-fashioned sideburns?"

"Oh yes, I saw him, on the video Sergeant Malloy was looking at. He froze the picture right about then and said he wanted to take the discs away. As evidence, he said."

"So," said Betsy, "things are looking dark for Joe."

Godwin stood silent, frowning.

They were in Crewel World. They should have been laughing and high-fiving each other, as the customer who had just left had spent nearly a thousand dollars on a hand-painted needlepoint canvas and the silks and wool necessary to stitch it. Instead they were baffled and having to rethink things.

"I think we should call Joe and warn him," said Godwin.

"It's probably too late for that," said Betsy.

The phone on the checkout desk rang, and she answered it. "Crewel World, Betsy speaking, how may I help you?"

"Is this Ms. Devonshire?" asked a man's voice.

"Yes?"

"I'm Nurse Amos Brighton, at Hennepin County Medical Center in Minneapolis. We have a patient here who has asked me to contact you on his behalf."

Betsy's first thought was a terrified, *It's Connor!* "Who—who is it asking for me?"

"His name is Joseph Alan Mickels. Do you know him?"

She pulled the phone away from her ear and stared at it.

Godwin asked, "What is it? What's the matter?"

She waved him off and said into the phone, "Yes, yes, I do. What happened? Why is he in the hospital?"

Godwin gasped and began waving a hand to draw her attention, which she ignored.

"He has suffered a gunshot wound."

"Oh my God! Is it serious? How did it happen?"

"What? What? What?" demanded Godwin, but she put up a shushing hand toward him.

"Are you a relative?" asked the nurse.

"No, just a friend."

"I'm afraid I can't discuss the details with you, in that case. You'll need to contact a relative."

"Can he have visitors?"

"Since he asked for you, yes, in perhaps another hour."

"Why did he ask for me, do you know?"

"No. I'm just the messenger."

"Well . . . thank you," Betsy said and hung up.

"What, what, what?" demanded Godwin.

"It's Joe. He's been shot. He's downtown at HCMC. No further details available."

"Joe? Oh, that's wonderful! I thought it was Connor!"

She sat down heavily behind the big desk and thrust her

fingers into her hair. "No, it's not wonderful! Don't you see? I think in my heart I wondered if maybe Joe did it, that he's a murderer. But I was wrong. Here's proof I was wrong."

"So what now?"

She leaped up. "What's the matter with me? I've got to go see him."

Chapter Twenty-three

BETSY took Highway 7 to I-494 to 394 downtown, frantically searched for and finally located a parking spot, then found her way to Joe's room in the hospital. But once there she to wait until someone else had finished talking with him. She strode impatiently up and down the hallway outside his room. Finally she saw the door open and Mike Malloy come out looking angry. Well, sure: His case against Joe had just been blown away. He gave her a curt nod and strode off down the corridor.

She took a deep, calming breath and let it out, then took another. She felt the tension in her shoulders ease and opened the door. Joe's bed had lifted him to a sitting position. He was pale as a ghost, with dark shadows around his deep-set eyes. He seemed very interested in the pale green wall opposite his bed until she realized he wasn't really seeing it. He was taking rapid, shallow breaths.

He was wearing a hospital gown that draped over only

one shoulder. The other was covered with a thick bandage that ran far down his chest. The head of his bed was entirely surrounded by differently sized monitors clicking and beeping, reporting blood pressure, pulse, oxygen levels and God knew what other bodily functions. A kind of abstract metal tree rose over his bed, and from it three fat plastic bags hung, two clear and one dark red. Tubes ran down from them into his left arm and the back of his hand. A translucent tube of an alarmingly big diameter came out from the bandage and dripped a slobbery red into an oblong glass jar marked off in centimeters.

"Hello, Joe," she said softly, surprised into compassion.

"Huh. Took you . . . long enough," he muttered weakly.

"I came as quickly as I could. What on earth happened?"

"Visiting my e-cig store . . . in Uptown, a . . . bandit came in . . . shot me."

"Just like that? He just walked in and shot you?" She came closer to his bed.

"No, no, course not," Joe said, vaguely annoyed. "It was a stickup. I tell my employees to . . . just hand over the cash . . . when . . . armed robber comes in, don't . . . fight. So Liza put up hands, an' I put mine up . . . He took the cash, fired once in the ceiling, then . . . shot me."

"Why? Did he say anything?"

"Said, 'Oh, it's you . . . effer.'"

Effer? Then she realized he was using a euphemism for a very bad word. "So he recognized you, and shot you on purpose. Thank God you're not dead!"

He gathered himself and said, "If God was really on my side, he would've made the dickhead miss altogether." Joe smiled, just a little, at scoring a point. His face began to take on a look more like the fierce old eagle he normally resembled.

Betsy changed course. "I assume Sergeant Malloy was here to get a description of the robber."

Joe rasped, "Hell, no, this happened . . . Minneap'lis. Talked to Minneap'lis police. Mike came to see . . . 'f this man was after me." He glanced up at her, saw her incomprehension, and said, "Third one still standing."

"Oh, so he sees it, too. Harry, then Maddy, then you. What do you think?"

Joe sighed twice, then coughed very feebly, which clearly hurt him so badly that he laid a hand gently on the big bandage, and closed his eyes. After a few moments, he said, "Think . . . 'bout it. Someone so desperate . . . kill three people to get th' property? But . . . proves himself killer when . . . closes on't. Have to sell it to pay lawyer." Joe smirked crookedly. "Stupid."

Betsy should have thought of that. "You're right, of course. So why did he shoot you?"

Joe put his head back and closed his eyes. "I don't know."

"Did you recognize him?"

"Couldn't. Wore black nylon stocking over . . . head."

"Still, what did he look like? Was there anything familiar about him? Could he have been someone you know?"

Joe's eyes didn't open, and after a wait, Betsy began to think he'd fallen asleep. But then he said, softly, "Stocking mashed . . . face, crooked." But then he frowned, thinking. He continued, even more softly, "He didn't talk ghetto, but I think . . . Gotta peek at 's wrist, and t'skin . . . very dark.

So . . . maybe . . ." He did stop then, and his breathing gentled into sleep.

"Thanks, Joe. I'll let you rest now."

"So where did this happen?" asked Connor, who had come down to the shop after Godwin called him with the news, and waited there for her to return, appalled at this turn of events.

Betsy said, "At his store in Uptown."

"So not a high-crime area."

"No, not particularly."

Godwin put in, "A fun place to go for entertainment."

"Yes, I remember," said Connor, looking at Betsy with a smile. The two of them had gone to Uptown once for an Asian fusion dinner and salsa dancing.

Godwin said, "Um."

Betsy turned to him and said, "Something else?"

"Yes. Did you hear about Maddy's will?"

"No. I assumed she had one, but don't know its terms. I didn't know she had a will. What about it?"

"This is rumor, so if it's entirely true or not, I can't say. But I hear she left all or most of her property to Chaz Reynolds."

Betsy felt a great sinking of her heart. "Oh dear."

"What, aren't you happy for him?" asked Connor.

"Joe Mickels thinks the person who shot him was a black man."

"Stop it!" whispered Godwin, awed. "But wait, no, Betsy, not Bershada's boy! He wouldn't, he just wouldn't!"

Connor said, "This is very bad news—if it's true. I wonder if Mike knows yet."

"Who told you?" Betsy asked Godwin.

"Leona, over at the Barleywine. I went there for lunch."

"Who told her?"

Godwin was clearly surprised by the question. "I didn't think to ask," he said. "She said it like"—he paused, then made a pretty good attempt at imitating Leona's matter-of-fact voice—"'Chaz Reynolds is gonna party like it's nineteen ninety-nine. Maddy O'Leary left him all her worldly goods.' She didn't say it like it was a half-assed rumor but like it was really true. I said, 'Good for him, putting up with her for years like he did,' and she laughed and went to bring me my sandwich."

"I wonder where Leona got that piece of information," said Connor.

"I could call her and ask," said Betsy. Suiting action to words, she pulled out her cell phone, found the Barleywine number, and pressed Dial.

"Leona," she said a minute later, "how did you find out about Maddy's will?"

"By eavesdropping," said Leona. "Mike Malloy was in here with Chief Haugen yesterday, and when I brought their sandwiches I heard Mike say he had talked with Maddy's attorney, who said Chaz was the 'principal legatee' who got most of the property but hardly any of the money. The money is divided in half, one part going to the Golden Valley Humane Society and the other going to the First Baptist Church of Minnetonka." Leona chuckled. "It took me a minute to get the order right and then again when I was putting it on the table so I could overhear all the details."

"So pretty close to the horse's mouth," said Betsy. "Thanks, Leona."

"I've got a beer tasting coming up next month, on the fifteenth. Tell Connor to mark his calendar."

"Will do. Bye." Betsy hung up and relayed Leona's announcement about the beer tasting to Connor.

"Ah," he said, pleased. "I hope she's brewing that spring ale she had last year."

"Betsy," Godwin broke in, anxious to get back to the subject at hand, "are you seriously thinking that Chaz is a murderer?"

"I find it hard to think so—and I dread what Bershada is going to do if Malloy comes after him. But Malloy . . . I don't know. He liked Joe a whole lot for this, but now Joe's in the hospital, shot by someone who may only have been pretending to be a robber."

"Coincidences do happen, *machree*," Connor pointed out.

"Is it a coincidence that of the three bidders on a piece of property, two are dead and one is in the hospital with a bullet wound?" asked Betsy.

"Well," said Connor, "it rather depends on who winds up with the property. Is it some fourth person who was squeezed out of the bidding early on?"

Godwin said, "Also, each one of them was hurt in a different way. One was bashed on the head, one was poisoned by nicotine, one was shot. Is that how murderers work?"

"No," said Betsy thoughtfully. "I've read in several places that if criminals find a method that works, that's what they keep using. It's called an MO, modus operandi, and detectives use it to track career criminals."

"But on the other hand, it's kind of hard to think you're trying to track three different criminals," pointed out Connor.

Betsy threw her hands up in the air. "I know, I know," she said. "Is it one, two, or three people? This is really frustrating!"

BETSY decided she had to learn where someone could get nicotine. The most obvious way, of course, was to buy it in e-cigarette stores.

Connor volunteered to go out and gather information in one of those stores, and perhaps buy a sample or two of the nicotine mixture.

After he left, a woman came in to order finishing for her counted cross-stitch pattern, a "summer montage" that featured a slice of watermelon, a seashell, an ear of corn, a rose blossom, a birdhouse (with bird), a beehive, a straw hat, and other summery items in realistic colors set in squares and rectangles. The result was complex and attractive. It was one of a set of four montages—the others were autumn, winter, and spring. Mrs. Hardy had done the others; this was the last. Each had cost her a little over thirty dollars for the pattern, Aida fabric, and floss, but now, like the others, it was going to cost her nearly two hundred dollars to get it properly finished.

"You want it like the other three?" said Betsy, writing the order. "Washed and stretched, laced, plain three-quarter-inch white mat, two-inch-wide gold frame, right?"

"Yes," said Mrs. Hardy. "I get so many compliments on the spring one—just like I did for winter and autumn. I so appreciate your suggestion that I display just one at a time, so my eyes don't get tired of seeing them."

"You're welcome. This should be ready in three weeks. Any idea what your next project will be?"

"Godwin signed me up for that hardanger class you're offering. I've always wanted to try it. You do hardanger, don't you, Betsy?"

"I'm afraid not. I've taken three classes in it, and so far I've got one half finished bookmark and a strong determination not to try it anymore. But you do such beautiful, intricate counted cross-stitch, I'm sure you'll have no trouble with hardanger."

"Well, we'll see, we'll see."

A few hours later, she and Godwin were closing up shop when Connor entered. He had two small plastic bags hanging from one hand and was smiling.

Without saying a word, he upended the bags on the library table. Eight or nine bottles of different opaque colors with squeeze-nipple tops rolled out: orange, green, red, yellow. Godwin hastened to keep them herded together. Betsy stooped to pick up a midnight blue bottle that had gone off the edge of the table.

Blue Ox Vapor, the label read. On the side of the label was stacked a series: 0mg, 6mg, 11mg, 18mg, 24mg, each with a pale blue dot beside it. The 24mg dot had a black dash inked onto it.

"They come in different strengths," said Connor, seeing her looking at the list. "If you'll look at the others, you'll find one at thirty-six milligrams. That's the strongest blend you can buy. But hear this: That strongest mix would still be only two point four percent nicotine."

"That's all?" said Godwin, picking up the red bottle. "Not even a measly two and a half percent?" He put it down and picked up a yellow one. "Yeah, this one's thirty-six milligrams." He turned to Betsy. "Would that be strong enough to kill someone?"

"I don't know," said Betsy, and she asked Connor, "What did they tell you at the store where you bought this?"

Connor said, "When I bought the thirty-six milligram, the salesclerk warned me that if I spilled any on my hand I should wash it off right away. I asked what might happen if I didn't, and he said it would soak through my skin, and if I spilled a lot, like half the bottle, my fingers would start to tingle, and my heart would go flippity-flip, and I'd get a bad headache. I said, then what? I'd fall down dead? And he laughed and said not a chance. You can't buy a deadly dose of nicotine in a vape shop, he said."

"Well . . ." said Betsy. She put her hand out, fingers open, and waggled it back and forth. "I'm sure he's been told that. I'm also sure that if someone has a weak heart, he might be fatally stricken, or if a toddler drank a whole bottle, she might die." She put down the Blue Ox bottle and picked up two more. "Strawberry flavor," she read aloud, and she unscrewed the bottle to take a sniff. "Alice is right, this smells delicious," she noted with a grimace.

"Did Maddy have a weak heart?" asked Connor.

"I don't know—but I don't think so. She certainly never acted as if she was in fear that her heart was about to quit."

"You got that right," said Godwin with a grim smile.

"So we're back to Joe Mickels?" asked Connor.

"Why?" asked Betsy. "If a customer couldn't buy a lethal dose of nicotine, why would you think Joe could?"

"Isn't it possible he was mixing his own brand of vapor liquid? As a wholesale purchaser, doesn't he have access to things the general public doesn't, such as pure nicotine?"

"You ask good questions," said Betsy. "How about we do some research this evening to see if we can find answers?"

Godwin said, "I can do research, too, please?"

Betsy smiled at him. "All right, good idea. How about you and Rafael research Harry Whiteside from a business angle? How much was he worth? What properties and companies did he own or control? What did the people who worked with him think of him? But poke gently; don't step on anyone's toes, especially if they work for the Wayzata police."

Godwin snatched up a ballpoint from the checkout desk and began writing down Betsy's instructions: ". . . people who worked with him," he concluded, nodding. He looked up at Betsy. "And don't step on toes," he added with a grin.

Seeing a hint of mischief in his eyes, Betsy said, "Godwin, this is important. If you screw up—" She looked across at Connor. "If any of us screw up, we may irreparably harm innocent people."

"Yes, you're right, of course," said Godwin. "We'll be careful. I promise."

Chapter Twenty-four

CHAZ was waiting at the door to Crewel World Monday morning. He was standing under a black umbrella—it was pouring rain—and was wearing a dark blue suit, dark red shirt, and silver tie.

Betsy unlocked the door and invited him in. "You look terrific!" she said.

"Thanks." He half closed his umbrella and shook it out the door, scattering redundant raindrops onto the sidewalk. He brought it back in and leaned it against the wall. "I've got a meeting with a lawyer this morning. I wanted to let you know, if you haven't heard already"—he grimaced against the probability that she had, given the reach of the Excelsior grapevine—"I'm inheriting a great deal of property from Maddy."

"Yes, I had heard. Not in any great detail, though," she hinted.

"Two large apartment buildings in Minneapolis," he

said, holding out one hand and pressing down on the fingers as he counted, "a corner grocery store with two apartments above it in Saint Paul, a building in Hopkins that's an empty store and a hair and nail salon on the first floor with four apartments on the second floor, two houses here in Excelsior, three houses in Wayzata, a dry cleaner and a lumberyard in Golden Valley, a gas station–mini mart in Minnetonka, and . . ." He had to pause and think. "That little set of three row houses over on North Water Street!" he concluded triumphantly.

"That's a lot of property, Chaz," Betsy said. "But they're spread out all over the place."

"Yes, I know," he said, "but I've already been managing most of them—some of them for a long while. I know the tenants, I know the problems—like the row houses need new roofs, and one of the apartment buildings has plumbing that seems to date back to the Civil War. And taxes? Whoosh! I've been telling Maddy we may have to raise the rents—I mean . . ." Suddenly, he looked near tears. "Dammit," he muttered as he struggled for control.

"Oh, Chaz, this must be at least as hard for you as it is good news." Betsy reached to touch him on the arm.

"Yes, it is. I mean, you're right. One part of me is celebrating because I'm actually rich, independently wealthy, and another part of me would give up any chance to own any of it if only Maddy would come storming into the office and chew me out for not getting the estimates for those roofs collected yet."

He drew a ragged breath. "But done's done. Mom said you wanted to ask me something."

Betsy turned away, pain gripping her heart. Chaz's distress

was palpable. How could she ask him a question that would add to it?

"What, what's the matter?" he asked. "Go ahead, tell me what it is. I have to get going. I have to be in that law office in forty-five minutes."

"All right." She turned back around. "Where were you on Friday afternoon?" The day Joe Mickels was shot.

"Oh jeez, you, too?" The words were jesting, but there was anger in his eyes.

"I guess the police have already asked you that."

"Damn straight." He took a calming breath. "Mom and I were on Skype with my sister Leeza, who is on her honeymoon in Key West."

Betsy was delighted and threw her arms around him. "Oh, that's so wonderful! Thank you!"

He didn't hug her back. "You're welcome. Now I gotta go." He made a sound that could have been a laugh, turned on his heel, scooped up his umbrella, and left.

BETSY called Excelsior's City Hall to see when she could get a peek at Maddy's will and was told it did not become public property until probate was complete, which would take at least four to six months, maybe longer.

A while later she sat down with Godwin at the library table. Betsy had her long notebook out, and Godwin had a small, fat spiral notebook in front of him. Each had a mug of tea.

"Okay, whatcha got?" asked Betsy.

"Harry Whiteside was a very rich man, his total worth somewhere around twenty-five or thirty million, maybe more. He owned property in four states, but primarily in Minnesota. He did big jobs and small ones. His last small one was at the University's hazardous waste disposal facility, replacing the pipes in the fire-extinguishing system. His last big one, which isn't finished, is building an industrial park up near Mille Lacs.

"He wasn't a crook—not legally. But there are people angry with him, some so angry that they've filed lawsuits against him. There have been four lawsuits in the past three years, and he won them all—he has a very good law firm on retainer. But his last lawsuit was a dilly."

"Who sued him?" asked Betsy.

"His son Howard."

Betsy stopped writing. "Howard? Are you sure?"

"Absolutely." Godwin handed over several multipage printouts and a screen shot.

It took Betsy, no economics whiz, a while studying the documents to understand what had happened. Harry had approached Howard to design an industrial park near Lake Mille Lacs in central Minnesota. Early in the negotiations, Harry asked Howard for some preliminary drawings. Howard complied—and Harry promptly turned them over to another contractor who signed a contract for thousands less than Howard was going to charge. The contractor's mistake was in making his plans too obviously derivative of Howard's drawings.

Howard saw the online advertising for the park and promptly sued. But Harry's law firm, through a feat of legerdemain Betsy couldn't quite understand, got the case dismissed "with prejudice," which meant Howard couldn't find another court to bring the suit in for essentially the same offense.

The screen shot was of an article from a Scranton, Pennsylvania, newspaper about an "outburst" in a courtroom where a hearing had begun in the lawsuit. Major fines were imposed on all parties, the heaviest on Howard and Harry Whiteside. "Objects were flung and a chair was broken," wrote the reporter.

"I'm surprised Hamilton and Hector didn't know about this," said Betsy.

"I guess if you move to different parts of the country and deliberately don't stay in touch, this sort of thing can happen. For example, the headline reads that the lawsuit was brought by Stonebridge Design, Incorporated. It's possible that the other two brothers didn't know Stonebridge was Howard Whiteside."

Betsy looked back into the papers. "Yes, Howard incorporated under that name only two years ago. So that would make it possible." She nodded to herself as she began to write a note. "It looks as if we have another motive for murder right here."

"So what did you and Connor find out?" Godwin asked.

"Even as the owner of an e-cigarette store, Joe couldn't buy pure nicotine. Only the factories that have a use for it, like making insecticides or bottling the flavored diluted nicotine, can buy the pure stuff. University medical departments and research labs can buy it, too. But not members of the general public, even if they sell vapor liquids. It's like buying cyanide or arsenic; you can do it, but you need a license, and a good enough reason to get a license, like working as a scientist in a research lab."

BUSINESS at Crewel World began its comeback that day. Seven customers came in the morning, five of them determined to buy something new, something complex, something challenging. Betsy and Godwin sold three hand-painted canvases to one regular, two to a man neither had ever seen before, and two to Jill Cross Larson. They sold two Dazor lights, four pairs of Gingher scissors, twenty-six cards of overdyed silk floss, three dozen skeins of cotton floss, six spools of Kreinik metallic, four packs of needles, three pairs of magnifying glasses, several yards of Aida cloth in eleven, fourteen, and eighteen count, and nearly a yard of Cashel linen. The rush of customers was so great that Betsy had had to call in a part-timer. By noon the cash drawer was plump and the charge card reader was, in Godwin's words, "smokin'!"

Bershada came in right at noon and said, "Betsy, may I take you to lunch?"

Godwin said, "Go, go, go! Milly's here, and I'm so pumped, I can handle anything."

"All right," Betsy said.

Bershada left her needlework bag under the library table, for when she'd return for the Monday Bunch meeting.

The rain had made the sunlight sparkle as if on a new-made world. The air was fresh and cool and smelled of new green growing things. Lake Minnetonka, across the street, twinkled blue and silver. A robin was in full song from near the top of a budding tree.

"Times like this, I forgive Minnesota for its winters," said Bershada as they crossed the street at Lake and Water—they were heading for the Barleywine.

They paused inside the door. Bershada had set a fast pace, and Betsy was a little winded. The place smelled strongly of beer (it was a microbrewery), cooked meats, fresh-baked bread, and steamed vegetables, with subtle undertones of herbs—Leona grew her own and used them generously in her recipes.

The floor was flagstone, a little uneven under their feet. A long bar to the left was made of dark carved wood. Behind it were slabs of clear glass, and behind them were the tall steel "kettles" that held the several brews. On the right were three booths left over from when the place was a simple country café, and at the back was a low counter and three stools; the Barleywine now had Wi-Fi for customers to use.

Bershada led the way to the back booth, slid in with a sigh, and said, "Chaz called me on his cell."

"Is he angry with me?" asked Betsy, sliding in across from her.

"I think he's not sure. He was upset. He thought you were on his side. I had a talk with him when he came home from court—did you know he's inherited about half of Maddy O'Leary's properties?"

"Yes, he was listing them for me this morning. Houses, businesses, all kinds of things. But he didn't say anything about money. Didn't she leave him any?"

"She didn't need to. Chaz has been putting money aside since he got a paper route in high school. The two of them were on the same page about money. You think Joe Mickels is a miser? Those two could give Joe Mickels lessons—and she gave him some good investment advice. She knew Chaz had more than enough to keep things going until his inheritance started paying off."

"Will they let Chaz continue managing her properties until the estate is settled?"

Bershada nodded. "Yes, and they'll pay Chaz a good salary."

"You said he's getting about half of her properties?"

"Yes, some of the rest are going to her church, some to other charities—who will probably sell them. It's a whole big business, managing properties, and it takes experience they probably don't have. The executors of her will—there are three of them, from a company with the super-imaginative name of Twin Cities Property Management, Incorporated—asked Chaz some questions. One question he couldn't answer, about a bill for window replacement in a cabin up in Pine County. Chaz knew nothing about a cabin, so he couldn't help them with that. He's wondering just how much property she died owning."

Betsy smiled. "Maybe it's half the homes in Duluth. It will be interesting to find out." Her smile faded. "Now for the hard question. Bershada, did Chaz think his race had anything to do with my asking for an alibi?"

Bershada bit her lower lip, then nodded, her eyes sad. "Yes, he took it as a sign of prejudice, which totally knocked him sideways, because he thought you and I were friends. I told him it wasn't prejudice at all, just your desire to get to the truth, but he doubts me."

"Oh gosh, the poor fellow! I couldn't believe Chaz

would do such a thing. It's just that Joe said he thinks the man who shot him was black, and the only black man I know who is in any way attached to this mess is Chaz."

Bershada asked sharply, "Is that true?"

"Yes. Don't you know I don't ask hard questions of people without a good reason?"

"I should know it, but I guess . . . But . . . You'd think this country would have gotten over that racist sickness a long time ago. We're way better than we used to be, but the virus remains, and it will ambush even me once in a while, often enough that I have to keep my guard up,"

Betsy looked sad now, too. "I'm a fixer—you know that. I see a problem, I want to find a solution. It frustrates me that I can't fix this one."

"You are fixing it, you and millions of others, all decent, caring people. I do my part by being decent and caring, too. In the words of the old song, 'We Shall Overcome.'"

Betsy reached out and took her friend's hand.

"Ahem," said someone, and they looked up to see a young man looking back at them, small notepad in hand. "Are you ready to order?"

They looked down at the neglected menus on the table—when had they been put there?

Bershada said, "I want that salad with little shrimps in it, vinegar and oil dressing. Diet Coke to drink."

Betsy said, "That sounds good, but I'd like an Arnie Palmer instead of a Coke."

The young man nodded, made a note, swooped up the menus, and walked away.

The two women looked at each other and laughed.

"Who needs menus when you come in here as often as

we do?" asked Bershada. Then she grew serious. "I know you're trying to prove Joe Mickels is not a murderer—"

Betsy drew a breath to disagree, but bit her tongue instead.

Bershada continued, "But if it wasn't Joe, then who do you think killed Maddy?"

"I don't know. Not Chaz, of course, I never thought him capable of murdering Maddy, but I'm glad he has a solid alibi."

"You seriously don't know who the murderer is?"

"I seriously do not."

ON Tuesday, Rafael and Godwin were in their living room overlooking beautiful Lake Minnetonka—but the view was lost on them. They were listening to their speakerphone setup. It was two in the afternoon, and Godwin had taken a late lunch to offer moral support to Rafael. The Davisson auction was in its final day, and numismatists from around the state were tuned in either by computer or phone. Davisson's actual building was small and remote, so this wasn't the kind of auction that had an auctioneer chanting for raises on bids.

Nevertheless, Rafael was deeply, intensely listening to a quiet voice calling out the raises as he heard them over the phone or read them on a computer screen.

The Cnut coin was next up for bids.

Rafael had rethought the Cnut coin and offered a bid forty dollars above the current bid of six hundred fifty dollars.

Godwin murmured, "Oooh, that's good, offering less than fifty more!"

The voice said, "We now have a bid of six hundred and ninety dollars." But a few seconds later, he said, "We now have a bid of seven hundred and sixty dollars."

Rafael made a face, raised his hands and his shoulders, shook his head, and then relaxed all over. He was done.

After about thirty seconds, the voice said, "Are there any more bids?" and soon after, "Sold for seven hundred and sixty dollars."

"Never mind," counseled Godwin, "there will be another Cnut, better and perhaps for less money."

"Next," said the voice on the speakerphone, "we have the Edward the Confessor penny, York mint, Extra Fine condition. Current bid is four hundred dollars." There was a pause that went on and on, and Rafael started to smile—the four-hundred-dollar bid was his.

But then the voice said, "We now have a bid for four hundred and fifty dollars."

"Ohhhhhh," groaned Godwin.

Rafael grimaced but said, "I'll bid five hundred dollars."

The voice said, "We now have a bid for five hundred dollars."

This time the silence went on for what seemed like several minutes but was just about thirty seconds.

The voice said, "Sold for five hundred dollars."

Godwin said, "Hurray! But you should have said four hundred and seventy-five, Rafael."

"No, because you saw what the forty-dollar raise did. Fifty dollars said I was *serious.*"

Godwin shrugged. He didn't understand the subtleties of such things, but Rafael obviously did. Rafael hung up the phone and let out a long sigh.

"You aren't going to bid on the James?" Godwin asked.

"No, I'm spending too much as it is. I need to stop myself before I come up short on next month's association fee."

Rafael was by far the wealthier of the two men, so it was unlikely he could spend a few hundred on coins and be unable to pay May's association fee.

There was a delicate balance between the two on financial matters, because of the difference between their earnings. It was Godwin, with his substantial trust fund, who was currently making the mortgage payments on their condo. By expending a large chunk of money on something as important as their dwelling place, he felt less "kept" by Rafael, who bought most of the food—Godwin did most of the cooking—and paid for the condo's association fee and any upkeep, plus utilities, plus all their taxes and insurance, and took them on most of their vacations. Rafael came from wealth, managed his own investments, and was probably worth three or four times what Godwin was.

It was descriptive of their relationship that either felt free to call for an adjustment of this arrangement if he felt it was necessary.

BACK at work, Godwin found Betsy sorting through an order of floss. He stopped to admire Rainbow Gallery's new colors in the Treasure Braid line, Awesome Gold, Orange, and Pumpkin. Though it was spring outside, these autumn colors made his fingers itch to stitch something in the Halloween line—and actually, it was more than time to start a fall-themed project. Godwin liked complex needlepoint pieces, which took months to complete.

He picked up the Fyre Werks cards of floss in fluorescent autumn colors. Oh my, yes, it was time to pick something for autumn!

He went to the canvas doors hanging on the wall. Wasn't there something he'd pinned up just the other day? Ah yes, here it was, not a Halloween theme but a river-in-fall theme, with colorful trees reflected in the water, the bright reds and oranges mixed with green pine and blue water, and more subtle blending than is usual with needle-point. Oh yes, this would keep his mind and fingers busy.

Then he looked at a lower corner of the taped canvas and yanked his hand away from the tacks holding it on to the door. Whoa! Nearly three hundred dollars! Even with his employee discount he'd have to give up a couple of outings and that fancy dinner he'd been planning if he were to buy this. Maybe he could find something similar in counted cross-stitch.

He turned away to find Connor looking at him. "Hi, Connor, is there something I can help you with?"

"I want to try to knit a Scottie dog using eyelash yarn. What do you think?"

Godwin considered this. "I love eyelash yarn, the cloud-like effect you get, like whatever you're knitting is set in a fog, all blurred edges. The problem is, sometimes you can't see your stitches after a couple of rows, and you end up knitting by feel. So when you put it down, you can't remember where you left off and you make mistakes. Of course, a lot of the time it doesn't matter, since you can't see the stitches anyway, so if you're doing straight stitch or knit one, purl one, that's okay. But I'd think after that marathon of knitting we did for the auction, you'd be off knitting."

"Yes, you'd think that. But in my case, you'd be wrong. So sell me some."

"Sure."

After the transaction was made, Connor took the little bag of floss and went to talk with Betsy, who was busy incorporating the new threads onto the appropriate spinner rack or into one of the little drawers of DMA and Anchor cotton floss.

"I did some more research on nicotine," he said to Betsy. "It's possible to extract it yourself from tobacco leaves, if you're a chemist with the right equipment. The liquid you get when you boil tobacco, as from a cigar or cigarettes, is deadly, but it's dark and has a very strong odor. You don't have to be in the southern United States to grow it; there are tobacco farmers in next-door Wisconsin, convenient if you want to slip into a field and steal a few leaves—which are enormous, by the way, as big as rhubarb leaves, though longer and narrower.

"You have to obtain a license to buy the pure stuff, and it's difficult to obtain. The University of Minnesota has one, though they were very reluctant to tell me what they use the nicotine for and not at all willing to part with even a small sample of it."

Then he changed the subject. "I'm on my way out to do a little grocery shopping. I'm thinking to fix a British-style curry for dinner, so I need a sharp-flavored apple and a box of golden raisins. Oh, and I love you."

"I love you, too. See if you can find a Honeycrisp apple. You'll have to buy one that comes from down under, as the local variety is long gone from the stores at this time of year. They don't keep, which is their only fault."

Chapter Twenty-five

On Wednesday, Godwin came home from work to find Rafael sitting silent and motionless in semidarkness in the living room.

"What's the matter? What's happened?" he asked.

"My sister is on her way here from the airport—and she's very angry at me."

Godwin flipped the switch that turned on the lamps. "Your sister? Which one?"

"The oldest, Pilar." He leaned forward, hands over his face.

"Why is she angry?"

He straightened, dropped his hands to show Godwin his angry, depressed face. "Because, *mi gorrión*, I told her—I told the whole family—that we're getting married."

"Uh-oh." Godwin knew his partner's family, while not anti-gay generally, were rabidly anti-gay in Rafael's case. The last male twig on his family tree, he was considered the only hope of carrying on the family name. His grandmother had kindly suggested he marry a woman and keep a boyfriend on the side, just as her husband had kept a mistress—or two—on the side. She did not have to mention a certain oft-married but childless uncle with his one lifelong, very close male friend—or the spinster cousin with her series of roommates, all female.

So Rafael was not exactly an outlier; the gene was there. On the other hand, despite his family's record, he was not prepared to sacrifice some unfortunate woman's happiness on the altar of propriety, or himself for his family's desire to continue the name, and had told Godwin this.

"What's in a name?" said Rafael, plagiarizing shamelessly. "My sister has two sons and three daughters. They have the family's blood, so it's not as if it will vanish into the dustbin of history if I do not offer a son to the world."

"Wouldn't it be a hoot," said Godwin, seeking to lighten this depressing subject, "if you did marry and your wife had six daughters?"

For some reason, Rafael didn't think that was funny. "Then she would continue having children until there was a handsome, healthy son," he said, and Godwin thought he said it in all seriousness. "I would not sacrifice you for anything less."

Now, with his sister's visit imminent, he stood and said, "Prepare for fireworks, *mi gorrión*. She is a tiger when she is angry."

Godwin went into the kitchen to contemplate a dinner menu. What would a very angry upper-class Spanish woman deign to eat? Especially if prepared by her brother's fiancé?

Godwin decided on a simple meal of tomato-basil soup, Cobb salad, and a grilled chicken breast sprinkled with herbs. And, if they were all still alive at the end of the meal, a lemon sorbet with wafer cookies.

The oven was hot, and he was rubbing the herbal mix into the meat, when the doorbell rang. Godwin heard the front door open. Rather than just press the intercom, Rafael had decided to go down and greet his sister at the main entrance, and escort her up to their apartment. That was probably a good idea, it would give Rafael a chance to gauge the strength of her anger.

A few minutes later, though the walls were thoroughly soundproofed, Godwin could hear a woman's penetrating voice coming up the hall. He couldn't understand the words, but he recognized the rhythms of Spanish speech. And the extra-rapid tempo made it clear that she was, in fact, angry. Very angry.

The door opened. "*Ni siquiera eres un verdadero hombre!*" she was shouting. Godwin's grasp of Spanish was poor, but after a few seconds he got *verdadero hombre*. Real man. Oh dear, this was not good. Was it himself or Rafael she was accusing of not being authentically male?

Rafael spoke gently to her, and Godwin put the chicken into the oven, washed his hands, and fearfully went into the well-appointed living room to see who he was up against.

First of all, she was beautiful. Slender and tall, nearly as tall as Rafael, with sleek black hair pulled back into a very large bun at the nape of her neck, she had white, flawless skin. Her huge dark eyes were lined with lots of false lashes, her full mouth was painted bright, shiny red, and her long, slender neck held her head high. She was wearing leggings and boots that barely covered her ankles, a close-fitting lightweight coat with a clever collar, and thin, tight gloves. Everything she had on was black, even her button earrings.

She was peeling off her gloves, and Rafael was standing behind her, waiting to help her off with her coat. When she shrugged it off her shoulders, the blouse under it was a soft black velvet that looked very simple but likely cost hundreds of dollars—Godwin had an eye for expensive clothing.

The entire time she had been looking at Godwin. At first, her magnificent dark eyes had widened as if in surprise, then narrowed.

Rafael, draping her coat over his forearm, said, "Pilar, this is Godwin DuLac, to whom I am engaged. Goddy, this is my big sister Pilar Gallardo."

If looks could kill, Godwin would have dropped to the hardwood floor. The woman's eyes glittered as they abruptly focused on the beautiful ruby ring that twinkled on Godwin's left hand.

She pointed to it like a vampire spying a crucifix. "*Como pudiste, Rafael! 'El Anillo de Soto' es un tesoro familiar, es invaluable, debe permanecer en la familia, en nuestra familia, no tienes derecho a dárselo a nadie!*"

Godwin looked helplessly at Rafael. He said, "She wonders how I dare give you a family heirloom, the Soto Ring." He said to her, gently, "*Es mio, Pilar, y ahora del hombre a quien amo.*" To Godwin, he translated, "The ring is mine, and I have given it to the man I love."

"*Que amas?*" she shrieked. "*Es una locura! Esto no es normal! Vas a destruir el linaje de nuestra familia! Como vamos a explicarle esto a nuestras amistades?*"

Rafael said to Godwin, his voice still gentle, "She says I am insane and not normal, that what we are doing will destroy my family. She wonders how she will explain this to her friends."

Godwin felt his own anger rising. "Why does she have to explain anything to her friends? They are her friends, not ours! What do we care about them? It's our life, and we love each other."

Rafael nodded. "You are right." He turned back to his sister. *"Tú no tienes que explicarle nada a nadie, Pilar. Es mi vida, amo a Godwin, él me ama a mí, y vamos a casarnos."*

Eyes blazing, she shouted, "*Vas a matarla, a la Abuela, lo sabes, no?*"

Color was rising in Rafael's face. "This would kill our grandmother? She is stronger than either of us! She has survived worse, including her husband, including you, even including *your* husband!"

Surprisingly, Pilar replied in English. "I wish you dead! I wish I could kill you myself!" And she launched herself at Rafael, her fingers curved into claws. He threw up both arms to fend her off but staggered back under her weight, then sideways, falling into Godwin. She was screaming like a wildcat.

Godwin fell onto the floor, striking his head on a corner of the couch. Suddenly, his vision blurred and the sounds in the room grew softer. With an effort, he rolled onto his stomach and pulled himself free of the tangle that was Rafael and Pilar.

"Whoa," he murmured. "Wow. Man, oh, man." He staggered to his feet and looked back at the pair, wrapped around each other, striking at random, she screaming Spanish invective, he growling replies. Godwin went wobbling into the kitchen. He opened the refrigerator and got out a liter bottle of water, staggered back into the living room, unscrewing the cap as he went. The two siblings were shouting, screaming and hitting, kicking. Rolling, they thumped against the coffee table and the couch. There was a sound of fabric tearing.

Godwin coolly upended the bottle over the two of them. Two shouts rose up, different in timbre from what had been going on, and the couple broke apart.

Pilar shrieked, "*Estas loco!? Que estas pensando!?*"

"Well done, *mi gorrión*!" shouted Rafael, getting to his feet, as water rolled past his ears. He glanced with indifference at Pilar, struggling to her knees. His nose and cheek were bleeding, and his shirt was torn at the collar. He came to shake Godwin's hand but winced when Godwin squeezed back, pulling his hand free to look with a grimace at a deep scratch on it.

Then he went to his sister, stooped, and put his hands under her shoulders to lift her to her feet. There was a red mark on her forehead, and her bun had come undone, spilling her long hair down her back. She brushed down her leggings and looked with dismay at the tear in the side seam of her velvet top.

"We have not put our hands on each other for long time," she said in English.

"It was rude of you to speak Spanish in front of someone who could not understand you," he said.

"Is that why you tear my clothes?"

"I was trying to get your fingernails out of my eyes."

"Ha! I wish I had blinded you! You are too stupid! You are not thinking—" Out of vocabulary, she lapsed into

Spanish. *"Tu deber es primero con la familia, y asegurarte de que nuestro apellido continúe, nos estas quitando oportunidades para el futuro! Porque no haces lo que dice la Abuela? Cásate con una mujer, ten un hijo, y él podrá continuar el apellido!"*

Rafael turned to appeal to Godwin. "She says my grandmother is anxious that I marry a woman long enough to sire a son, so that the family name can continue."

Pilar said, *"Si, si. Y divorciate despues si quieres, pero ten ese hijo."*

"Then," translated Rafael, "I may divorce her if I wish, but sire that boy!"

"Yes, yes," said Pilar, "have that boy!"

"What's it to you?" Godwin asked her. "Don't you have any boys of your own?"

"I have two boys." She held up two fingers. "Two. But the *importante* boy must come from him," she added, pointing to Rafael.

"Why?"

"Family," she said, opening her arms wide, then raising and lowering them, to encompass the world. "Family is everything. The name is everything. Our family name is *everything*."

"We are a family," said Godwin, going to put an arm around Rafael.

"No, no, no!" said Pilar, waving a hand as if to erase what she was seeing. "That is crazy—*loco*—to think that!"

"Pilar, Pilar, enough," said Rafael. "You are tired from your long airplane ride. You are tired from striking me in the face. Your hair has fallen down."

"Eeee!" she said in a squeaky voice. She reached to the

back of her head to gather her long crow black locks, twisting them around her hand and expertly tying them into a knot at the back of her head, tucking the ends inside it.

"Listen to me," said Rafael. "Take your suitcase to our guest room and change out of that destroyed shirt. There is a bathroom at the back of the bedroom you can use to clean up. I will also clean my face and change my shirt, which you have torn. Meanwhile, Godwin will salvage what he can of dinner—"

Godwin made a squeaky noise of his own and ran for the kitchen, which was just starting to fill with the scent of overcooked meat.

He heard Rafael say in the living room, "We will eat a little something, and then maybe we can talk like civilized people. Okay?"

"Show me this guest room," she said in a wounded, imperious manner.

THE chicken was beyond repair, so Godwin discarded it. Everyone's appetite was already dampened, so the soup, salad, a crispy loaf of French bread, and the lemon sorbet with wafer cookies was about all anyone wanted. More than enough; not even half of it was eaten.

The conversation was in English, desultory and quiet, and after they'd finished with their meal, Godwin took the dishes into the kitchen to be put into the dishwasher. With an ear cocked for sounds of combat coming from the living room, he put the dishwashing pellets into the cups and started the cycle. He went into the living room to find brother and sister sitting quietly, Pilar on the couch and Rafael in an easy chair watching darkness overtake the big, beautiful lake out the window.

"Is a silly name for a lake, no?" said Pilar. "Min-ee-tunk-a."

"It's Minnetonka, an Indian name," said Godwin. "It means Big Water."

"Is the biggest lake in this state?"

"No, it's number nine, or maybe ten, I forget. There are many lakes in Minnesota. Our license plates brag that there are ten thousand, but actually there are way more than that."

"Your license plates lie?" she said, amusement in her voice.

"No, long ago they made a guess, picked a big number, and now are stuck with it. That's my theory, anyhow."

"There are new lakes forming and old lakes dying all the time," said Rafael. "It is impossible to keep track. But that is not why you are here, to count our lakes. You have made your demand, and I have declined to obey. We are at an impasse."

"What is this 'impasse'?"

"*Punto muerto*," said Rafael.

"No, no, no," said Pilar, with a triumphant smile. "I have arrange things at home for you. Consuela Montserrat is your bride."

"What? What are you saying?" demanded Rafael.

Pilar continued as if he hasn't spoken. "You remember her, she was best friends with our cousin Maria Eugenia. Very nice woman, her years are but twenty, she is pretty, she look like her mama, she have six brothers, so you see she is perfect! And when I go home, I shall . . ." She paused to translate her Spanish thoughts to English. "I shall *release* the news that you are promise to, to *diarios*—the media!" She produced the word with an effort of thought, pleased to have succeeded. "The TV, the radio, the newspapers, no? Yes! Then you *must* marry her."

Rafael said nothing, but when Godwin looked at him, it was as if his partner had turned into a pale marble statue.

So Godwin spoke for him. "You can't do that!"

"No?" she said, pleased. "You jus' watch me, buster!"

Godwin burst into laughter.

Insulted, she retreated again into Spanish. "*Rafael*," she began, rolling the *R* until it screamed for mercy, "*Rafael, se nota que no estás pensando con claridad! Eres un irresponsable, y por lo visto necesitas que te recuerde cuál es tu deber ante la familia! Tú bien sabes que es tú responsabilidad que la línea familiar continúe de manera honorable, decente y bajo la Ley de la Iglesia.*"

Rafael grew serious, leaning forward out of the chair. "You will not do this thing," he said to his sister in a voice made of icicles. "You will not arrange my life for me."

"You cannot stop me unless you kill me!"

Rafael looked about to rise, and for just an instant Pilar looked frightened, as if she'd gone a step too far and he might indeed reach for her with murder in his heart.

But he spoke calmly, although there were razors in his voice, "If one word of my engagement to anyone but Godwin DuLac reaches the media, I will make a release of my own, of a set of e-mails I received from your Franco."

"What has my husband to do with this?" she said with disdain.

"We used to be friends, Franco and I, before he understood I am gay. He was then, and remains, unfaithful to you."

"So?" she said, but less certain.

"So not long ago he was very close to a certain woman, and still may be. He bragged about her to me. He sent me a picture of the two of them smiling at me. She is called Si-Si, do you know of her?"

All the color drained from Pilar's face.

"I see you do. She is notorious, is she not? Franco is like many men of our class, who marry for advantage, not love. But this, this is too much; she is promiscuous to an infamous degree, she discolors all she touches." He looked at Godwin. "Is 'discolors' the correct word?"

"I think the word you want is 'taints.'"

Rafael looked at his sister. Now she was the one sitting pale and frozen. "I think we have again reached a *punto muerto.*"

Chapter Twenty-six

THAT same evening, Betsy called Mike Malloy at home. "May I ask a favor?" she asked.

"Tell me why I should do you a favor," he growled.

"Having a hard week?" she asked.

"All my weeks are hard. What's making this one hard is that Joe Mickels's alibi turned up."

"You mean the man he was interviewing for a job?"

"That's the one. Wayzata PD found him up in Duluth. He agrees he went to a late dinner with Joe, didn't like the terms of employment he was offered, and turned him down."

"Well, that's good, that's progress!" Then she remembered he liked Joe a whole lot for the murder of Harry Whiteside. "Still . . ." she said.

"What do you want?"

"I understand you've got some video of the reception over at Mount Calvary, and Joe's on it."

"Can't *nobody* keep their mouths shut anymore?" he complained, intentionally colloquial.

"Apparently not. But is it true? You actually saw Joe there and going into the janitor's closet where the bags were kept?"

"In the video footage he's there, all right."

"But not going into the closet."

"You can't see the closet on the camera. He was near it, going toward it, we got that much."

"Mike, can I watch the videos?"

"What for?"

"I want to see who else was near that closet door. Have you watched all three of them?"

"Of course I have."

"Did you see anyone else on the footage who is significant to the case?"

"Sure, I did. Chaz and Bershada Reynolds were there; both the Larsons, Jill and Lars. My wife and oldest daughter were there. Sergeant Larabee of Wayzata PD was there. Hell, Harry Whiteside was there."

"Harry was there?"

"Sure, why not? He came to all kinds of events. Looking for more clients. Letting people see him talking to important clients. You know, being a big shot. Showing the flag."

"I don't remember seeing him around," said Betsy, who went to a number of "events" herself. Then she had a second thought. "Well, I might have. I didn't know him and I don't remember anyone introducing him to me. Unless he wore a name tag, I wouldn't have recognized him if he stood right beside me."

"I didn't see you on the videos at Mount Calvary," Mike said.

"That's because I wasn't there," said Betsy. "I was doing taxes. But what I want to ask is, may I come over to the station and borrow those discs?"

"No, you may not. But you can come over and watch them at the department."

"When?"

"How about right now?"

He was being sarcastic, but she decided to take him at his word. "Thank you, I'll meet you over there shortly."

IT was a little after six when Betsy drove up to the little brick and white stone building that was Excelsior's Police Department.

Betsy went into the air lock that was the entrance to the station. She got out her cell and called Mike. "I'm out front," she said.

"I'll be right there," he said.

A minute later, Mike came up to the thick glass that looked into the station and pressed or levered something that made a door to the inside open with a clack. Betsy went through, and Mike escorted her to his little office with the twin desks pushed up against each other. There was no one at the other desk.

"Where's Elton?" asked Betsy.

"Home eating dinner," said Mike.

"Mike, I'm sorry to get you out like this. But you offered, and I'm grateful you agreed to let me see the recordings."

Mike said, reluctantly, "Well, sometimes you come up with things, I have to admit."

On Mike's desk was an old gray laptop computer, and beside it were three dark brown plastic computer disc cases. One was open, and a disc was shoved halfway into the side of his keyboard.

Mike sat down on the office chair behind his desk, gesturing at the armless wooden chair next to it.

Betsy pulled it around to sit next to Mike. He pushed the disc the rest of the way in. The computer gulped and twinkled and displayed a menu with only one item on it. Mike moved his mouse to bring a fat arrow to the item and clicked on it.

His computer grumbled and hummed, and suddenly they were looking at the big rotunda that was Mount Calvary's church hall. There were six or seven people there, nicely dressed for church in light spring coats, all adults. Along a far wall was a long table with a white tablecloth on it, ornamented with two punch bowls, one full of something orange, the other full of something pink. Between the punch bowls were various platters displaying very small crustless sandwiches, crackers with dabs of cheese topped with slices of something dark, probably olives, and small cookies. Plastic glasses rose in towers behind the punch bowls, and while Betsy watched, two women came to dip ladles into the bowls.

Meanwhile, the room was filling up. Betsy leaned forward. She saw Joe accepting a clear plastic cup of orange punch and one of the little sandwiches, tucking a tiny napkin into a curled little finger. He wandered off around the room. She followed him until he went out of camera range.

She recognized several of her favorite customers, then Jill and Lars, without the children.

"There's Harry," said Mike, touching the screen.

"Where?" she asked, leaning forward.

"There," he said, touching the screen again. Harry Whiteside, tall and silver haired, in a dark topcoat, turned away from the camera then turned back. He seemed to be looking for someone. Then he wandered out of the camera's range.

He looks like Heck, she thought.

The room became increasingly crowded, and it was harder to pick out individual faces. She thought she saw Alice, but the figure turned away and didn't reappear.

The recording lasted a little over an hour, the crowd thinning slowly at first, then more rapidly. By the time it was down to the cleanup crew, it suddenly cut off.

"Seen enough?" asked Mike, pushing a button to expel the disc.

"Does one of them show the door to the janitor's closet?" she asked.

He rattled his way among the plastic boxes and picked one. "None show the closet door," he said, "but this one comes closest."

He popped the disc into the computer, which grumbled again, and suddenly the church hall was back on Mike's computer screen.

Mike touched a spot on the screen. "The door is just about two, two and a half feet from here, this way." He moved his finger out and up off the screen.

Betsy studied the screen and located herself in the scene. "Yes," she said, "right over there is Kari's office." She touched the screen up and to the left of where Mike had touched it.

She focused in on that part of the screen and just watched. Alice came near it, Joe came near it, Harry came near it, several other people Betsy recognized came near it. Harry came back a second time, went off camera in its direction for a short time, perhaps fifteen seconds, then came back. He was smiling, as if someone had told him a cruel but funny joke. Then Joe came back, thrust a hand into his pocket, and went off camera and was gone longer, nearly half a minute. When he came back he looked around as if for spying eyes.

Uh-oh, thought Betsy.

Then Alice came back. Betsy saw her reaching out, as if for a doorknob, as she went off camera in the direction of the janitor's closet. She backed away from it, frowned at it, then turned and walked away.

"It seems to me," said Betsy, "that Alice is behaving as suspiciously as Joe or Harry."

"Harry's dead, and Alice has no motive I've been able to find."

"Hmmm," said Betsy, and she went home discouraged.

WHEN Betsy came down the next morning a few minutes before opening-up time, she found the shop lit and dusted, smelling of fresh coffee, the teakettle singing to itself in an undertone. Godwin was sitting at the little round table in the back of the shop, a cup of tea in front of him. He was looking very pensive.

Betsy made a very sweet and milky cup of coffee for herself and came to sit across from him.

"What's on your mind?" she asked.

"Oh . . ." he began, then sighed.

She asked, alarmed, "Is the marriage off?"

"Oh yes," he said but not unhappily, and she took a drink of coffee, unable to reply.

"Oh," he said, looking at her, "not our marriage, the other one, the one his family arranged for him in Spain, to a woman named Montserrat—isn't that a Spanish mountain?"

"Goddy!"

"All right, all right. Let's see, where to start. When we drove Pilar to the airport to wait for a plane that will begin her journey home, she and Rafael talked. She had to change in Chicago, I think. She wasn't angry anymore."

"No, sweetie, that's the end of the story, not the beginning. Who is Pilar?"

"She's Raf's big sister. She came on behalf of the family, I think. Trying to talk him out of marrying me."

"Was she difficult?"

"Difficult?" He raised pale eyebrows at her, making his light blue eyes open very wide. "Oh, Betsy, 'difficult' is entirely too mild a word to describe her. She was a screaming harridan. She actually attacked Rafael, knocked him down, tore his clothing half off him, tried to scratch his eyes out."

"Are you serious?"

He nodded, frowning painfully at the memory. "Knocked me down, too. Collateral damage, but still. Gave me a knot on my head." He touched a place above his left ear tenderly. "It was a total war. She frightened me to *death*! I managed to crawl away, then actually had to pour cold water on her to make her let go of Rafael."

Betsy felt uncertain laughter start to bubble up and severely choked it down, sending down a big swallow of coffee to drown it. "What about this woman, Montserrat?"

"Apparently Pilar thought that if she announced their engagement in the papers, Rafael and this woman's engagement, he would be shamed into going to Spain and marrying her."

"She *announced* it? Before she *talked* to him?"

"No, it hadn't actually been announced; she just told us her plans. Thought the fix was in because she—or maybe the whole family—did apparently get the unfortunate woman to agree to marry him. She's supposed to be very pretty, and she's got six brothers."

"What does six—oh."

Godwin nodded, now amused himself. "They really, really want Rafael to father a boy, to carry on the family name. Do you think there's a title in his family somewhere? Maybe if enough people die childless, Raf can be Sir Rafael. Maybe that's what's got them so excited. Rafael was instructed to take back the ring from me and to be sure to wear it when appearing before his grandmother at home in Spain." Godwin straightened in his chair and flourished his left hand, which twinkled. "*Which* he is not going to do!"

"So how did he persuade Pilar to abandon this plan and go home by herself?"

Godwin looked uncomfortable. "Blackmail," he said.

"He is going to blackmail his *grandmother*?"

"Oh no, she is halfway already to being on his side; says after he fathers a boy, he can divorce the Montserrat and come back to me. Or he can stay married to her and keep me like a mistress on the side. Whichever."

"Oh, Goddy!"

"Not to worry, he refused absolutely. Said he would not do that to an innocent woman. Or me."

"So who is he blackmailing?"

"Pilar. Her husband is some kind of rutting pig, and he's not at all faithful to Pilar—which amazes me, seeing how beautiful *and* how vicious she is. Anyway, he had a clandestine affair with a notorious woman—and made the mistake of bragging to Rafael about it—sent pictures and everything. Rafael said he would release Francisco's e-mails to the media the day after she releases the news of his engagement to the mountain." Godwin smiled, an ugly smile, and hid it behind his cup of tea.

"Oh, Goddy! But wait, if she's notorious, isn't everyone already aware of it?"

"Raf told me that it's like the English royals and Hollywood stars back in the day. People around them knew, but not the public. It was never in the papers."

"And Rafael has threatened to tell the papers."

"Yes. I know, it's all too, too utterly shabby!" He frowned unhappily. "Needs must," he mumbled.

"But it's over, right? She's going home and will not do anything further."

"It looks that way. But I hate what Raf had to do. I hate it."

"Poor fellow." She reached for his hand, and found it cold. "Come on, let's take your mind off it by opening up."

An hour later, checking her e-mail, she found a message from Heck Whiteside.

Ham's in town. He has agreed to talk to you if Howie and I come along. We want you to come to our father's house in Wayzata. The address is 1250 Lakeview Street, and we're meeting there at eight o'clock tonight to talk about an estate sale. Ham says he'll give you half an hour, so don't be late.

It was signed, *Heck.*

"Should I go?" Betsy asked, in succession, Connor, Godwin, Jill, and Mike Malloy.

All said she should go, even Mike. And all, even Mike, asked for a report of the conversation.

Chapter Twenty-seven

WAYZATA is a beautiful little town, though its Indian name is not spelled the way it is pronounced: Why-zet-ah. Its main street, unlike Excelsior's, runs along the lakefront, and its shops along the inshore side are attractive and upscale. Behind the main street, the land rises in steps, and those homes lucky enough to face the lake are beautiful and costly, without being overbearing, vainglorious mansions.

It was dark when Betsy arrived at the late Harry Whiteside's house, on a big corner lot up three "steps" from the lakefront, too dark to see anything other than that the house itself was white stucco and at least two stories tall.

The driveway started at the back of the lot and curved around to a broad parking area. There were three outsize vehicles taking up all the space, so Betsy pulled beyond them to find another space set forward in front of a two-car garage.

She got out and went back to a broad front porch—well, a back porch, really, since the front must face the lake. The porch was as broad as the house and marked with arched stucco pillars.

She rang the doorbell. The chimes inside were three deep notes, *ding*, *dang*, *dong*.

The door, made of polished vertical boards with a little window guarded by wrought-iron filigree, was promptly opened by Heck. "Well, howdy, Ms. Devonshire, glad you could make it!" he said, his Texas accent a little more on display than it was during their conversation at her shop. He was wearing a red and gray plaid flannel shirt of western design, plain jeans, and old cowboy boots. Betsy suspected his wardrobe choice was an overreaction to being away from home, like an American discovering patriotism while in France.

"I'm glad you offered me this opportunity to meet all three of you," said Betsy, coming into the house. They were in a roomy reception area with tile paving and a small wrought-iron chandelier overhead.

Heck came around behind her to help her off with her white cloth coat. He hung it in the coat closet and gestured at her to precede him through a big, gourmet eat-in kitchen into the living room. There she stopped in her tracks. An even more beautiful room!

It was big, and done all in shades of gray. The floor was shining wood stained dark gray, the square-cut couch was light gray, as was the severely modern occasional chair, and the walls were a medium gray. Very light and filmy silvery gray curtains were pulled back from the gigantic square of glass that was the wall facing the lake. Beside the one window was a huge square of plywood covering what was undoubtedly a twin opening now lacking glass.

In front of the couch, which faced the windows, was a highly polished chrome coffee table. It and the couch rested on a big rug woven in a geometric pattern of dark taupe and white. To the right, suspended on the wall, was a long gas fireplace with a surround of small rectangular stones a darker shade of gray than the walls. Tiny yellow flames danced through black gravel down its length, and hanging above it were two large framed architectural drawings of commercial buildings on pale gray paper. On the left side, the entire wall was a floor-to-ceiling bookcase made of matte black metal. The books in it provided touches of color. Small lights on the ceiling spotlighted the bookshelves, the coffee table, and the architectural drawings.

As Betsy stepped farther into the room, she glanced back the way she'd come and saw on the wall a large Impressionistic painting of Marilyn Monroe's head, done in shades of black, gray, and white, except for her lips, which were a brilliant red.

"Wow!" said Betsy, turning back around slowly to take a second look. Someone had paid a professional interior designer a lot of money to put together this room. Outside the front window the land fell away. There were a few mature trees in black silhouette flanking the window, and houses with glowing windows were down the hill. The main feature in view was the dark, restless surface of the lake, and the darker sky with clouds moving swiftly across a half-moon high in it. The view was wonderful, in tune with the room's message of masculinity, power, and money.

"You like it?" asked one of the other two men standing

near the windows. He was just a little taller than Heck, slimmer, older. He and the other man, even taller and very skinny, but not so much older, had dark hair and features very much like Heck's. Clearly, the men were his two brothers, Howard and Hamilton.

"Impressive," said Betsy.

"But perhaps lacking a woman's touch," said the thinnest brother with a wry smile. He was wearing a dark blue suit with a faint pinstripe and a dark tie, also pinstripe, but from side to side. A short glass, half full of whiskey-colored liquid and ice, was in one hand.

"I'm Hamilton Whiteside," he said.

"I'm Howard," said the other, who was wearing a very thick brown pullover and brown corduroy trousers. He held an identical glass in his hand.

"The house is for sale, of course," said Hamilton.

"Would you like to make an offer?" asked Howard, only half seriously.

Betsy laughed. "No, I don't think so. For one thing, it's not my style. For another, I don't think I could afford it."

"Come over, sit down," invited Hamilton, gesturing at the couch. "Would you like something to drink? We have beer, wine, gin, scotch, Campari, and—" He glanced at Heck.

"Diet Coke, and something called 'spicy ginger ale.'"

"The ginger ale, please," said Betsy, hoping it was what she thought it might be, and in any case thinking it was the best of the choices.

So she took the tall, ice-filled glass of the pale stuff when Heck brought it to her, and she smiled. "Thank you," she said, and she took a taste. It was what she hoped; she recognized the taste, not too sweet and very gingery. "I'll come to your estate sale to buy all of this you have." Betsy had found WBC Craft Sodas at a now-closed craft beer store in Saint Louis Park and was sadly disappointed when she couldn't find the Spicy Ginger variety she'd quickly come to love anywhere else she looked.

"There's a whole case of it back beside the refrigerator," said Heck.

"I'll take it."

"Write that down," said Hamilton to Howard, gravely.

Betsy drank some more, then realized a silence had fallen. They were waiting for her.

"Ah," she said, looking for a coaster on which to place her sweating glass.

"Just put it on the table," said Heck. "It can take it."

She obeyed, then went into her purse for her long, narrow notepad and a pencil—ballpoint pens sometimes failed her when she was trying to get something down on paper quickly.

She looked up and around at the three of them, all still standing, and got up to go to the egg-shaped occasional chair, which was under the window. She moved it near the coffee table and sat down. It was surprisingly comfortable. "Will you all sit?" she asked.

"Sure," said Heck quickly, and they moved to the couch. It was more than long enough to hold the three of them.

"I'm interested in the kind of person your father was," she began. "Howard, you're the oldest; presumably you knew him best. He was a very successful businessman. But what was he like as a man? What were his hobbies? Did he fish? Play golf? Own a motorcycle?"

"He liked to fish," said Howard. "When he was a kid, he

used to spend summers with his grandparents up somewhere in Pine County in a cabin on Pine Lake—imaginative names you people have for landmarks. He took me up there a couple of times to see the old place, which was about the size of this room and had a roof that was missing half its shingles. It actually had an outhouse, which he thought was a fine feature." He made a sideways mouth at the memory.

Hamilton said, "I remember that! Somebody else owned it, and he wanted to buy it from them and restore it. But they wouldn't sell it. He kept raising his bid for it, but they had hopes some company was going to build a lodge up there and refused to sell it to Dad."

Heck said, amused, "An outhouse? An actual two-holer?"

Howard said, "Yes, and he was going to *keep the outhouse*. Wanted us to go on vacation up there. Said roughing it would be good for us, because it was good for him." He shook his head.

Betsy hid a smile behind her glass of ginger ale, and took a drink.

Hamilton said, "I saw where the hopeful owner finally died, but now someone else has it and tore down the old place to build a new cabin on it. So I guess we can be grateful we dodged that bullet."

Betsy asked, "Did your father know who the newest owner is, the one who built a new cabin?"

Ham looked thoughtful. "I don't think so—I never asked him."

"Could it have been Maddy O'Leary?"

"Why Maddy O'Leary?" asked Hamilton. "Who is she?"

"She and a man named Joe Mickels were bidding on the

Excelsior property," said Heck. "And you know Dad when someone was trying to keep him from something."

The brothers looked at one another. Then Howard said slowly, "If Dad thought someone bought that cabin in order to keep him from having it . . . Especially someone he was already quarreling with."

The others drew long faces at the thought. But Heck said, "There's no way to know that, is there?"

Hamilton said, "Sure there is. A search of listings of property owners on Pine Lake would tell you that. The county—and I'll bet you a dollar it's Pine County—would give you the names. Easy peasy." He said to Betsy, "They call me Ham."

Betsy made a note. Then she said, "What do you think was your father's strongest personal strength, Howard?"

"Tenacity," said Howard at once. "He tried for years to acquire that rotten old cabin. Said his grandfather built it with his own hands. And call me Howie."

"Fine, Howie. Was he friendly? Honest? Temperamental?" At that last word, all three stirred. Howie snorted and hid his mouth with his hand.

"Easily stirred to anger?" suggested Betsy, and this time all three of them snorted. She made a note. "Is it possible he poisoned Maddy O'Leary?"

"Hey, no, no, no," said Howie, surprised at her. "Where'd you get an idea like that?"

"It's Dad who was murdered," said Heck, equally surprised.

"She's also been murdered," said Howie.

"And you think our father killed her?" Ham's tone was incredulous.

"No, the cops think Joe did it," said Howie. He was looking quizzically at her.

"I was originally thinking there was one murderer who killed both Maddy and Harry," said Betsy. "And that still may be the case. But Joe has an alibi for your father's murder. I'm looking for someone else who was angry with him."

"You've come to the wrong source," said Heck. "None of us knows diddly about who Dad was dealing with currently."

"Now hold on," said Ham. "If you're looking for who was tight around the jaws, get a list of who he was doing business with, and you'll have a list of who was mad at him."

"Well," said Betsy, "he dealt recently with Howie."

"He asked me to help him design a building he wanted to put up in Excelsior," said Howie. "I turned him down. No fight, no quarrel, I just said no."

"I'm talking about before that, the time your father took elements of an industrial park design you started doing for him and hired someone else to execute a new design based on your drawings. And you sued him for doing that."

"What are you—how do you—where did you—?"

"Do you deny that you are Stonebridge Design?" asked Betsy.

"Uh-oh," said Ham in an amused voice.

"So you knew about it?" Betsy asked him.

"A chair thrown at the judge in his courtroom? Yes, I'd read the story. But I didn't know that was you, Howie—or Dad. But I should have; it sounds a whole lot like him. And you." Ham was smiling broadly.

"That's enough!" said Heck. "This is serious."

Everyone looked at Howie, whose face had gone red with fury. He took a long, noisy breath through his nose, then said, "Yes, that was me. I couldn't believe that a dad would do that to his own son."

"Not all dads," said Ham. "Not even most dads. But our dad? Sure, why not?"

Betsy said, "I know Heck has an alibi for the night your father was murdered. Do the rest of you?"

"Now she sounds like a cop," said Ham, amused. "And yes, I have an alibi. I was in my office at home researching some upcoming litigation—which I should be home doing more of right now—while my wife kept freshening my coffee mug."

Ham, Heck, and Betsy looked at Howie. He threw up his brown-sweatered arms and tried to make a joke of it. "Well, how the hell was I to know I'd need an alibi?" he demanded. When they didn't laugh, he continued, "If I'd known, I'd have stayed at home! But I had a fight with Abby, and I went out for a drive, stayed out all night."

"Did you go to a hotel?" asked Heck. "Or to a friend's house?"

"It was three o'clock in the morning before I cooled off enough to think about finding a place to bed down. I looked like a bum—I'd been working in the yard, I was all over dirt and blisters, I didn't want to show my face anywhere. So I went to the work site and slept in my car, went home around eight to find Abby sick with worry, and we made up." He shrugged. "We hadn't had a fight like that for years."

"So the investigators here in Wayzata wonder if you picked that fight," said Betsy.

Howie stared at her with respect. "Their very words," he said.

"If he didn't want to show his dirty face at a hotel," suggested Heck, "then why would he show it on an airline?"

"If we're talking premeditated," said Ham, "you stash a change of clothing in your trunk beforehand, clean up in the airport bathroom. Then change back and roll on the floor of the parking garage before you go home."

"What are you trying to do to me?" Howie shouted at Ham. "Get me hanged?"

"Minnesota doesn't have the death penalty," said Betsy.

He turned an angry face to her, then suddenly laughed, a harsh, ugly sound. "This is stupid!" he shouted. "You're all stupid! I didn't murder my father!" He made a sound dangerously near a sob. "I never killed any human being in my life!" He turned away from them all. "I'm not staying here for this! She's not a cop, she can't arrest me! I think we're done." He gestured at Betsy. "It's over. This was a mistake, agreeing to talk to her. We're done, you're done, all right? Heck, show her out!"

"Hold on, pardner, hold on just one minute," said Heck. "Ham didn't mean anything—right, Ham?"

"That's right," said Ham, with a placating smile. "No reason to fly off the handle. I apologize. We've got a problem here, and we need to work together to solve it. I don't think you murdered Dad, all right? Seriously, I don't."

"Me, neither," said Heck. He looked to Betsy for an agreeing comment.

But Betsy didn't give him one, instead drank some more ginger ale. "What time did you leave the house after the argument?" she asked Howie.

"Answer her," warned Ham when Howie appeared about to explode again. Ham was looking very lawyerly.

Howie blew out the big breath he'd taken in order to resume shouting. He took a lesser one. "All right, all right, let me think." He turned to look at the long line of little flames in the fireplace. "It was almost dark. I remember being surprised by that. I was working outside and didn't realize how dark it was getting—you know how that happens."

Ham and Heck made soft sounds of agreement

"The argument started at a late dinnertime—she'd called me in about four times before I *did* come in, and I came to the table looking like the wrath of God, and she told me to at least go wash my hands. But dammit, I was hungry and I grabbed a chicken leg—and she knocked it out of my hand. I was pissed. I picked it up off the floor and took a bite, and she yanked it out of my hand and threw it in the garbage, and we were off to the races, the kids crying and hiding in their rooms, me totally out of control." He took a breath and blew it out through pursed lips. "So I don't know, it was probably after eight when I stomped out." He looked at Betsy. "Okay?"

She said, "Your home is in the Eastern time zone, so here in the Midwest it would be after seven. You'd need time to clean up, get to the airport, get a ticket, fly to Minneapolis, then get from the airport to Wayzata. The medical examiner has set the time of death somewhere around eight thirty, give or take forty minutes. So . . . you're okay, if she's right—and you're right—about the time." She wrote briefly in her notebook.

"There, see?" said Heck, grinning. "See?"

"All right, all right, you're right, I guess," said Howie, looking a little ashamed of himself. "But dammit . . ."

"Yes, you are right," said Betsy. She had let this get out of hand because she had underestimated how volatile one of them might become when he realized he was suspected of murder.

She said, "I'd like to shift focus from you back to your father. He seems to have been quick to anger, willing to use physical force."

"That's him exactly," agreed Howie, and the other two nodded.

"But what about more subtle ways of aggression?" she asked.

"I don't understand the question," said Howie. "Subtle aggression? Is that like when a person hugs you to death?"

"I'm thinking practical jokes—like he did to you, Heck, when you were a kid on the job."

The men's almost identical puzzled expressions cleared up.

"Oh, that," said Heck. "Is a practical joke a kind of aggression?"

"Of course it is," Betsy said. "You make a fool of someone, he may laugh, but he feels injured. You're showing him you're smarter than he is, more clever."

"I think almost everyone working on a building site plays practical jokes," said Howie.

"So do soldiers, so do cops, so do cowboys," said Heck. "It's part of the rough-and-ready mentality, I think."

"Attorneys as well," put in Ham. "Only ours are sneakier, of course. Sometimes a victim never realizes he's been played."

"But did Harry like practical jokes played on him?"

"Now, that's a whole different story," said Heck. "He'd lay for anyone who pulled one on him. Didn't find them funny the least little bit."

"That's right," said Howie, nodding.

"But he liked to play them," said Betsy.

"Sure he did," said Howie. "All his life, and some of them were damn mean. But so what?"

Ham said, "She's thinking about that woman, what's her name, O'Leary, Maddy O'Leary. Someone sneaked poison onto her knitting yarn, remember? A really filthy practical joke. And Harry was very angry that she outbid him. And if she'd already done him out of the cabin . . ."

"No, no," said Heck. "She died from that poisoned yarn. That's not exactly a little ol' practical joke. And anyway, she died *after* Dad."

"The trap was laid before Harry was killed," said Betsy, and a silence fell.

Finally, Heck murmured, "Well, damn."

But that was it; without saying a word, the trio seemed to draw together, to make a pact to say nothing more. The man, after all, was their father. Betsy tried to ask a few more questions, but she got monosyllables in return.

"Maybe we had better wrap this up," Betsy said at last. "I am grateful to all three of you for allowing me to come here and talk with you. I hope there are no hard feelings and that you'll allow me to contact one or more of you if I have additional questions."

There was a little murmur of reluctant agreement, and Betsy collected their current contact information.

She thanked them again.

Heck walked her through the beautiful kitchen, retrieved

and helped her on with her coat, but when he opened the door, rain was falling in a steady patter.

"Oh, rats," sighed Betsy. "I knew I should have worn my raincoat."

"Where's your car?" asked Heck, peering out into the rain past the three SUVs.

"Over past the end of the porch," said Betsy, gesturing. "In front of the garage."

"Oh, well, come on, there's a door to the outside through the garage. I'll let you out there. Less of a hike."

"Thanks," said Betsy.

A sudden silence fell as they came back into the living room. Heck smirked at his brothers and said, "Raining. Letting her out through the garage."

He hustled her across the room, out a dark gray door, into a hallway. Betsy got a glimpse of an office through an open door halfway along, then reached for a doorknob at the end of the corridor.

"Wait!" ordered Heck. "It's dark and there's a step down." He went around her to open the door.

"Ow!" He went into a dark space beyond the door, and a second later a pair of overhead lights came on, and she saw him grasping his right hand. A tiny trickle of blood was just barely visible through his left fingers.

"What happened?" Betsy asked.

"That damn door bit me!" He was smiling, but it was a painful smile.

He'd gone down a step, and Betsy saw a big concrete block a couple of inches below the threshold. Betsy looked at the door, which was standing open. It looked uninjured.

Heck said, "Here, let me look at that doorknob." He

bent down to examine it. "Looks like there's a screw loose," he said. "And I don't mean in me."

Betsy came for a look. There was a small, dark stain on the underside of the bright brass knob, on the area where it fastened to the flange that came through the door latch. It was partly covered by fresh blood, and the flat head of a screw was standing up a fraction of an inch through it.

"I'd better fix that before it gets someone else," said Heck.

"It already has," said Betsy. "And I think we'd better leave it alone. The police need to be called right away."

"They do? Why?"

"Because that dark stain already on the screw is probably blood, and I think it was left there by the murderer."

Chapter Twenty-eight

AT breakfast the next morning, Connor asked, "So the police investigator wasn't as excited about the bloody doorknob as you were?"

"No, but he did take samples."

"What are they expecting to find?"

"Probably that Harry Whiteside cut his hand on the knob."

"But you don't think so."

"I think if Harry cut his hand, he would have cleaned himself up, then wiped the knob, then fixed the loose screw. That house was immaculate, everything in order, no books stacked on tables or the floor, no dishes in the sink, nothing dirty or dusty. The kind of person who likes cleanliness and order is not going to leave a hazard like that doorknob unrepaired. It's my opinion that the murderer cut his hand going out the door. I did persuade the investigator to look around the garage for more blood traces. I looked, too, and didn't find any.

"But you see, I don't think they'll get any usable evidence from the blood they did find at all. Heck Whiteside also cut his hand on that door, so the blood sample is mixed, and DNA testing won't prove anything useful." She looked down at her two soft-boiled eggs in the little blue dish. "Rats," she mumbled.

Downstairs, she found Godwin just starting to open up. He was unusually quiet, and she let him go unquestioned until at last, the opening up finished, she asked, "Something on your mind, Goddy?"

"Well, yes. But, there is, um . . . but . . ."

"Oh dear. What now?"

"Well, I don't know which one of them had this brainstorm, Raf or Pilar, but they talked about it on the way to the airport, and most of it was in Spanish, and it was late when we got back, and I sort of forgot about it until this morning. So I remembered and asked. And so now he's told me what they think they've cooked up. And I don't know if I like it. I mean, maybe it's all right, but I never did think I'd be a parent one day." He went to the library table and dropped into a chair with a sigh.

She joined him there and said, "A parent? I don't understand. You mean he got talked back into doing that? He will after all go ahead with the plan and marry Ms. Montserrat, and try to get custody of the child when they divorce?"

"No, he's not going to marry Ms. Mountain."

"Who, then? And what if it's a girl?"

"We talked about that, earlier, that he might have to

breed a long string of girl babies before they got to a boy. But no, that's not the plan at all."

"Then I really don't understand."

"We'll still get married. But then . . . things like in vitro and, and a surrogate." Godwin drew up his shoulders, his face showing his distaste for the idea. "Because the way he and his family think, it has to be his biological son, not an adopted child. And so, of course, we will be the ones to raise it."

Betsy sat staring at him while the silence went on and on. He just stared at the collection of stitching tools in a bin in the center of the table.

Finally, she said, "What are you going to do?"

"I don't know. Rafael's halfway to being pleased with the idea; he thinks it's clever. But somehow the idea of me being a daddy—well, it just never occurred to me. I knew a long time ago that I wouldn't ever . . . you know, with a *girl*, so I just accepted that to be the way it was. And I put a brave, bad face on it, because after all, babies are loud and messy, and you're up all night and ishy *diapers* and icky *potty training* and crying for no reason and *expensive* . . . so I told myself that was okay for some but not for me. Besides, I wasn't ever going to be old enough to be a *father*. Fathers are old, and I'm always so . . . *young*." He looked at her, his expression so pitiful and yearning that her heart turned over.

"And now, the man you love is suggesting the two of you do this thing that will upset that applecart," she said. "What did you say to Rafael when he told you?"

"I hugged him so he wouldn't see the look on my face and said I had to get to work early. I've been here for nearly an hour. I'm trying to think, and I can't think. What can I say to him?"

Betsy took several minutes to gather her thoughts. "First of all, you mustn't lie to him. You have to talk to him, tell him you have deep reservations about this plan. You could begin by saying you don't think you'd be any good at parenting—"

"Well, I wouldn't! I mean, look at me! I'm frivolous! I'm vain! I like pretty clothes and nice vacations and everything neat and clean, sweet and peaceful. Except at parties, I like loud parties and drinking too much and then sleeping till noon the next day. You can't do that with a baby!"

"It wouldn't stay a baby forever, you know. They grow up quicker than you think. But then, of course, you're faced with new problems: dating, and driving, and getting into a good college."

Godwin's eyes widened. "Oh my God, you're right! Suppose he drops out of school, takes drugs, and falls in love with absolutely the wrong person?"

"Suppose she's a girl, this child of yours?"

He waved that off with one hand. "No, not likely. There's something they can do, some processing of the sperm that makes it extremely likely it will be a boy."

"What if he's gay?"

Godwin stared at her, then bloomed all over. "Wouldn't that be the biggest hoot in the *world*?" He laughed. "I don't think dear Pilar thought about *that*!"

Then he sobered. "So you think I should tell Rafael what I think."

"I think you must, because you are not to go into this unwillingly. Remember how your father reacted to learning you were gay? Think how this child will react to a father who dislikes him for a reason he cannot understand?"

Godwin's mouth fell open, then his face crumpled. He jumped to his feet and ran into the back room. Betsy heard the bathroom door slam. She went there but heard noisy weeping and retreated. Neither of Godwin's parents spoke to him, hadn't seen or communicated with him in any manner since he was fourteen and they'd thrown him out into the street.

She had cut him to the quick with that single careless remark.

She felt tears of her own beginning, but the front door began to play "Yes! We Have No Bananas," and Jill came into the shop with the children, Emma Beth, Airy, and Einar. The children ran to her for hugs and loud greetings—she was Emma's godmother and informal aunt to them all.

But Jill saw something in Betsy's face and said, "What's wrong?"

"It's Godwin. He's in a real pickle, and I don't know what to tell him."

"Get the coloring books," ordered Jill, and Betsy went into a bottom drawer of the checkout desk for the big plastic box of crayons and three coloring books.

In another minute the children were settled at the library table telling stories about the pages they were coloring—or scribbling over, in Einar's case—while Betsy drew Jill out of earshot and swiftly gave a condensed version of Godwin's predicament.

"Where is he now?"

Betsy grimaced. "In the bathroom, crying his eyes out. It's my fault. I brought up his parents, who didn't want him once they learned he was gay. If he is burdened with a child he doesn't want . . ."

Jill nodded. "That wasn't a very clever thing to say."

"I agree, I should have thought harder before I spoke. But on the other hand, he needs to really think this through before agreeing to help Rafael raise a child. He thinks children are pretty awful."

"Does he? Does he really?"

"Well, he said so, in so many words, just a few minutes ago."

"Hmmmm," said Jill. "Watch the children for me." She walked into the back room.

Betsy went out front and found Einar, already bored with his coloring book, beginning to scrawl on the table.

"Here now, sweetie," said Betsy, taking the crayon from his hand. "I have a different job for you."

Einar puckered up as if to cry and reached for his crayon, but Betsy lifted it higher. "Would you like to pop bubbles?"

"Bubbles!" shouted the child.

"No, not really bubbles," said Betsy. "This is something different." She went to her desk and opened a middle drawer. Under a clipboard was a length of bubble wrap.

"Yay!" cheered Airy—his real name was Erik, but Emma Beth had called him Airy when they were both very young, and the nickname stuck.

"Awww, baby stuff!" scoffed Emma Beth and went back to coloring a crowned frog in her book. She was very good, even adding shading to the frog's foreleg.

"No, it isn't!" shouted Airy. "Me, me, give me some bubbles to pop!"

So Betsy cut the piece into two unequal pieces and gave the bigger to Airy, who immediately began to pop his between thumb and forefinger. Einar watched him for a few seconds, then began popping his own piece. It took him under a minute to master the technique, and then, successful, he growled a low, dirty laugh, "Hurrr, hurrr, hurrr."

Betsy stared at him, amazed. She'd never heard such a sound from a little child before. It was practically a baritone.

"Isn't he just the cutest thing?" said Emma Beth without looking up from her book, obviously quoting some adult.

Remarkable," said Betsy.

Snap, *crackle*, *pop*, went Airy's plastic wrap. He was an expert at popping the wrap.

Pop . . . pop . . . pop, pop . . . pop, went Einar's. "Hurrr, hurrr, hurrr."

Betsy retreated to the other side of the box shelves that divided the shop in half. There she found Jill and Godwin seated at the little round table, talking in low voices.

"Oh!" Betsy said. "Excuse me!"

"It's all right," said Godwin, offering her a watery smile. "We're just talking. I think . . . I think I'm starting to understand what I'm going to do."

Betsy looked at Jill, who smiled and nodded. "It's going to be all right. Goddy is a good man; he's just a little frightened at all this happening so fast. It was thoughtless of Rafael to make an agreement with Pilar without consulting him first. But it will go much slower now; these things take time, lots of time. And he'll have all the time he needs to think about it, talk about it, make sure he knows what he wants, and what Rafael wants, and that they're on the same page."

"Oh, Jill, you're so *wise*, so *sensible*, I just love you to *death*!" said Godwin.

There came the angry wail of a small child, and Jill got up to go see what atrocity had occurred in the front of the store. Her mere appearance stopped the wail in its tracks.

"Wow," said Godwin, looking through the opening at her. He said to Betsy, "Do you think she'll give Rafael and me lessons?"

THAT crisis over, Betsy told him about her adventure with the Whiteside brothers last night. She sighed a bit over the unfairness of discovering the tiny sample of blood only after it had been hopelessly mixed with Heck's. "I'm as sure as I can be that the first drop of blood was left by the murderer, but now there's no way to prove that."

"Somebody, probably you, will think of something else that will break this case wide open," Godwin predicted.

But it was Jill who lifted her spirits when she said, "They can test mixed DNA samples. They do it all the time; they just separate them. That's how I knew my second child would be a boy."

"What do you mean?"

"I mean a baby's DNA gets into the mother from the womb through the umbilical cord. She's sending oxygen and food to the baby, and the baby is sending fragments of itself to the mother. A blood test will pick up those fragments, and a technician can separate the DNA in them from the mother's DNA."

Betsy said, in a very quiet voice, "Really?"

"Google it. DNA technology is galloping headlong down the road, past what you're wishing it might do. They've been doing it for years."

Betsy went to her computer and asked her search engine to tell her if it was possible to separate mixed DNA samples. Indeed, yes, said several sites, though sometimes in language that gave new meaning to the term "scientific explanation": The terminology used in some of the scientific abstracts she read—"loci," "contributor genotypes," "biostatical software"—was enough to give her a headache.

Jill, reading over Betsy's shoulder, said, "See? In a case like Wayzata's, only two samples are in the mix, none of it fragmentary or degraded. That means it'll be relatively simple to separate them. And since one of them is Heck Whiteside, who is currently present and can give a fresh sample, it'll be even easier, using one they pull from him for comparison."

Betsy began to smile. "God bless the scientists who keep getting better and better at using DNA," she said. "Do you think it would be interfering if I called Detective Larabee and told him about these advances in DNA testing?"

"Oh yes, I think it would. He's better educated about DNA than you and I are. I would be very surprised if he isn't well aware of the separation technique."

"Then he'll be able to test that second sample of DNA against all the suspects in Harry's murder."

"I'm absolutely sure he'll do that," said Jill.

* * *

JILL had been gone for about forty-five minutes, having left with one hand holding a fistful of beautiful Silk and Ivory floss in a small plastic bag, when the door began to play "Yes We Have No Bananas" and Joe Mickels came in. He was looking triumphant, and he said to Betsy, "You're fired!"

Godwin scolded, "Who do you think you are, Donald Trump?"

Mickels frowned at Godwin, then laughed, a sound rarely heard. Certainly neither Betsy nor Godwin had heard it before.

"Whatever is the matter with you, Joe?" Betsy asked.

"They arrested the man who shot me!" said Joe.

"Not Chaz, surely!" exclaimed Betsy.

"No, o' course not! I never thought it was him. It's Herman Glass. He used to be a tenant of mine. He's a student at Rasmussen College, and to finance his education he was selling drugs out of his apartment. When I found out about it, he asked me to give him a break, so I didn't call the cops on him, I just evicted him. He called me names anyway. Then he decided selling drugs wasn't his forte, so he started pulling stickups. When he walked into one of my stores and saw me there, he took advantage of the opportunity and shot me."

"The dastard!" said Godwin.

Joe turned and looked at him. "What did you say?"

"Dastard."

"What is that, a ladylike version of bastard?"

"No, it's a word of its own, dates way, way back, medieval. It means a contemptible, sneaky coward."

"Dastard," repeated Joe, trying it out on his tongue.

"Dastard," agreed Godwin. He had a curious fondness for old-fashioned words—and old-fashioned music, and cartoons, and radio shows, too.

Joe turned back to Betsy. "But that's not what I'm here about. They found the man I had dinner with the night Whiteside was killed, so I've got an alibi for his murder, so I don't need your help anymore."

"What about for Maddy?"

He shrugged. "They'd have to prove I had access to pure nicotine, and they can't, because I don't. QED, I'm in the clear."

Betsy nodded. "Very well, I won't spend any more time trying to prove you didn't kill Maddy O'Leary."

He turned serious, even morose. "I take it you will bill me for your expenses?"

"I don't charge for my investigative services. I thought we were clear on that."

He brightened. "Yes, you did say that, didn't you? I'm glad to have that confirmed. Good day to you."

He turned and stumped out.

"Not a 'thank you' in a carload," remarked Godwin. "But maybe we should be grateful he didn't poke you in the eye with a sharp stick."

BETSY took the cordless shop phone into the back room and called Bershada. "Is Chaz there by some chance?"

"No, why?"

"Because apparently there's a cabin up on Pine Lake in Pine County that might have had its windows broken by a vandal. I'm wondering if that cabin belonged to Maddy. Does Chaz have access to a complete listing of her holdings?"

"I think he does, or knows how to get one, at least. A cabin up in Pine County, you say?"

"On property that used to belong to Harry Whiteside's grandparents."

"Oh my Lord! Where did you find out—never mind! I'll ask him and call you back."

"Thanks, Bershada."

SERGEANT Frank Larabee wrote up an order directing the Hennepin County medical examiner to take a sample from the body of Harry Whiteside suitable for DNA testing. He also ordered samples to be taken from Hamilton Whiteside and from the Merry Maid woman who cleaned Harry's house and from Harry's friend Martin LeBeau (who had dined with Harry the week he died), and for all samples to be compared to the separated DNA samples taken off the doorknob shank in Harry's house. All had denied cutting a finger while in the house, but the blood sample was very small, and it was possible they hadn't noticed. Or they were lying.

Meanwhile, Sergeant Larabee was rounding up files on known burglars active in the Wayzata area and checking their alibis. Someone had injured his or her finger on that loose screw, not badly, but enough to have left a usable sample of blood behind. He had a hunch that it was Heck's brother Howard who cut himself walking out after slamming his father on the head and breaking one of the big front windows (not in order to get in, just in a fit of anger, or maybe to make the police think that was how a thief got in), turning over chairs and tables, and maybe stealing a few things from the house—there wasn't any inventory available to prove that—to make it look like the work of a burglar. Howard had his father's temper, and there were years of quarrels between them—that business of the dismissed lawsuit still rankled. Howard had tried to shrug it off as water over the dam when Larabee spoke to him, but it hadn't been difficult to see the anger still smoking in Howard's closed fists and tight vocal cords. And he didn't have an alibi worth spit.

Larabee was pretty sure he'd be able to arrest Howard Whiteside as soon as the results came back.

He was about to close up shop when his phone rang.

"Larabee," he said on picking up.

"Sergeant Larabee, this is Betsy Devonshire—"

"Oh jeez, what is it now?"

"Have you had that mixed blood sample separated and tested?"

"It's being done. But I'm not going to share the results with you."

"That's fine. I'm sure you're being very thorough and testing every possible person who might have been in that house."

"You got that right."

"Including Maddy O'Leary."

"Maddy—? What makes you think I should test a dead woman's DNA?"

"She wasn't dead when Mr. Whiteside was killed."

"Ms. Devonshire, I'd really appreciate it if you wouldn't call me up to tell me how to do my job." He hung up on her.

What a crazy, interfering, ignorant woman! Not only wasn't she a cop, she wasn't even a licensed private investigator!

He finished locking the files away and went off to spend ninety minutes in the gym, fifteen minutes of which he'd spend looking at himself in the big mirror in various poses. His chest was coming along well, but he needed to do something to tighten those glutes.

WHEN Betsy closed shop and went upstairs that evening, Connor wordlessly indicated she should go look in the dining nook.

Standing proudly in the center of the round table was a bouquet of two dozen roses, with an additional half-bushel of baby's breath and some kind of large-leaf foliage. The roses were the large, pale ivory kind with deep pink edges to their petals. Best of all, they were the scented variety, filling the air with a heavenly odor.

"What's the occasion?" Betsy asked, flashing a delighted smile at him.

"They're not from me," he said. "But there's a card."

Betsy approached and found a small card tucked in among the blooms. She opened the tiny envelope and read the message inside: *Thank you for your efforts on my behalf. Joe Mickels.*

Betsy laughed. "Goddy was wrong. He does know how to say thank you."

Chapter Twenty-nine

"So, you're off the hook, right?" said Connor over supper. They had had to move the rose bouquet to the living room; it was so large that it impeded sight lines, even the placement of dinnerware. Connor had actually had to go over to Leipold's for an especially large vase.

"I suppose I am. So why don't I feel like it?"

"I don't know. Why don't you?"

"I think because I have a theory about what happened. But I don't have any proof. It makes me uncomfortable, not having proof."

"You're saying that for your own peace of mind, you need to continue sleuthing."

She sighed. "Yes, I guess that's what I'm saying."

"All right, it's your decision, and I understand what's driving you. Do you want to tell me whom you suspect?"

"N-no, I don't think so. Without proof it's just a theory."

"I'm not going to find myself in a scenario where you're dead and I don't know whom to blame?"

She laughed. "No, absolutely no danger of that."

"I'm glad to hear it. What do you want to do next?"

"I need to find out how someone on my list of suspects got hold of pure nicotine. It's not easy to come by. But it doesn't take a large quantity, so suppose I really, really wanted just a little, a couple of teaspoons or a tablespoon of it. Where would I have to go?"

"Contact the people who produce it, I suppose. Where does it come from?"

"Well, from tobacco, of course." She held up both hands. "I know, that isn't what you're asking. It comes from laboratories, from chemical factories. I'll have to do a search to see if I can find someone who works in the manufacturing end willing to talk to me."

It seemed startlingly easy at first. There was actually a company in Minnesota that advertised it made and sold nicotine (among other things)—and its factory was in Minnetonka, right up the road. But when she tried to phone them the next morning, their phone number had been disconnected, and Google Maps seemed never to have heard of them. They'd gone quietly out of business, leaving no forwarding address.

So she backed up and called an e-cigarette store. Where did they get the "juice" they sold? That led her to a distributor. Several distributors, actually; but at first her questions seemed to lead them to think she was an undercover activist, and they refused to give her any information.

Her line of questioning became more polished as she

went along—she'd even connected with a laboratory that made nicotine for commercial use, but they didn't want to tell her anything about it. Then, finally, a distributor gave her the name and phone number of the public affairs officer in a chemical company in Virginia—of course, prime tobacco country.

Jill had once told Betsy she'd make a good con woman because she was a good liar. So, since her various approaches to the truth weren't working, she decided to lie.

There were several female crime fiction authors in the Twin Cities area. Betsy picked one, and when she got the PR fellow on the line, she introduced herself as that person. She continued, "I'm writing a mystery in which my victim is killed when her husband pours a little liquid nicotine on her favorite sweater. She absorbs it through her skin."

"Say, that's pretty mean," the man responded.

"You bet. But would it work?"

"Oh, sure."

"Good. But I've been having trouble finding out how he might get hold of the stuff without leaving a trail. Retail and wholesale e-cigarette dealers only get the mixes, and the strongest mix is still only three percent. What kind of job or occupation can I give my murderer that will allow him to get hold of one hundred percent nicotine?"

"He could be a chemist, of course. But that's a little obvious for your purposes, right?"

"Yes, that's right. I've discovered that when a medical examiner conducts the initial test for drugs on a body, nicotine is one of the basics. That surprised me."

"It surprises me, too. Well, okay, in order not to leave a

trail, he's going to have to steal it, unless he takes classes in chemistry at a university under a fake name."

"No, I think stealing it is best—fastest, anyway."

"Sure, I get it. Maybe he's a painter and gets a job painting the walls of a factory where they manufacture the vapor mixes." The man seemed to be getting into the spirit of Betsy's quest. It was surprising how many people had a trace of the criminal in them. Probably not a good thing, except for the bottom line of mystery authors.

"Have you handled pure nicotine yourself?" asked Betsy.

"Oh yes. Not often, but yes. You have to be careful; it doesn't take a lot to make someone damn sick."

"So my idea of putting it on an article of clothing is good."

"It would have to be something that comes into direct contact with the skin, and for a prolonged period of time. That sweater idea is good. Underwear might be better. Gloves would be good, too. Where are you calling from?"

"Minnesota."

"Oh yeah, a land of winter sports. Pour it onto her socks, send her skiing, find her body on the slopes." He really was getting into this.

"Is there a tobacco smell she might notice?"

"No, it's just about odorless. Colorless, too."

"The stuff you buy for e-cigarettes seems to be like syrup," said Betsy.

"That's an additive to make it burn. And another to make it smell good. Nicotine is only a little thicker than water. But it oxidizes fairly rapidly, so your killer would have to do it so it dries not more than a day or two before your victim puts the socks on. Oh, and here's an idea: Have your murderer be a maintenance man, working in a lab. He could find an almost-empty bottle of the stuff in a wastepaper basket."

"Scary to think someone would just toss a bottle away without at least rinsing it."

"It's illegal to pour it down a drain. Much better to put it in a landfill."

And on that note, Betsy thanked him and hung up before he could ask her to send him a copy of the book when it came out.

She barely had time to serve a customer who wanted to buy the magnificent counted cross-stitch Eagle Owl pattern from Riolis, when the phone rang.

"Wow, you really are a sleuth!" Chaz exclaimed when she answered. His previous anger toward her seemed to have disappeared. Betsy thanked her stars for Bershada, who obviously had been able to calm his resentment over being thought a suspect.

"Why, did she own a cabin up on Pine Lake?"

"She sure did! Bought it five years ago from a party named Makepeace. It had a raggedy old cabin on it, which she tore down and replaced with a log house. All modern conveniences, plus a river rock fireplace. It's on the shore of Pine Lake, so she built a little boathouse that you can paddle your canoe right into. And it was vandalized back in February, windows broken, couple cans of paint emptied into it. Froze the pipes, which broke the toilet. Over fifteen thousand dollars in damage."

"Can you find out if there was an owner named Whiteside, back in the fifties?"

"Oh my God. You're thinking—oh my God. No, I don't believe it."

"But you'll find out for me?"

"Yes, but you're wrong, Betsy."

"For your sake, I hope I am."

BETSY was restless in bed Sunday night. Some fragment of information was nagging at her, and though she chased it all over her brain, she couldn't catch up and get hold of it. "Laboratory," she murmured to herself. And, "Landfill." She finally fell into an uneasy slumber and dreamed all night of houses on fire. She woke up from a dream of someone setting fire to the back door of her own building and causing major smoke damage to the contents of her shop. The dream was so vivid she went all over the apartment, sniffing for evidence of smoke, thinking something must have triggered those dreams. But there was nothing but clean air.

So she pulled on her swimsuit and some clothes on over it, grabbed a change of underwear, and went off to water aerobics.

Over time, people had dropped out of the Early Bird class at the Golden Valley Courage Center and new ones came in, the instructors changed, even the kind of aerobics changed. Tabata was now all the rage, with its twenty seconds of action and ten seconds of "rest" (marked by gentler movements, not standing still). Yet it still all took place in the very large, heated, Olympic-size pool, with its flat platforms at increasing depths, under a pair of enormous glass windows with a stained glass pattern that looked like a map of several rivers converging here and there.

Betsy had been going to this aerobics class for years. It started at six thirty and went for an hour, which made it perfect for people with day jobs. Oddly, most of the current participants were senior citizens. Connor had joined her for a few classes then decided he preferred to sleep in and get up only in time to have her breakfast cooking when she got back home.

A Russian immigrant, Michael, with a hearing problem and not much command of English, was a newer member of the class. He had multiple physical problems as well and often just stood in one place, clumsily shuffling his feet and feebly moving his arms while everyone else was doing cross-country ski or jumping jack movements back and forth across the pool.

On the other hand, another newcomer, Sarah, was tall, young, and strong. Betsy was jealous of her ability to move swiftly and smoothly through the water while Betsy puffed and struggled.

An old, familiar, and much-liked couple, Peter and Ingrid, were no longer members of the class. Peter had had a stroke, and Ingrid dropped out to care for him; Betsy missed them both.

But there remained the heated water and the movements, and focusing on those elements gave her a break from everything else.

A small whiteboard was fastened to a section of wall between the windows. There was a new riddle written on it for each day's class. Today's was: *What happens when you don't pay your exorcist?* As usual, the answer was not written on the board, and Betsy spent several minutes trying to think what it might be.

Samantha—Sam—was running the class today. She was a new instructor, not fond of Tabata, and her method was to get a movement started and then let it run awhile—other people who taught the class switched off very frequently, not letting the muscles settle into a routine. But Sam liked to give each set of muscles a thorough workout. Once she picked up the rhythm, Betsy's mind was free to work on the riddle.

And suddenly, she knew the answer and laughed out loud. Lifeguard Amy had earlier acknowledged she knew the answer, so when Betsy arrived at Amy's side of the pool, she gave her guess, and Amy said, "Correct!"

Perhaps it was the mental exercise of the riddle, or the oxygenation of her brain from vigorous exercise, but on her drive home, Betsy thought she understood at last what her dreams had tried to tell her last night. Her shop didn't have those pipes that carried water that sprayed during a fire. A serious fire would have destroyed her whole building. But the University of Minnesota's waste-handling building did. Their pipes had needed replacement. And Harry Whiteside had contracted to replace them.

To Betsy's mind, that was a very large clue.

She got home to find Connor preparing to pour pancake batter into a heated pan as soon as she opened the door. A few minutes later, while sitting at the table, she was putting butter and syrup on those very pancakes. "What happens if you neglect to pay your exorcist?" she asked Connor as she tucked into her breakfast.

"I don't know, what?"

"Think about it."

"You've the devil to pay?" he guessed.

She laughed. "Good guess, but no."

He sat down to his own breakfast, and silence fell for a few minutes. Then he began to laugh. "You get repossessed?"

She laughed back at him. "That's right!"After breakfast, Betsy retreated to the bedroom to change into her work clothes. She put on a two-piece suit in a medium yellow that had very faint patterns of large pink flowers woven into it. She wore yellow heels with it that were more comfortable than they looked.

Connor approved. "You look like a morning in spring."

"Thank you. Connor, could you do something for me?"

"Anything, *machree*." The English spelling of an Irish word that means "my heart," it was his favorite nickname for her.

"I need to visit the hazardous waste disposal building on the U of M campus. But I need an excuse."

"And you think I might come up with one?"

"Well, can you?"

"Not off the top of my head. What's there for you to see or find out?"

Armed with her fresh insight, she was not willing to explain her theory.

"Does Mike Malloy know about this?" he asked.

"No—well, I don't know. I haven't said anything to him."

"Why not?"

"Well . . . I guess the thing is, I want to do this myself."

"My dear, dear heart," he said, coming to take her by the elbows. "'Pride goeth before a fall.' It seems to me you either have to lie—which is never a good thing to do to innocent bystanders in a criminal investigation—or tell the truth and be rebuffed. I suggest you take the third choice, the high road, and talk to Mike."

"But he—he doesn't like me."

"That's not true. He respects you, but you make him nervous. He wishes you'd stay out of his business, or at least get a license. You're a wild card, and law enforcement officials don't like wild cards. When you do things that break open a case, he probably has a hard time explaining you to the chief, to prosecuting attorneys, to defense attorneys, to judges, maybe even to his wife." He was smiling warmly at her, and her heart turned over—who else in the whole world could criticize her, warn her, advise her all in a couple of sentences, and make her like it?

She put her arms around him, and he took her in a warm embrace. They stood that way for a couple of minutes, until the threat of tears went away, and she stepped back.

"I'll call Mike today," she said.

Chapter Thirty

"GOOD morning, Mike," said Betsy on the phone.

"What do you want now?"

"I have an idea, but I need your help."

"What kind of help?" he asked, warily.

"I think I know who killed Maddy O'Leary."

"Yeah? Who?"

"Harry Whiteside."

"Harry Whiteside? But that's not possible! He died before she did!"

"Yes, but that yarn was poisoned before he died. He was at Mount Calvary's Lenten service—or at least at the reception afterward—and he approached the closet where the knitting bags were being kept. And he hated Maddy, had hated her for a long time. He saw an opportunity to get at her, an opportunity he was sure was safe—"

"What are you talking about, what was safe?"

"A chance to get hold of a deadly poison without having to buy it. A chance theft no one would think to blame him for. He did some work at the University's hazardous waste disposal building."

"And this has something to do with his work at the hazardous waste place?"

"It could."

"How?"

"One of the last jobs Harry did was to replace the pipes in their fire-extinguishing system. So he was there. The term 'hazardous waste' can cover things like poisons used in laboratory research testing, which they do a lot of at our university. You can't pour radioactive material or plague germs or poisons down the sink. You need that kind of waste professionally handled; that's what places like that are for. The question is, could someone just passing through get hold of a dollop of something he could use to kill?"

"Hmmmmm."

"Right."

"So maybe I should go have a look at this place," said Mike.

"And you'll take me with you."

"The hell I will!"

"Mike, I brought this to you. I think I deserve a reward for that."

"I'll send you a dollar in the mail. Two dollars if it plays out."

"You want me to go over there by myself?"

"You wouldn't get past the receptionist, probably."

"All right, you're probably right. So please? Didn't you say yourself I sometimes see things other people miss?"

There was a long silence, followed by a heavy sigh. "I'll call you back."

"Thank you very much." *It'll probably take him an hour to think of a way to tell me to butt out*, she thought, disgruntled.

"Anything else?" he asked in a sarcastic voice.

"Um . . . actually, yes."

"What is it?"

"Do you know if Sergeant Larabee has gotten the results of that DNA test he was running on the blood found on the doorknob at Harry Whiteside's house?"

"Yes, no matches."

"What? None at all?" Betsy was incredulous. How could she have been so wrong?

"That's what he says. Why, whose did you think it would match?"

"Maddy O'Leary's."

There was a silence of several seconds. "Mike?" she asked.

"I'm here. Why in the *hell* do you think that blood would be Maddy's?"

"Well, I'll tell you," she said, and she did. Then the penny dropped—as her father, who was British-American, would put it, meaning she saw the whole picture. "He didn't test her DNA, did he?" she asked.

"No. I saw the report, and no, he didn't. I'll give him a call later today."

"What's the matter?" asked Godwin, when she'd hung up.

"Oh, that dreadful man!"

"Who, Mike? I've already told you he's hopeless!"

"No, not Mike, that detective over in Wayzata, Larabee. Mike's going to talk to him. I hope he can get results. The other thing is, there's a place I want to visit, over at the U, but I can't think of an excuse to get in there, and Mike doesn't want to take me." *Jeepers*, Betsy thought, *I sound like a spoiled nine-year-old who's been told she can't go to the zoo.*

"Never mind," she said aloud. "I'll find a way. I just need to practice a little patience. Tell me, what's going on with you and Rafael?"

"So," he said, drawing out the word, "I screwed my courage to the sticking place—isn't Shakespeare wonderful?—and told him I had made up my mind a long time ago that I wasn't the parenting kind and the idea of taking on a baby scared me witless."

"Uh-oh," said Betsy. "What did he say?"

"He said he felt just the same way! Isn't that amazing? I was so shocked!"

"So you're not going to go through with it."

"Oh, but that's not decided yet for sure."

"What?"

"Well . . . you see, the more we talked about what a bad idea it was, the less of a bad idea it seemed. There are nurses and nannies and babysitters in the world, and when kids get older, they're in school all day, and there are even boarding schools where they go all the school year. So it's not like a twenty-four-seven job, is it? Rafael says that when he was a little boy, he saw his parents for about twenty minutes a day, sometimes less, until they sent him to a boarding school when he was eight and then to a prep school and then college, and he only came home for Easter and Christmas. And even then he saw more of his grandmama than his parents. He says he's surprised he can remember what they looked like, though I think he's joking."

"So it's back on again."

"Well . . . maybe."

"What do his parents say about this plan to use a surrogate to have a child?"

"Not a thing. They're dead. They died in a plane crash when he was twenty-three."

"Oh, that's sad."

"So maybe ours'll be one of those angelic kids, and if so, we're thinking maybe not a boarding school."

"You are? That's good." Rafael would be the strict parent, and Godwin would be the indulgent parent, and the thought of Godwin being indulgent with a toddler made her smile for the rest of the morning.

"LARABEE."

"Frank, this is Mike Malloy."

"Say, little buddy, how's life over on the wrong side of the lake?"

"Not good. I read that report you copied to me on the DNA results from the Whiteside house."

"Yeah, looks like we're back to square one on that case. Too bad. I was betting on a match with Howard Whiteside."

"Why didn't you order up a test on Maddy O'Leary?"

"In case you didn't hear, the lady is dead."

"The ME stores samples from murder victims, and there's more than enough for a DNA sample to be taken."

"The lady had no reason to be in that house."

"I have information that would indicate otherwise."

"What information is that?"

Mike started to explain but hadn't said more than three sentences before he was interrupted. "That damn amateur you got over there planted that idea in your head, right?"

"That damn amateur, as you call her, has broken more than a few cases. She may be wrong, but her reasoning is solid. I think you—"

"I don't give a rat's ass what you think! We're doin' just fine without your help, especially if it comes secondhand from some old spinster seamstress who sells silk thread for a living!" And crash went the phone in Mike's ear.

SHE was barely through with the turkey salad Godwin had brought her for lunch when the phone rang.

"Crewel World, Betsy speaking, how may I help you?"

"It's the Safety and Environmental Protection Facility," said Mike.

"What is?"

"The hazardous waste disposal plant on the campus."

"Oh. And, am I coming with you to tour it?"

"Yes, I'll pick you up tomorrow morning, nine o'clock sharp. Don't dress froufrou, and don't ask any questions without asking me first."

After a startled pause, Betsy said meekly, "All right."

OVER supper that evening, Connor was pleased that his advice to contact Mike Malloy had worked out well. But he was a little more concerned about Godwin's talk about having an angelic baby. "No matter how angelic," he said, "there are times when you'd cheerfully leave them in a basket at the side door of an ophanage."

Betsy wan't sure what Mike meant by not dressing frou-frou. She contemplated the contents of her closet the next morning before picking a dark green lightweight wool dress with a modest hemline and filling its décolletage with a green and tan silk scarf. She put on gold earrings and a little gold watch and slipped into low-heeled tan shoes, transferring her notepad, wallet, lipstick, comb, cell phone, and other items to a matching tan purse that hung from her shoulder. She almost decided against perfume but thought she needed the reassurance of just a trace of good old-fashioned Chanel No. 5.

Connor said, "You look good enough to hire."

"Thank you," she said, smiling gently at him, and went downstairs.

The day was bright and cloudless, but the temperature hovered at sixty-eight. Of course, it was early, and the forecast was for it to rise to seventy-five.

Mike was very prompt. He drove up in a big old sedan that wasn't marked as a squad car, though it had the complex regalia inside—except there was no shotgun attached to the dash.

"Does this belong to the Excelsior Police?" asked Betsy, letting herself into the front passenger seat.

"Yes," said Mike in a tone that discouraged further inquiry. He pulled away from the curb, went up Lake Street to cross at the asterisk of streets, and then turned onto Highway 7 headed east.

"The man in charge of the facility is Dr. George Seely—a PhD doctor, of law. He's an adjunct instructor at the law school, but his primary job is director of the Safety and Environmental Protection Facility. The building is on the campus across from the University's TCF Bank Stadium."

"All right," said Betsy, getting out her notebook and beginning to write. "Did you ask him about Harry Whiteside?"

"Yes, and as a matter of fact, Dr. Seely knew Harry personally. They started pre-law school together. But Harry dropped out and went into engineering."

"Is that how Harry got the job of repairing the fire control system?"

"I don't know; we didn't get that far. I do know that Harry was in and out of the facility for over a week back in early March."

"Does Dr. Seely know you're bringing me along?"

"I told him I might bring someone with me, but that's all."

They got off the highway at University Avenue and went over to Twenty-third, around the stadium, and pulled up in front of a good-size, new-looking brick building with no windows.

Dr. Seely was evidently looking for their arrival, because he came out and leaned down to speak to Betsy, who rolled down her window. Mike produced his ID and badge, which Dr. Seely looked at for several seconds, though he did not take hold of it. He was a very tall man, with keen, dark brown eyes and a lot of nose. His iron gray hair grew down over his ears. He wore a pale blue dress shirt with the sleeves turned back and crisp black trousers.

"You'll need a special pass to park here or you'll get a ticket," he said, handing Betsy a red and white striped card about the size of an iPhone. She gave it to Mike, who put his badge away and hung the card from his rearview mirror.

Then they both got out of the car and followed Dr. Seely to the deeply inset entrance on a corner of the building. Seely had to press a card against a box on the wall to gain entrance.

He led them down a severely plain corridor with a high ceiling, past an office with a big window, to another door, and this time he had to slide a card down a slot to make the door unlock.

Then they were in a very large, oddly shaped room that looked kind of like a factory, only with no machinery, all hard surfaces. Paths were marked with narrow stripes of white paint on the gray concrete floor. Overhead were pipes: boxy green pipes, fat yellow round pipes, narrower red pipes, very narrow pipes in tan and black.

The air smelled faintly of . . . something. A kind of chemical odor, as if it had passed through a number of extremely efficient filters before being allowed in.

Off to the left was a room set with big panes of glass, and inside were three or four people at consoles facing the glass. The rest of the room was studded with big, sturdy-looking red metal doors. The whole place looked very clean.

Dr. Seely gestured at the doors and said, "We sort the incoming material according to kind—the really dangerous stuff goes into one of those rooms to be unpacked, which room depending on what kind of hazard it presents. Some materials, for example, react badly to moisture in the air. Some are dangerous to breathe."

Mike said, "I hope the people who work here are very picky about what they're doing."

"I try to make it so," Dr. Seely replied, smiling.

"What kind of hazardous material do you handle?"

"Anything, really. Disease germs, outdated prescription medicines, poisons, even small amounts of radioactive material. We have this whole building all to ourselves. It's an interesting job, and quite safe, if you're very careful."

"So, how do you dispose of such dangerous substances?"

"We sort it, seal it in drums, and send it to a special kind of incinerator that burns very hot, destroying everything, even the drums themselves."

"With extra-good scrubbers on the smokestacks," suggested Mike.

"Yes, indeed."

"Interesting that you knew Harry Whiteside from years back," Mike went on. "I'd like to talk to you about him."

Dr. Seely started to say something, then changed his mind and asked instead, "What's your interest in Harry?"

"I'm investigating a murder, and it's just barely possible that Harry is involved in it."

"Indeed? I thought it would be Harry's murder you were interested in."

"No, his murder is being handled by the Wayzata police. This is a second murder, of a woman, that happened around the same time. She was bidding against Harry for some property. Did Harry happen to mention to you anything about this bidding war?"

Frowning, Dr. Seely shook his head. "We didn't discuss business, except in very general terms."

"How did you come to hire him?"

"As I told you on the phone, we became friends here at

the U when we were both pre-law students. I went on to get my JD, and he got a master's in architectural design. We stayed in touch, but only casually—he was a difficult person, you see. I found him . . . manipulative and sometimes bad tempered. But he was also very amusing, witty, fun to be around.

"Well, as it happens, we ran across each other at a Golden Gophers basketball game back in February, and he mentioned that he'd installed a sprinkler system in a warehouse and his foreman—his *former* foreman, that is—had ordered half again the number of pipes needed for the job. Funny how that sort of thing can happen, his having extra pipes and us needing them."

"He didn't by chance know about your need for pipes before he told you this story?"

"Oh no, not at all. He told me the story first, and I said how interesting that was, because we needed new pipes to replace some corroded ones in our building. I suggested that perhaps the University could buy them from him at a discount, him being an alum, you see. Because most of the building and repair on campus is done by employees of the university. And he seemed open to that. Sometimes, though, we farm out a job, and it turned out that we needed to farm out this one. So I told him never mind and explained why, and he asked if he could submit a bid. I said he could, and I recommended his company, and he put in a nice, low bid and got the job."

"Was his work satisfactory?"

"Oh yes. But I'd forgotten what a son of a bitch he could be." Seely shook his head. "He complained the whole time because he had to carry an ID card and swipe a pass card every time he came in. 'You'd think you're storing nitroglycerin in here,' he said." Seely winked. "I didn't tell him we had a package of bubonic plague germs on the counter right under where he was complaining to me about our stringent security methods."

"Where in the building did the pipes get replaced?" asked Mike.

"Come on, I'll show you."

He led them past two very large doors beyond the glass room. They led into yet another big room, and at the far end of it a sliding door was raised. Betsy could see the back end of the trailer of a semi truck up against it. Parked near the trailer's back end was a bright yellow forklift truck.

"We're about to send out a shipment to be incinerated," Seely said.

"Where's the incinerator?" asked Mike.

"This shipment's going to Saint Louis."

"Kind of far from here, isn't that?"

"Well, there aren't many of those incinerators in the country, and the one that's nearer, in Illinois, is backed up. Believe me, things are packed very thoroughly. Our packaging can survive even a rollover."

"Good to know," observed Mike.

"Come on. The pipes were replaced in here, where we pack things up."

He led them through a door high and wide enough to easily accommodate the forklift. In the first room—there was a second room beyond it, where Betsy could see row upon row of big blue barrels—was a small enclosure with a big metal hood over it. "We open some packages in there," he said. "The ventilation system sucks up vapors very efficiently." He made a gesture that took in the whole room. "This is where Harry did his work for us."

Betsy looked up but didn't see any new pipes. Dr. Seely saw her looking and said, "He painted them to match." The room's ceiling had the same complement of many colored pipes as the other.

Its walls were lined on three sides by a deep shelf about waist high. On the shelf were shoebox-size packages wrapped in brown paper and a few open boxes holding small bottles in Ziploc bags.

Curious, Betsy dared approach the shelf—though she stopped short when she saw that each wrapped package had a big black-and-white HAZARDOUS MATERIAL sticker on it. She came back to stand near Mike. This was a dangerous place.

"It's safe to go for a look," said Seely, amused. "Just don't open anything."

"Don't even touch it," warned Mike.

Betsy went closer and saw that most of the bottles in the open boxes looked like prescription bottles, though one had a chemical formula on it: HCN.

Mike, who had come along with her, said, "What's HCN?"

"That's cyanide," said Seely.

"Whoa!" said Mike.

Someone with a sense of humor had put a green Mr. Yuk sticker on it, next to the skull and crossbones sticker.

"Do you get a lot of poisons?" asked Betsy, and Mike cleared his throat warningly.

Seely nodded. "We got a lot of everything. Mostly outdated medicines, though. When you think how much prescription medicines cost, it breaks my heart to see how much of it gets thrown away."

"I assume you keep careful track of things like that," said Mike. "I mean, someone could come by and just pick up a bottle of outdated penicillin and take it home with him."

"It would have to be someone who works here," said Seely. "We don't allow non-employees to wander around unaccompanied. And look at this." He went to the counter and pulled a two-page packing slip from one of the open boxes, one white and one yellow, "See, the sender writes down what's in the packet and how many bottles of it there are. And our packer checks it off, making sure the bottle matches the description and that the number of bottles is correct."

But Betsy had got the bit between her teeth, and she pressed, "Does anyone ever make a mistake? I mean, the shipper writes down three bottles and there are only two in the box?"

Seely gave Betsy a long look.

But Mike said, "That's a good question."

"Okay, sometimes—*not often*—mistakes are made," he said. He repeated it. "Not often, you understand."

Betsy and Mike nodded.

"How does it happen when it does?" Mike asked.

"The guy packing things up over in the lab—this is the lowest-grade job a grad student can have, you understand—goes to pack up three bottles and can only find two, and he'll scratch a line through the three and write two and initial the change. Or someone here, unpacking, finds two bottles and the invoice says three. It could be just a case of bad handwriting—a two looking like a three—but it could be a bottle got misplaced, or the chemist decided he needed one and took it back. Now my guy is supposed to call the lab and run down the person who did up the package, but it's time to quit and he's tired, so he'll draw that line through the number himself and make the three a two. It can happen. But you've got something specific on your mind. What do you think went missing from here?"

Betsy looked at Mike, who said, "A bottle of nicotine."

"OKAY, it's a possibility," said Malloy in the car on their way back to Excelsior, "but how do we prove it?"

"You'll have to go back through those packing slips," said Betsy. "That card Doctor Seely swiped coming in, he told us it tracks him, records the day and time every time he passes through. He said everyone, employee, subcontractor, everyone has to use that tracking card. You heard him tell us that Harry complained about having to swipe a card every time he came in. So you look through the packing slips that came in on the days he was here and see if there's not one for nicotine that has a line through the number of bottles."

"Do you know how much time that will take me? They must get dozens at least every day."

"I'll do it. Get me access, a search warrant, whatever it takes. I'm way long overdue for a vacation, Mike. Hire me and I'll spend it at the Safety and Environmental Protection building. I'm sure I'm right."

"And so what if you are? We don't need to do this, you know. Every possible suspect has been cleared; no one's in danger of arrest. According to you—and I agree with you—the likely perp is dead."

"But people will talk if this isn't cleared up. They're already talking. Half the town thinks Joe's gotten away with murder; the other half thinks Chaz did it. This can destroy their lives. You can't let this go, Mike. You can't."

BACK in his little office in Excelsior, Mike called Wayzata PD and asked to speak to the chief of detectives, Andy Taylor—and yes, he took a lot of hazing over his name, thanks to the old *Andy Griffith Show* that featured a small-town sheriff with the same name.

"I've got a little problem I'm hoping you can help me solve," Mike said after the usual introductions and pleasantries were exchanged.

"What's your little problem?" asked Captain Taylor.

"The investigator in charge of the Harry Whiteside case was given a piece of information, and because it came from a private citizen over here in Excelsior, he's dismissed it. Even after I suggested he follow up on it, he has taken no action. Now I'm well aware that we cops don't like interference in a case—"

"You got that right, for sure," interrupted Taylor, who did not sound the least little bit like his far friendlier TV namesake.

"On the other hand," Mike went on, "Larabee is stymied, and it's possible he's ignoring a very solid lead."

"Well, what is it?"

"That he should have the DNA of Maddy O'Leary compared to that blood sample collected at the Whiteside house." Mike explained Betsy's—and his own—reasoning for doing so.

"So why has he turned it down?"

"Because the suggestion first came from, as he puts it, an old spinster seamstress."

"Are you talking about that woman, Devonshire, who owns a needlework shop over in Excelsior?"

"Yes, sir, I am."

"Damn nosey parker interfering amateur."

"Yes, sir, that describes her pretty well. The problem is, she's right a lot of the time."

"Yeah, that's the word I've gotten about her. Not from my juice monkey, of course."

"Juice monkey?"

"Larabee. He's a weight lifter, and he's bulked up so fast the past year or so I suspect he's using steroids. Sometimes called juice."

"Ah, juice monkey. Now I see."

"And I've noticed that steroid use shrinks the brain while it swells the abs. Okay, I'll order that test. And thank you, Sergeant Malloy, for calling this to my attention. I'll let you know if it checks out."

"Thank you, Captain."

Chapter Thirty-one

A WEEK later, Mike got a forwarded e-mail with an attachment originated by the undergrad the University had hired to comb through the file of packing slips at the Safety and Environmental Protection Facility.

Is this what you're looking for? the young woman had asked Dr. Seely.

And, sure enough, the attachment was a color copy of the yellow packing slip used by the University. It showed that three one-ounce bottles of nicotine—two full, one reduced to .63 ounces—were sent to be safely disposed of, but the numeral 3 had a diagonal line drawn through its box and the numeral 2 written in beside it. The box was further crowded by an illegible scribble meant to be someone's initials.

The date on the slip indicated that the box had been packed on March 9 of this year and opened at the facility on March 11.

Harry Whiteside had worked at the facility from March 7 through March 17.

Mike called Dr. Seely.

"I was about to call you," Dr. Seely said. "I checked the security records, and Mr. Whiteside was here the day the packing slip was changed. Moreover, no one I've spoken to can identify the initials on the changed slip."

Mike would have preferred to check out the initials himself, but considering the careful attitude of Dr. Seely, that would be duplicating an already thorough effort.

So as far as he was concerned, Harry Whiteside was guilty of the murder of Maddy O'Leary. He went into his computer and pulled up the file on the case and added a brief note to Dr. Seely's report, printed out the whole thing, and hand carried it down the hall to Chief Haugen's office.

Chief Haugen was a tall man nearing fifty, thickening in the waist. A square-faced towhead with very chilly light gray eyes, his blond hair was almost unobtrusively turning white. He was taciturn by nature, and he merely nodded at Mike coming into his office.

Mike said, "Good afternoon, sir," and put the report on the chief's desk.

"He was a quick study," said Mike, after Chief Haugen read the report. "It only took four days for Harry to discover the weak spot in the control system that made it possible for him to take a little bottle of nicotine without being detected."

"But did he take it?" asked the chief. "Has the stolen bottle been found in the vicinity of Harry Whiteside?"

"No, and we won't find it," said Mike. "Anyone with a

room-temperature IQ would know to get rid of it in a way that it would never be found. Anyway, if you think a search should be made, the person to ask is Sergeant Larabee of Wayzata PD. It's his case. I hope you don't want me to ask him, because he blew up all over me when I suggested he have Maddy O'Leary's DNA compared to the blood sample sorted out from the mix found on that doorknob. I had to go over his head to their chief of detectives, Taylor, and ask him to order it. I almost think Larabee's madder at me because they found a match than he'd be if they didn't."

"What made you think to suggest Maddy O'Leary's DNA might be in the Whiteside house?"

Mike fell silent for a few seconds. Then, because the chief was amazingly perceptive and Mike was basically honest, he said, "A private citizen talked to me about it."

"Is she a resident of Excelsior?"

Mike sighed. "Yeah, she is." Haugen kept looking at him, so he reluctantly continued. "This woman found out that Harry Whiteside got a job replacing some pipes in the hazardous waste disposal building on the U campus. Harry and Maddy O'Leary have been at loggerheads for years, and when she got in ahead of him on the Water Street property, he was over-the-top pissed. At that hazardous waste building he saw a banquet of poisons just sitting there waiting for him to select one. So he decided he didn't have to share the world with her anymore and acquired some liquid nicotine, which he poured onto some yarn she was going to knit in public at that toy auction."

"That's this woman's theory."

"Well, yeah. But the evidence supports it."

"Is she the same person you took with you to that hazardous waste facility? And who suggested that we check the packing slips?"

"Well, I was already thinking we should do that."

"That was your thinking."

"Yessir." Then he added hastily, "But I'll admit she thought of it, too. Actually, maybe she thought of it first."

"And you think maybe I should call a news conference and explain all this to reporters, making the two of us look like fools who needed the help of this amateur to solve a murder."

"Yessir, except you can leave out the part about us looking like fools by leaving out her role. That's what I'd suggest. Sir."

"Why should we do this? Why not just say the case is closed?"

"Because there's gossip all over town that maybe Mr. Mickels or Mr. Reynolds got away with murder, and I think it's irresponsible of us to allow that if there's any way to clear them."

"Uh-huh, you were thinking that."

"Well, she's thinking that, too. And, okay, she told me I should think of it. But it's true, I had someone tell me to my face it's a shame we haven't arrested Mr. Mickels."

"And you agree with her conclusions."

"Well, I've come to the same ones."

"With her help."

"Ah, well, yes."

"Maybe I should let you go and hire her instead."

Mike forced a chuckle and said, "You can make the offer, but she won't even get a PI license. So no way will she agree to carry a badge." Then he offered his best crooked smile to show he knew they were both joking.

But it was also true. No way would she make it as a cop.

And a good thing. He and Elton had had enough trouble with Jill Cross Larson when she was a sergeant on the force; there was no way Elton could endure working with a crazy lady like Betsy Devonshire. Yes, she was a very clever lady, and sometimes a big help on a difficult case, but Betsy Devonshire was the proof that clinched his argument that females didn't belong as cops. She didn't think like a cop, and she didn't like the rules and restraints they worked under. Much better, to his way of thinking, that she stay in that needlework shop of hers and be free to only poke her oar in once in a widely separated while.

Betsy Devonshire, PI? That might be helpful, if only because the training would teach her the rules she would nevertheless continue to ignore. Detective Sergeant Betsy Devonshire? As if!

IN what had become a required ritual at the end of each case, Betsy Devonshire sat at the head of the library table in Crewel World while the Monday Bunch surrounded her, and Godwin sat at the foot.

"All right, girl," said Bershada. "Give."

"First of all, neither Chaz nor Joe had anything to do with these two deaths."

"We knew that!" said Bershada.

"About Chaz, yes," said Godwin. "About Joe, not so much."

"So who did murder them?" asked Phil. "Did the same person do both of them in?"

"Of course not!" said Valentina. "Don't you remember that there were two very different methods? One was, like, break in, break things, break the man's skull; the other was sneaky. That *must* mean two different murderers."

"Now, not necessarily," said Alice. "It could have been that the murderer needed different methods because the victims were so different."

Jill said, "Perhaps if we just sit quietly, Betsy will tell us how it happened."

The others gave abashed laughs, then fell silent and looked at Betsy.

She said, "There's going to be a joint news conference tomorrow morning over in Wayzata, with Detective Sergeants Mike Malloy and Frank Larabee speaking, with backup from Chief Haugen and Chief Weil. They are going to announce that they are 'satisfied' they have identified the murderers of Maddy O'Leary and Harry Whiteside—and it's each of them. Maddy murdered Harry, and Harry murdered Maddy."

There was a stunned silence around the table.

"I don't see how," said Emily. "How could Mr. Whiteside murder Maddy after he was already dead?"

"He poured the nicotine onto Maddy's yarn while it—and he—was at the music reception at Mount Calvary in the afternoon. Then he went home and surprised Maddy vandalizing his house, and she killed him."

"*Maddy* was the one who burglarized him?" asked Valentina.

"Why?" asked Emily. "She wasn't poor; she didn't need any of his stuff."

"I'm sure it will transpire that she took nothing. She

was exacting revenge for his vandalizing her cabin up in Pine County."

Blank looks all around. Finally Doris ventured, "What cabin?"

"That cabin was the precipitating—if precipitating is the word I'm after—" She paused, then nodded, deciding it was, and continued. "Maddy and Harry have been at odds for a long time. They often ended up bidding on the same job or piece of property. Harry was richer, but Maddy was more clever—or at least less willing to aggravate and provoke the people she was working with. They might have gone on like that for years. But then Maddy found a piece of property for sale up in Pine County. It was on a lake that wasn't already surrounded by cabins, so it was nice and private. There was a raggedy old cabin already on the property, which she tore down and replaced with a beautiful one with indoor plumbing and electrical wiring.

"The problem was, that property and primitive cabin was originally owned by Harry's grandparents, and he had happy memories of summers spent up there. His plan was to buy and restore the cabin, complete with kerosene lamps and an outhouse. He tried for years to get it, without success—but Maddy happened to be up there a few years ago when the owner died suddenly, and his family immediately put it on the market. She snapped it up. People wondering where she went for her annual two weeks' vacation should have looked at lakeside rental cabins.

"Harry thought she deliberately outmaneuvered him to deny him his grandparents' land, but I can't find any evidence of that. Still, she was probably pleased when he accused her of it.

"Then, when she outbid him on the Water Street property, he totally lost his temper, went up there, and smashed the windows of her cabin. Chaz remembers Harry asking her about repairing some broken windows. He knew of no broken windows in her rental property and was surprised at her furious reaction. Harry was letting her know he was responsible for the damage to the cabin. So she went to his Wayzata home and began breaking things."

"How did she get in?"

"Talk to Chaz; he'll tell you about how she taught him to bypass locks a tenant would put on without permission."

"Why would he need to do that?" asked Emily, diverted.

Bershada said, "Chaz told me that sometimes people move out without leaving the keys. Sometimes they don't want their landlords to investigate because they're doing something illegal in their unit."

Betsy said, "My problem is tenants making copies of their keys and handing them out to unauthorized people.

"But the point is, Maddy knew how to bypass locks." Betsy made a sad face. "I've seen Harry's place; it's gorgeous and very expensively decorated. She could have done—she may have done thousands of dollars of damage very easily.

"But Harry walked in on her while she was there. And a very short fight ensued. Maddy wasn't injured. She probably had something in her hands she was using to break things and she struck him on the head with it. I don't know if she meant to kill him; it's possible she hit him in self-defense. But whatever, she left him dead on his kitchen floor."

Jill said, "And you know she's the one who did this—how?"

"She came in here the Friday before the auction with more knitted toys, remember?"

They all nodded.

"And she had a Band-Aid on her finger."

Godwin said, "Yes! I remember because the Band-Aid was red, white, and blue, and I'd set the door to play 'Hail to the Chief.'"

Betsy said, "And whoever murdered Harry cut her finger on a projecting screw on a doorknob. A DNA test proved the blood left on the screw belonged to Maddy. That test proved she was in his house and there is no way on earth he would invite her to come for a visit. So why was she in there?"

Betsy sighed. "But Harry had already poisoned her yarn with nicotine he stole from the University's hazardous waste disposal facility when he went there to repair their fire-extinguishing system."

"Mmmm-mmmm-mmmm," said Bershada. "Nasty. Serious anger problems in both of them."

Phil said, "But at least the anger was limited in its direction: strictly at each other."

"The really hot anger was," said Betsy, "but both of them were well-known for shouting at other people, some of whom didn't deserve it. All three of Harry's sons, for example, moved out of state to get away from him. And poor Chaz put up with an awful lot from Maddy, some of whose tenants would move out when they heard she'd bought their apartment building. Harry and Maddy were both accomplished, talented people, but they were by no means governed by sweetness and light."

"Awwww," said Cherie, "I was kind of hoping we'd hear

from you that there were going to be people arrested and sent to jail. Instead, we get . . . nothing."

"We got plenty!" disagreed Phil. "We got a neat little package of two mean people destroying each other and no innocent bystanders killed in the process. Well . . ." he conceded, "Joe Mickels is still standing."

"He's going to get his Mickels Building at last," said Emily. "Good for him. Now maybe he won't be sad anymore."

"LET'S begin again," said Doris to Godwin and Rafael. They were in the pair's condo and had just finished a light supper of poached salmon and vegetable soup, served with wine. "How much do you want to spend on this wedding?"

"I don't think we ought to start with a budget," said Godwin. "I think we should decide what we want and find a way to pay for it."

"Well, I think we should have a budget," interjected Rafael. "Some weddings cost tens of thousands of dollars, which I think is ridiculous. Is the object of this ceremony to see how ostentatious—is that the correct word?—we can be? Or is it to celebrate the legal joining of our lives while our friends celebrate, too?"

"The legal joining of our lives," sighed Godwin. "What a sweet way you put it, Rafael."

"So of course we will do it in the presence of God and the company we invite, and so it should be beautiful. There should be flowers and perhaps balloons, and bright colors, and good food. And we will wear something appropriate—yes? Or festive. Which do you prefer, *mi gorrión*?"

"If it is to be formal, we should wear tuxedos. If you want to go festive, we could wear bullfighter costumes—"

"Not bullfighter costumes, because we are not bullfighters. No costumes. We are not making believe; we are Rafael and Godwin, two real men doing a real thing."

Doris hastily drew a line through something she had written. "I think tuxedos are nice, unless you want to go full formal and wear tails."

"Tails?" said Rafael.

"It's very formal menswear," said Doris. "White shirt and tie, white vest, black trousers, and a coat that has a back that is very long and split in half at the bottom. Orchestra conductors wear them. The outfit probably has some other name, but I've always heard it called tails. Of course, if you want to go that far, then you have to get married in the evening, as it is incorrect to wear tails during the day."

Godwin stared at her admiringly. "How clever of you to know that!"

"I've been studying up on weddings. Miss Manners has been very useful."

"I think we want an afternoon wedding," said Rafael. "So tuxedos, all right?"

"All right," said Godwin. "But maybe with rainbow cummerbunds?" He made a gesture indicating the size and location of a cummerbund.

Doris laughed. "That sounds like fun."

"And my tuxedo black, Raff's white?"

Rafael nodded. "But then I want my . . . my cummerbund to be lavender."

"Yes!" cheered Godwin. "And matching bow ties, lavender for you and rainbow for me!"

Doris made some more notes. "Now," she said, "about location. The wedding's a little more than a year away, so it's possible not all the good places are taken."

"We want it indoors—remember?" said Godwin.

"I remember. Did you know you could use the Minneapolis Institute of Art?"

"Wow, that would be fabulous." He turned to Rafael. "Just imagine a photo of the two of us at the top of those stairs leading up to the old entrance. Do a video, starting long-distance, from the bottom and gradually coming up and up, closer and closer . . ." His eyes closed, and he smiled.

"In the rain," Rafael said.

"Oh. Well, we could shoot that on another day, when it's not raining, unless it's not raining on our day. Still . . ." He looked at Doris. "Where else?"

"Well, there's Loews Minneapolis Hotel downtown. Their Stone Arch Ballroom has seventeen-foot-high ceilings and can seat four hundred, and they have other, smaller rooms. And an on-site catering service that can do plain or fancy. I didn't ask for a quote, but they sound pricey. But for real extravagance, there's the Saint Paul Hotel. Beautiful location, however."

Doris named several other places, from an arboretum to a retired railroad station. Then she said, "Look, I'm not a professional. I don't want to plan your wedding for you, just help you make important decisions, tell you what your options might be. What I think you should do is contact a professional wedding planner. Sunrise Styling looks great, judging from their web site, and they specialize in gay and lesbian weddings. Ariane Criger is another. They have venues, catering, photographers, everything at their fingertips. I want to stay involved, help you make decisions—keep you, Goddy, from sitting up the night before dyeing white doves lavender; and you, Rafael, from holding the reception at McDonald's. Does that sound good?"

"No lavender doves?" sniffed Godwin, pretending to be heartbroken.

"No Quarter Pounders?" mourned Rafael—then he laughed. "All right, Dorita, you are to accompany us to our planning sessions and wear a big hat with a long pin in it, so you can prick us in our backsides when we start failing to do this properly."

Doris's eyes shone. "You two are so wonderful!" she said.

JOE Mickels sat up late in his modest Excelsior office. He was calculating the value of assets he could draw money from, considering the disposition of other assets, moving money into accessible accounts. Those people running Maddy's estate would have no wish to involve themselves in the complex and time-consuming building project over on Water Street, so they would—probably fairly quickly—put the option to buy on the market. And he was not going to be caught short again.

He could see it in his mind's eye, rising above the surrounding buildings. Maybe copper clad—or was that too ostentatious for little old Excelsior? But not plain glass; he wanted something ornate. And over the main entrance a massive granite lintel with letters cut deep: THE MICKELS BUILDING.

He was no longer feeling his age. He felt young and vigorous and energetic. Maybe he should invite Betsy Devonshire to the grand opening.

It was close to bedtime. Connor was in the bathroom, brushing his teeth. Betsy was in bed but reading—rereading, actually—Jerome K. Jerome's famous comic novel, *Three Men in a Boat.* A best seller over a hundred years ago, it was still very funny. Betsy was making the bed jiggle with her chuckles when Connor crawled in beside her.

"*Machree*," he said, "I have something to ask you. Something important."

Betsy immediately put the book down. "What is it?"

"All this talk of marriage has reminded me that I haven't asked you to marry me for several months. So I ask again: Will you marry me?"

"Oh, Connor . . ."

"Is it because you don't love me enough?"

"I love you with all my heart, you know that."

"Then what's holding you back?"

"I've tried marrying, twice. And failed at it both times."

"You haven't tried it with me."

"You've tried it before. And it didn't work."

"I think my marriage failed because I was so often and for so long at sea. But I'm home from the sea now."

"I think my marriages failed because I'm lousy at picking men to marry."

Connor looked so stricken that she said at once, "Don't you see? That's why I haven't married you! I love you, I love who you are, where you came from, what you can do, everything about you! I love having you in my life; you are very good to me and for me. But I'm scared. I don't trust my own judgment. I'd be devastated if you left me. And for some stupid reason, I'm scared witless that if we marry, you'll leave me. And I couldn't bear that, I couldn't!" She felt herself beginning to weep and started to turn away.

But he gathered her into his arms. "Oh, my dearest darling, my own heart, how could I leave you? You are everything to me." He began to kiss her gently, stroking her face, her hair, her back, then more ardently, insistently . . .

Later, all tension gone, she purred, "You are such a comfort to me."

"And you to me. So let's make a bargain. If I am still here a year from now, and you are still with me, then we will reopen the question. Until then, I will not ask you again. All right?"

"All right." A year. In a year, surely she would know.

"Sophie" Knitted Amigurumi Cat Pattern

Designed by Diane Davis

"Sophie" is a fluffy little avalanche of white with a patchwork of gray and tan on her ear, back, and tail. She'll be great company while you're reading one of the Needlecraft Mysteries by Monica Ferris!

FINISHED SIZE:

Approx. 7" long by 3" wide

MATERIALS REQUIRED:

Worsted weight yarn—approx. 65 yards in Main Color (MC), 10-15 yards in Gray (A) and Tan or Gold (B)

Satin ribbon for collar (approx 9")

Embroidery floss or yarn for embroidering face (Optional: Small plastic cat eyes and nose)

Stuffing material

Size 3 double pointed needles
Plastic needlepoint or darning needle

ABBREVIATIONS:

CO: Cast on
K: Knit
P: Purl
M1: Make 1 stitch
M1K1: Make 1, Knit 1
skpo: Slip 1 stitch as if to knit, knit 1 stitch, pass the slipped stitch over
K2 tog: Knit 2 stitches together
w&t: Wrap and turn
PU: Pick up
dpn: Double pointed needle

SPECIAL STITCHES USED:

M1—Used to increase stitches. Make 1 stitch, lift right leg of the stitch in the row below the next stitch to be worked and place it on the left needle, then work it as a normal knit stitch.

W&T—Used in short rows to avoid "holes" in your work. When knitting, knit required stitches, pass yarn to the front, slip next stitch to the right needle, pass yarn to the back, slip stitch back to left needle and turn your work. When purling, pass yarn to the back, slip next stitch to the right needle, pass yarn to the front, slip stitch back to the left needle and turn your work.

Double Knitting—In this pattern, we'll use double knitting to combine all of the stitches onto one dpn before binding off. However, instead of using separate strands of yarn for front and back layers, we're going to use just one strand of MC, switching to B when we reach the left ear. *Purl one stitch from the rear needle, knit one from the front, continuing in the same pattern across the needles.* When you reach the B stitches, let MC trail out between the MC and B stitches (you'll need it again when you're ready to bind off). Continue in B for remainder of row until all stitches are on one dpn.

HINTS FOR COLOR WORK (INTARSIA) KNITTING:

- When switching from one color to another, wrap the two strands around each other to minimize holes or gaps between color patches.
- When knitting intarsia in the round, there are many times when your working yarn will end up at the wrong end of the patch you're knitting. When this happens, knit up to the color change, slip stitches to be knitted from one needle to the other and turn your work. (These spots are noted in the pattern instructions.) Pick up the working yarn and purl back across the stitches, then turn your work again and slip the purled stitches back to the right needle. Carry your MC behind the stitches and continue with your next color.

BODY

CO 26 st in MC, divide between 3 dpns (10 st on dpn1, 8 st each on dpn2 and dpn3). Connect in the round, making sure your stitches are not twisted.

Rounds 1–2: K all

Round 3: Dpn1—K3, M1 K4, M1, K3 (12 st); Dpn2 & Dpn3—K2, M1, K4, M1, K2 (10 st on each)

Round 4: Dpn1—K4 in MC, attach color A and K3, attach color B and K2, MC K3; Dpn2 & Dpn3: K all in MC

Round 5: Dpn1—K3 in MC, slip next 6 st, turn, P3 in B, P3 in A, turn and slip those 6 st back to working needle, K3 in MC; Dpn2 & Dpn3: K all in MC

Round 6: Dpn1—K4 in MC, K2 in A, K2 in MC, K3 in B, K1 in MC; Dpn2 & Dpn3: K all in MC

Round 7: Dpn1—K4 in MC, slip next 7 st, turn, P5 in B, P2 in A, turn and slip those 7 st back to working needle, K1 in MC; Dpn2 & Dpn3: K all in MC

Round 8: Dpn1—K2 in MC, K5 in B, K3 in A, K2 in MC; Dpn2 & Dpn3: K all in MC

Round 9: Dpn1—K3 in MC, slip next 7 st, turn, P5 in B, P2 in A, turn and slip those 7 st back to working needle, K2 in MC; Dpn2 & Dpn3: K all in MC

Round 10: Dpn1—K3 in MC, K3 in A, K4 in B, K2 in MC; Dpn2 & Dpn3: K all in MC

Round 11: Dpn1—K3 in MC, slip next 7 st, turn, P5 in B, P2 in A, turn and slip those 7 st back to working needle, K2 in MC; Dpn2 & Dpn3: K all in MC

Round 12: Dpn1—K3 in MC, K3 in B, K4 in A, K2 in MC; Dpn2 & Dpn3: K all in MC

Round 13: Dpn1—K3 in MC, slip next 7 st, turn, P5 in B, P2 in A, turn and slip those 7 st back to working needle, K2 in MC; Dpn2 & Dpn3: K all in MC

Round 14–16: Dpn1—K all in MC; Dpn2 & Dpn3: K all in MC

Round 17: Dpn1—K5 in MC, K2 in B, K5 in MC; Dpn2 & Dpn3: K all in MC

Round 18: Dpn1—K4 in MC, K4 in B, K4 in MC; Dpn2 & Dpn3: K all in MC

Round 19: Dpn1—K4 in MC, K5 in B, K3 in MC; Dpn2 & Dpn3: K all in MC

Round 20: Dpn1—K4 in MC, K5 in A, K3 in MC; Dpn2 & Dpn3: K all in MC

Round 21: Dpn1—K4 in MC, slip next 5 st, turn, P5 in A, turn and slip those 5 st back to working needle, K3 in MC; Dpn2 & Dpn3: K all in MC

Round 22: Dpn1—K5 in MC, K3 in A, K4 in MC; Dpn2 & Dpn3: K all in MC

Round 23: K all in MC

****NOTE:** Knit rounds 24–28 in MC**

Round 24: K3, skpo, *K6, skpo* 3 times, K3 (28 st)

Round 25: K3, skpo, *K5, skpo* 3 times, K2 (24 st)

Round 26: K3, skpo, *K4, skpo* 3 times, K1 (20 st)

Round 27: K3, skpo, *K3, skpo* 3 times (16 st)

Round 28: K3, skpo, K2, skpo, K2, skpo, K2, slip last stitch, pass over 1st stitch in the round (12 st)

Round 29: In Color A: K2, skpo, K1, skpo, K1, skpo, K1, slip last stitch, pass over 1st stitch in the round (8 st)

TAIL

Continue with the 8 stitches on the dpns

Round 1: K all in A

Round 2–16: All 3 colors should be trailing out the hole where the tail will be. For the remaining rows, hold together two of the strands for one round, and change combinations for each round.

Round 17: *K2 tog* in A only, repeat from * 3 times. Cut a length of yarn and thread a plastic darning needle. Pass stitches from needles to the yarn and pull tight to close the end of the tail. Fasten off and weave ends down inside tail. (Tail doesn't need additional stuffing.)

PAWS (TWO)

CO 10 st in MC, divide between 2 dpns to give paws a flatter look. Connect in the round, making sure your stitches are not twisted.

Rounds 1–15: K all

Round 16: Skpo, K1, skpo twice, K1, skpo. Cut a length of yarn and thread a plastic darning needle. Pass stitches from needles to the yarn and pull tight to close the end of the paw. Fasten off. Stuff lightly to within a ½" from the closed end of the paw and shape paws around your thumb, giving them a slight downward curve. Sew paws to underside of body approx. 8–10 rows from neck opening. After paws are attached, stuff body to desired fluffiness.

HEAD/CHEST

Determine center of front neck opening, count 8 stitches to the right. This is where you will begin picking up stitches for the Head/Chest section. Pick up 26 stitches around the neck opening, moving clockwise as you look at the opening. Distribute the stitches on 3 dpns with 8 st each on left and right front sides (dpn1 on the right as you look at the opening, dpn 2 on the left) and 10 stitches on dpn3 across the back of the neck opening. Knit all of the stitches on dpn 1 (K8), which will bring you to the center of the neck opening, and begin the short rows. (The short row section will only be worked across dpn1 and dpn2.)

Rows 1&2: Dpn2: K2, w&t, P2; Dpn1: P2, w&t, K2

Rows 3&4: Dpn2: K3, w&t, P3; Dpn1: P3, w&t, K3

Rows 5&6: Dpn2: K4, w&t, P4; Dpn1: P4, w&t, K4

Rows 7&8: Dpn 2: K5, w&t, P5; Dpn 1: P5, w&t, K5

Rows 9&10, 11&12, 13&14:**
Continue adding a stitch each pair of rows until all 8 stitches on each dpn are wrapped and turned.

****Row 14—Note:** You will end the 14th Row at the center of the chest, then K the next 8 stitches on dpn2 to make the front rows even on both sides. Transfer 1 st from the ends of dpn1 and dpn2 to dpn 3, giving you 7 st on dpn1 & dpn 2, and 12 on dpn3.**

Round 15: Begin knitting in rounds, starting with dpn3. Dpn3: K11 in MC, K1 in B (beginning of color work for ear section); Dpn1: K1 in B, K6 in MC; Dpn2: K7 in MC

Round 16: Dpn3: K10 in MC, K2 in B; Dpn1: K2 in B, K5 in MC; Dpn2: K7 in MC

Round 17: Dpn3: K9 in MC, K3 in B; Dpn1: K3 in B, K4 in MC; Dpn2: K7 in MC

Round 18: Dpn3: K8 in MC, K4 in B; Dpn1: K4 in B, K3 in MC; Dpn2: K7 in MC

Round 19: Dpn3: K7 in MC, K5 in B; Dpn1: K5 in B, K2 in MC; Dpn2: K7 in MC

Round 20: Dpn3: K6 in MC, K6 in B; Dpn1: K6 in B, slip last st on dpn1, K first st on dpn2 in MC and psso, K6 in MC (7 st on dpn1); Dpn2: K6 in MC (25 st)

Round 21: Dpn3: K6 in MC, K6 in B; Dpn1: K7 in B; Dpn2: K6 in MC (25 st)

NOTE: At this point you will need to stop and stitch the facial features and stuff the head and chest before seaming the top. Don't forget to add a few whiskers!

Round 22: There are now 13 stitches on dpns1 & 2, and 12 stitches on dpn3. Turn work so that dpn3 is closest to you, and hold the front needles parallel to it. Starting with the first st on dpn2, double knit the front and back stitches (P st from dpn1 & 2, K st from dpn3), alternating until all stitches are on one needle. (1st 6 from each dpn will be in MC, remaining 7 will be in B).

Row 23: Turn work so the back of the neck is closest to you. K2tog, binding off the row as you go. Fasten off and weave in ends.

FINISHING TOUCHES:

- Stitch along where ears meet the head and over the top seam between the ears to give them more definition. Tie off at back of head and weave ends in.
- Tuck tail around the side of the body and stitch if desired, or let it hang naturally.
- Add a "collar" of satin ribbon with a bell or charm on it for a sophisticated touch.